"This novel had serious 'O autumn! O tea kettle! O grace!' vibes, a kickass soundtrack and the most wonderful love story. I loved every bit of it."   —**Kerry Clare, author of** *Asking for a Friend*

"*Make Me a Mixtape* is packed full of witty banter, the best music references and an amazing, vibrant cast of characters. I loved complicated, talented and a little bit surly Allie, a former punk rocker struggling to come to terms with her past while figuring out what to do next with her life. Ryan is a complete cinnamon roll who admires, supports and challenges Allie to be her best self. I was rooting for these two music nerds from the first page!"

—**Farah Heron, author of** *Jana Goes Wild* **and** *Accidentally Engaged*

"An absolute delight! Whiteford's combination of a Black Cat girlfriend and Golden Retriever boyfriend and a witty and vivid voice creates a charming romance. *Make Me a Mixtape* feels nostalgic and left me with that same warmth you get from putting on your favorite vinyl record."

—**Ruby Barrett, author of** *The Friendship Study*

MAKE ME
A MIXTAPE

MAKE ME A MIXTAPE

JENNIFER WHITEFORD

DOUBLEDAY CANADA

Doubleday Canada and colophon are registered trademarks of Penguin Random House Canada Limited

LIBRARY AND ARCHIVES CANADA CATALOGUING IN PUBLICATION
Title: Make me a mixtape / Jennifer Whiteford.
Names: Whiteford, Jennifer, author.
Identifiers: Canadiana (print) 20240327829 | Canadiana (ebook) 20240327853 |
ISBN 9780385689175 (softcover) | ISBN 9780385689182 (EPUB)
Subjects: LCGFT: Romance fiction. | LCGFT: Novels.
Classification: LCC PS8645.H5485 M35 2024 | DDC C813/.6—dc23

This book is a work of fiction. Names, characters, places and incidents are products of the author's imagination or are used fictitiously. Any resemblance to actual events or locales or persons, living or dead, is entirely coincidental.

Cover design: Lisa Jager
Cover and interior art: (café) MM memo, (cassette) GreenSkyStudio, (woman) Katakari, all Shutterstock; (notes) Graficriver/Adobe Stock Images

Printed in Canada

Published in Canada by Doubleday Canada,
a division of Penguin Random House Canada Limited
and distributed in the United States by Penguin Random House LLC

www.penguinrandomhouse.ca

10 9 8 7 6 5 4 3 2 1

Penguin
Random House
DOUBLEDAY CANADA

To Megan Butcher
Thank you for ruining me for absolutely everyone else.

OCTOBER

We Belong

Chapter One

Allie Andrews could not have cared less about her neighborhood's charm and beauty as she stomped the streets of Brooklyn in a terrible mood.

It was October, and the corner bodegas of Park Slope were bursting with mums and marigolds, apples and pumpkins. The trees that lined the blocks were dropping their muted, rosy leaves onto the sprawling sidewalks. The autumn sun poured its golden light over the bustling crowds. But to Allie, it looked as if Brooklyn was showing off, as if it was trying too hard to impress someone on a first date.

She'd lost the spirited game of rock-paper-scissors that decided who would deliver the coffee order called in during the last few minutes of the afternoon shift. It was a small order—one latte, two cookies—so it hardly seemed worth leaving the cozy café to navigate the crowded streets. On top of that, Solidarity Studios was her least favorite place for deliveries. The podcast company was on the fourth floor of an old building—no elevator—on an irritatingly beautiful corner in one of the hippest sections of the borough.

Looking at the fashionable outfits of the people around her, Allie felt distinctly grungy by comparison in her dirty sneakers and secondhand dress. Wait, it was worse. She'd also forgotten to remove the dark-green café apron tied around her waist. A streak of foamy oat milk was still smeared across the pocket on her left hip.

As she approached the building, she dodged a woman wearing a neon-yellow beanie, carrying a pumpkin and laughing with a tall purple-haired man. Allie stumbled to the edge of the sidewalk, holding the coffee aloft. Annoyance fizzed up inside her.

It took three jabs of the buzzer before the ancient front door would properly release. Allie trudged into the lobby and over to the stairwell, shuffling around the cup of coffee and bag of cookies so she could hold the railing as she climbed. She stopped on the first landing and listened for footsteps. Silence. She was alone.

The only thing this place had going for it was its excellent acoustics. Ascending slowly, she sang the opening lines of "True Colors" by Cyndi Lauper.

The song was released years before Allie was born, but it was so familiar she felt as if she'd written it herself. She sang softly for the first verse, but by the time she reached the chorus, she was belting it out with her full voice. She slowed her pace, hoping for more time with Cyndi before she had to step out of the stairwell and back into her real life.

Despite her deep love for Cyndi (or "Ms. Lauper" as she'd breathlessly addressed the pop star once when she'd seen her in the bathroom of a pizzeria in Carroll Gardens), Allie had never been a "Girls Just Want to Have Fun" person. She respected the song, sure. It was an enduring hit, and she understood why people connected with it. Heck, even *she* sometimes wanted to have fun when the working day was done. But for her, it didn't hold a candle to "True Colors." There was real emotion in the ballad that you didn't get in the pop hit. "True Colors" was about being accepted by someone, loved without condition.

She reluctantly exited the stairwell and yanked open the door that led to the studio's reception area.

Still humming under her breath, Allie checked the order slip and made her way down the hall toward Recording Room 4. The place was unsettlingly quiet, with just a few unfamiliar faces working at computers visible through glass walls. Despite the frequent orders they received from studio employees, she hadn't recognized the name this time.

He had his back to her when she walked into the room. Definitely a new guy. She would have remembered him if she'd seen him before. He was a giant. Tall and broad, not in a muscular body-builder way, but still large enough that no one would mess with him on a dark sidewalk. He wore Blundstone boots, black jeans and a worn denim shirt stretched across his wide shoulders. His hair looked freshly cut, shaved at the back and sides with a longer section at the top neatly combed to the left.

She cleared her throat. "Hello?" She pulled the order slip out of her pocket. "Are you Ryan?"

He turned to look at her with a wide smile on his face. Allie felt an involuntary jolt in her belly.

Handsome.

He had a thick, tidy beard and a kind, open look in his eyes. But as soon as he saw her, his expression twisted into one of shock. The microphone in his hands tumbled to the floor with an unsettling snap. Allie was about to apologize for startling him, but he spoke before she could.

"You're Allie Jetski!"

Allie's eyes widened in horror. She almost dropped his coffee, but the microphone served as a cautionary tale. Instead, she shook her head wildly, and whispered, "*No.*"

"Yes!" He took a step toward her with his long legs and bent slightly to look into her face with intense focus. "You *are!* You're Allie Jetski. *Allie Jetski* is delivering my coffee. How about that?"

Allie froze, too shocked to respond.

This didn't happen. This had literally *never* happened. It was something she loved about New York. There were so many people, all absorbed in their own lives, anonymity was a given. Even if a huge celebrity appeared in the wild, everyone just pretended to ignore them. And she was absolutely not a huge celebrity.

He was still looking at her, expectantly. She noted again, now with annoyance, that he was disarmingly attractive. His well-groomed appearance and warm eyes were enough to immediately throw her off balance in a way that she hadn't felt in . . . well, in a long-ass time. She sighed. It didn't appear that he was going to accept her feeble denial.

"It's Allie Andrews, actually. I haven't been Allie Jetski for years."

He clapped his hands and straightened his posture, his face breaking back into its friendly smile. "Hot dang! I knew it was you. The Jetskis were my favorite band back in the day!"

She snorted with laughter. "Well, that's obviously a lie."

"No!" He put his hand over his heart. "No, I swear! I was just a kid when y'all were playing, but I saw you every time you came through Birmingham."

That explained it. His slight accent, his weird friendliness, his awareness of a band that no one in New York would remember or care about.

"Well, we were also just kids when we were playing," she told him, fidgeting from one foot to the other.

He laughed. "Well, y'all seemed like cool adults to me. I was nineteen when I saw you at the Hidey Hole."

The Hidey Hole.

Allie remembered it. A basement punk club where the entrance was literally a hole in the wall. She had a sudden, vivid memory of her former bandmate and best friend Jessi going through the hole/door ahead of her, muttering "If there's a fire, we're all gonna die." The acoustics in that place were amazing, though. Concrete walls, just like the stairwell she'd been singing in mere minutes ago.

Allie did quick mental math. "I would have been eighteen then, so there you go."

For the first time since his initial shock at her appearance, Ryan was bemused. "Huh!" He stared past her, and she felt as if she could see him reviewing history in his head. "Isn't that something? Memories are weird things. I could have sworn you were all leagues ahead of me in life."

Allie did not feel as if she had ever been leagues ahead of anyone in life. "It was a long time ago. Here." She thrust the coffee and cookies at his chest. He stared at them, as if he'd forgotten that's why she was there in the first place.

"Oh! Right." He took the items from her hands. He smelled nice. Like cologne? Aftershave? Essential oils? She didn't know what made men smell nice these days. She was sweating. Why was she sweating?

He dropped the bag of cookies onto the table beside him and shifted the coffee to his left hand, offering his right to her. "Ryan Abernathy."

She shook it, cautiously. Her heart rate accelerated as his soft, warm skin touched hers. "Allie—"

"Andrews." He nodded. "So you said. Hard to get my head around that, though."

"Try."

They looked at each other for a moment before he released her hand. One side of his mouth crept up into a small smile. A rush of adrenaline moved through her. This was too much. She immediately looked down at the ground, gaze landing on the forgotten microphone.

"That looks busted."

He looked at the floor and cringed. "Dang."

The black casing around the base of the microphone was clearly cracked. Allie could see the wiring inside peeking out. Ryan bent to pick it up. "Great. I've been working here for all of one week, and I'm already breaking things. You wouldn't happen to know of a repair shop nearby, would you?"

Allie did not want to play tour guide. What she wanted was to get back to the comforting familiarity of the café. But she was reluctantly taken in by his gentle, pleading expression. It didn't hurt to be helpful.

"Music Go Round is just up the block. If you walk downstairs with me, I'll point you in the right direction."

"Great!" He juggled his coffee from one hand to the other. "I'll save those cookies for later. Unless you'd like one, Jetski."

Every time he said it, the word was like a punch to her gut. Allie was already regretting her offer of help.

"I don't want your cookies."

They shuffled out of the recording room. Ryan locked the door behind them, a Solidarity Studios tote bag containing the broken microphone slung over his broad shoulder. He held the door open for her as they entered the stairwell.

"So, Allie Jetski."

"Andrews."

"Right." He flashed her a grin. "Andrews, sorry. Are you still into punk? Or did you mellow into a fan of classic country like all the other oldies in the scene?"

Allie had no idea what part of this jumble of assumptions she should respond to first. Then it occurred to her that she didn't owe anyone, least of all this friendly giant she'd known for all of two minutes, an explanation for her complicated relationship with music.

"Nope."

"Nope what?"

"Not into classic country."

"So, punk still?" He was walking beside her down the stairs, their footsteps echoing in unison. His shoulder brushed hers as they turned to descend the next section of the staircase.

She jumped away and shook her head. "Not really into punk, either."

"But you must still play music."

"No." They reached the bottom of the staircase.

"No?" He was incredulous. "How come?" They were less than a foot apart, standing in the tiny vestibule by the front door. She could see his chest rising and falling with each breath. Being close to him made her lightheaded. Allie took a deep breath.

She forced herself to look steadily into his eyes. "That," she said, pulling open the door and gesturing to him to go out first, "is none of your business."

Ryan held up both palms in mock surrender as he stepped forward, moving through the doorway, laughing. "Whatever you say, Jetski. Whatever you say."

She rolled her eyes and stepped out after him. The waning sun drenched the neighborhood in warm light like the final scene in some romantic movie that had nothing in common with her life. Why was Brooklyn being such a pain in the ass today?

She pointed west. "Walk three blocks that way and then turn right. You'll see the striped awning a few buildings along. The sign says Music Go Round. Hussein will help you."

"Thank you." All joking gone from his demeanor, he furrowed his brow. "Really. You're truly saving me here." He lifted one hand, as though he was about to reach for her. For what? Another handshake? Surely not a hug. Allie felt her own hands twitch. She wanted to reach for him, too. It didn't matter, though, since he seemed to think better of it and dropped his arm back to his side. Instead, she waved at him and turned to walk in the opposite direction, willing herself not to look back.

Once she'd safely rounded the corner, the fog of attraction seemed to lift. A cool breeze caused an eruption of goose bumps on her warm skin. She shook her arms and head vigorously, earning a strange look from a tall, bespectacled man walking a dachshund.

No matter how cute Ryan was, or how familiar he was with that magical part of her past, this guy was not worth the trouble. Her life was just fine now. Predictable and safe. The last thing she needed was someone upending all of that.

She walked slowly back to the café, sure of only one thing: the next time a delivery for Solidarity Studios was called in, she was getting someone else to do it.

Chapter Two

"Earth to Allie!"

Allie jumped, startled by Ren's words, which came with a snap of fingers close to her nose.

"Oh shit, what was I saying?"

Ren rolled their eyes. "I was asking about the new code for the alarm, but you were just staring out the window."

"Right, right." Allie shook her head. "Sorry. The code is 7865. The new system has four numbers instead of three. But it works pretty much the same as the old one. I can come downstairs when it's time to close up if you want help."

"Naw, I got it."

A group of women came in and approached the counter, chattering about oat milk versus coconut milk for lattes. Allie gave them a bright smile and took their orders while Ren moved over to the coffee machine.

Over the years, Allie had learned how to manage customers. With her thick brown hair and clear blue eyes, she had an approachable attractiveness that seemed to make people eager to chat. Sometimes too eager, but she was well practiced at retreating to the kitchen when she needed a moment to herself. She dressed her short, curvy frame in brightly colored jumpsuits and dresses and wore very little makeup.

Having an unfussy wardrobe and beauty routine was necessary for the early mornings and long days of food service work.

Allie may have drawn people in with her hardworking charm, but Ren was always the cool one. With their shaved head, lanky stature, and arms full of black-and-gray tattoos, Ren was someone who made customers think that the café must be intriguing in ways they could only hope to discover.

"What's with you, anyway?" Ren asked, once the customers had their lattes—oat milk had been declared the winner—and were seated in a far corner of the café.

Whenever Allie was upset about something and trying to hide it, Ren knew immediately. It bordered on creepy.

Allie sighed. "You ever have an encounter with a stranger and they act like they know you but they don't, really, and it's kind of annoying?"

Ren nodded. "All the time. I mean, you were here when that guy wouldn't stop insisting that I was the"—Ren formed air quotes with their fingers—"'Asian chick who won *Top Chef*.'"

"Oh yeah." Allie cringed. "Mindy told him not to come back."

Ren started wiping down the counter. "Did you have a bad customer today?"

"No. Just a weird delivery experience. It's fine, though. I mean, it wasn't like I was misgendered by a racist or anything."

Ren laughed. "That would be a tall order, given that you're white and girly."

Allie joined in Ren's laughter. She felt more steady, being back behind the counter, the familiar smell of coffee and baked goods surrounding her.

She'd been at the café for ten years now. Each day blending pleasantly into the next.

"Oh, for Pete's sake, could one of you restock the pastry case? We have customers who might actually want to eat something."

Allie turned around and locked eyes with her Aunt Mindy, who had appeared in the doorway between the kitchen and the front counter.

As though to counteract Allie's colorful clothing and Ren's edgy look, Mindy dressed daily in worn black jeans and tentlike gray linen tunics, usually with a black beanie on her head. Her face was creased into an almost constant scowl. She called it "resting hag face" and said it was the consequence of running a café in Brooklyn for decades. Her hair was completely white, and she only ever wore it in two braids. She'd had some very proud moments when people mistook her for aging punk icon Patti Smith.

Allie picked up a tray. "We were just about to restock. Take it easy."

Mindy frowned. "Take it easy yourself, smartass. I'll help you load up." She turned on her heel and marched back to the kitchen.

The café itself was an embodiment of Mindy's no-nonsense style. Sturdy wooden furnishings, smooth gray concrete floors, pendant lights with matte black shades providing the perfect amount of glow above each table. People were drawn in. Passersby could look through the window at the clean, humble space and think *That's the perfect place to read in peace with a latte.* The only color in the neutral space came from the deep-green tiles along the front of the service counter. Allie ran her hand along the cool surface when she walked by, following her aunt into the kitchen.

As she was filling a tray with tarts, cake slices and turnovers, Allie heard the bell on the front door sound. Mindy peeked out at the front and then leaned back into the kitchen, nodding in Allie's direction.

"Your boyfriend's here."

Allie smiled. "Oh, is he?"

"Yep. God knows, he never wants Ren or me to serve him. You'd better get out there."

"Well." Allie stood up, the tray now laden with fresh pastries held in front of her. "I won't keep him waiting, then." She stopped in front of Mindy on her way out of the kitchen. "How's my hair?"

Mindy smoothed Allie's short bangs and fluffed her long, dark waves. "It's great, since you're not wearing a hairnet like you're supposed to."

Allie rolled her eyes. "I literally just came back here because you were harassing me about the urgent need for pastries."

"Tell that to the health inspector."

Allie ignored this and made a beeline for George MacDonald, the man who loved her more than any other.

"Hello, George."

His eyes lit up as she greeted him. "Good afternoon, Allie. I thought I heard you back there. I hope I didn't disturb you."

"Never!" She smiled at him as she carefully filled the pastry case. "How was your birthday party? Sorry I had to miss it."

His eyes crinkled when he laughed. "Well, you know, they're never too wild these days. Just me and some of the other residents. The cake Mindy made was lovely."

George had just turned eighty-five. He lived in a seniors' apartment two blocks from the café. He didn't go far from home any longer, but he did come in for tea every afternoon. Allie was the only one, he said, who could make a perfect cup of Earl Grey.

She pulled his favorite mug off the shelf above the espresso machines and added the tea leaves to a strainer. While it steeped, she warmed some milk for him and set everything together on a tray. George was already sitting in his usual spot to the left of the main counter. She brought the tea over, and he gestured for her to sit in the empty chair across from him.

"So." He took a long sip from his cup and gave her a smile and a thumbs-up. "How many more songs do you have to go?"

"Three. I want to stop at thirteen. It was my dad's lucky number."

George nodded thoughtfully. "So what song is next?"

"Oh, it's a good one." She leaned forward, tugging the sleeves of her yellow flowered dress up over her elbows to keep them safe from any dregs of tea or milk that might splash onto the table. George's hands weren't always steady. "It's 'We Belong' by Pat Benatar. I think we've talked about her."

George squinted, looking past her. "Is she the one who did a song about the love battlefield?"

"Yes! That's right."

"I liked your version of that one. I had one of the nurses play me the original to compare. The acoustic guitar as the main rhythm was a good choice."

"Thanks, George." She beamed at him. "This other song, the one I'm working on now, it's even more dramatic. So fun to sing."

"Well, make sure I get to hear it when you're done."

"I'll probably work on it some more tonight." She glanced up at the clock above the counter. "I'm off in a few minutes."

George patted her hand. "Don't let me keep you. I'll be in tomorrow and you can tell me more about it. I think I like this Pat Benatar person. She's got something."

Before his retirement, George worked as a music archivist. While his own taste mostly stayed in the classical realm, he was curious about all types of music, and he was the person in Allie's life who was the most enthusiastic about the '80s pop song covers she'd been recording in her spare time.

Mindy appeared behind the counter and called out a greeting to George. He waved at her from his seat. They had known each other since before Allie arrived at the café ten years earlier, though George's daily visits hadn't started until Allie was a fixture. George and Mindy had a mutual respect that Allie found reassuring. It was like having parents who you knew liked each other too much to get a divorce, even though they had very little in common.

"Allie was just telling me about her new recording. Don't you think she should start a band, Mindy? Wouldn't that be wonderful?"

Mindy and Allie made eye contact and were silent for what felt like a very long moment. Finally, Allie spoke. "I've told you, George. No band for me. I wouldn't even know where to start."

She patted the old man's shoulder as she left the table, passing Mindy on her way to the kitchen. She could hear her aunt's nonslip Swedish clogs clomping behind her.

"Why do you do that?" Mindy asked, closing a recipe book and placing it back with the others on a high shelf.

"Do what?" Allie was suddenly very interested in her own feet. Her left sneaker had a stain on the toe from where she'd accidentally dropped a lump of coffee grounds headed for the compost. What would get that stain out? Vinegar? Bleach?

"You know what. Lie about your past."

Allie huffed and looked up at her aunt. "I'm not *lying*. I just don't feel like talking about it. It's depressing."

Mindy shook her head. "Of all the things that have happened in your life, it's the *band* that you find depressing?"

"Well, not *only* the band . . ." Allie was saved from further conversation by the ringing of the café phone. Mindy went to the front to answer it. Allie filled a glass with water and drank it slowly.

So what if she didn't want to talk to George about her band? Why was everyone suddenly so interested in her band? A memory of Ryan's delighted voice chirping "Allie Jetski!" made her stomach seize up. She shook it off and turned to put her glass in the dishwasher.

Everybody needed to mind their own business.

"I'm heading upstairs!" She didn't wait for Mindy or Ren to answer before she started up the back staircase to her apartment. After the day she'd had, she was desperate to be alone.

Allie's 300-square-foot studio apartment above the café was always comforting. Her bed in one corner, her bookshelf in another. Her clothes hung—in the order of her weekly outfit schedule—on a bar that Mindy had attached to the ceiling when she'd lived in the same apartment, many years before Allie had moved in.

She always wore the yellow dress and red sneakers on Monday. Her denim overalls and orange clogs were ready for Tuesday. The Bangles

T-shirt that she usually wore under the overalls was starting to get a little thin, so she was considering replacing it in the rotation with a Bananarama one Mindy had thrifted.

Along the wall close to the second window was her very rudimentary home recording studio setup. Allie felt her shoulders relax as she slid her favorite microphone into the stand and plugged its cord into her tiny soundboard. She clicked her mouse and brought her laptop to life. Her recording app was already open. Right where she'd left off.

Music wasn't what had failed her. It was all the other stuff that stressed her out.

Clueless male journalists asking her and her bandmates whether they all got their periods at the same time. Fans who insisted they had a place for the band to sleep that turned out to be a patch of dirty floor next to a never-emptied litter box. That one promoter who didn't have any cash and offered to pay them with pairs of jeans.

Jessi slamming the door of their practice space when she left for the last time.

Allie shook the memory out of her head and looked back at her screen.

The version of "We Belong" she'd been thinking about had a driving guitar part. Grabbing her treasured Martin acoustic, she tuned each string. Satisfied, she stood. Usually, she sat to play, but the forceful strumming that she wanted for this song would require the full movement of her body. It was a good thing. Playing hard and loud would give her a way to work out any lingering frustrations about her unnerving day.

Plugging a patch cord into the body of the guitar, she gave it a few loud strums to check the levels. Her mood already improving, she put on her headphones and clicked Record.

Chapter Three

The next morning, dressed in her new Bananarama shirt and old denim overalls, Allie bounced down the staircase and through the back door of the café. She was expecting to start her day alone in the kitchen as usual, but Mindy was already there, looming over the prep counter.

"Shit, you scared me!" Allie laughed. She pulled a yellow bandanna out of her pocket to tie around her hair before Mindy could tell her off.

"I need to talk to you about something."

Only then did Allie notice the odd look of concern in her aunt's brown eyes. She went still, her hands gripping the edge of the counter between them.

"What is it? Did someone die?"

Her aunt laughed and shook her head. "Allie, we're the last two people alive in our family. Who the fuck else could die?"

"Good point." Allie dropped her shoulders and then pulled a stool over to the prep counter and sat down. "Okay, go ahead."

Mindy sighed and tugged at the end of one of her tight braids. She shut her eyes for a beat longer than normal, then opened them, leveling Allie with a determined stare.

"I'm leaving."

"Leaving what?"

"The café. The city. Also the country."

Allie wondered whether she was the victim of a weird prank.

"What do you mean? You're going on a vacation? You've never gone on a vacation."

Mindy shook her head. "Not a vacation. I'm leaving for good."

Allie opened her mouth and then closed it again. Panic washed over her. She pressed her fingers into her temples. "I still don't get what you mean. Are you sick?"

Mindy leaned back against the wall, her hands shoved deep in the pockets of her gray linen dress. "I'm fine. I should have said that first. I apologize."

When Allie was eighteen, her mom, Mindy's younger sister, had died of cancer. But that hadn't actually been where Allie's mind had gone. Her mom and Mindy were so different, it took actual effort to remember that they shared genetic material.

"But then . . . what is happening?" Allie's stomach churned. Something had to be wrong. Something major.

Their lives had been the same for a decade. And Mindy's life had been the same for decades before that. Surely only a major disaster could disrupt their careful routines. From the moment Allie had stumbled into the café ten years earlier with a shabby suitcase and a tearstained face, Mindy had been there. Available, helpful, supportive.

Mindy leaned forward. One side of her usual scowl bent upward into a rare half smile. "I've never traveled. I've never done anything adventurous. I haven't even been out of the country. I didn't have a passport until last week. I'm sixty years old. My whole adult life has been here, in this place."

She looked at Allie and seemed to finally notice the distressed look on her niece's face. "Not that I haven't loved it! I have. I have loved being with you and working with you and being here in our space. But my mom was sixty-two when she died. And my dad was sixty-five. And all I can think these days is if I died tomorrow, how would I feel about how I chose to spend my life? I don't want my obituary to say *She owned a café and never went to Paris.*"

"Obituaries don't say what people didn't do." Allie couldn't help herself. Mindy, who normally would have scoffed at the pedantic statement, smiled again sadly.

Allie furrowed her brow, trying not to pout like a child. "So that's what you're doing, then? Going to Paris? What about the café?"

"Well," Mindy said, twisting her apron in her hands, "that's up to you."

"What?" Allie felt another shot of panic buzz through her.

"You get to choose. If I *did* die tomorrow, you'd inherit the building and the café and all my other assets. So if you want to take it over, I'll sign everything over to you now, without having to go to the trouble of kicking the bucket first."

Allie could barely process everything that she was hearing. "And if I don't want it?"

"Then I'll sell it to someone else. And when I *actually* die, you'll get whatever is left in my coffers."

"And you'll be in Paris."

Mindy shrugged. "For a while, anyway. It's funny, but somehow staying in one place for my whole life has made me a lot of international friends. Lots of people leave New York and go to even more exciting places. And they seem to all want me to come and stay with them."

"But if you give me the café, how will you have money? Where is your plane fare and food coming from while you're couch surfing?"

"I'm not a nincompoop, Allie. I've been saving for my retirement for years."

"Retirement?"

"Yes. You know when old people stop working? That's what we call it."

Allie took as deep a breath as her tense body would allow and tilted forward, eventually resting her forehead on the counter. "This is a lot to take in."

"I know." An unusual tenderness crept into her aunt's voice. She placed one warm hand on Allie's back. "But think of it as a good thing. If you take all this over, you're set. You'll always have a place to live and a place to work. The building was paid off years ago, so you're really in a good position. And I'll come back to visit. At some point."

Allie did not want to think about any of this. She wanted a time machine to take her back to twenty minutes ago, when she was admiring her hair in the mirror and clomping down the stairs for what she thought was going to be a perfectly normal day at work.

She straightened up and looked at the clock on the wall. "We have to start prep."

Mindy nodded. "Think about it. We can talk about all this more later. There's no rush."

Allie heaved one more huge sigh and opened the knife drawer.

Tomatoes. She needed to cut up some tomatoes.

—

Allie had never been more thankful for a morning rush. The sparkling fall sunshine and their breakfast special—pumpkin almond scone and a large coffee for seven dollars—meant that the café was jammed with patrons. Almost able to ignore the knot of unease in her stomach, she raced through the morning, assisting the counter staff with orders, pulling batches of scones from the oven and fiddling with the playlist Mindy had chosen when it somehow got stuck in a Crosby, Stills & Nash loop. No one needed that much Crosby, Stills & Nash.

By the time the midafternoon lull came about, she was over her initial shock and starting to grow irritated with Mindy for blindsiding her. When Ren arrived to take over the counter, Allie and Mindy ended up side by side, wrapping cutlery in napkins at the prep station.

"So, is this a sure thing? There's no chance of you changing your mind and just staying here?"

Mindy looked at her with a familiar no-nonsense expression. "Allie. You know me. When have I ever changed my mind after deciding to do something?"

She had a point. Allie hadn't even been born when her aunt had run away to Brooklyn and bought a whole-ass building with the inheritance she got from her grandfather. Everyone in the family thought that Mindy was out of control. Mindy hadn't let that change her path. The café had been open and basically thriving since 1985. Stubbornness could carry a person pretty far. Apparently, it was now going to carry Mindy to Paris.

"How long have you known?" The question occurred to Allie suddenly.

"Known?" Mindy kept her head down.

"Yeah. How long have you known that you were going to leave?"

"Oh. I'm not sure, really."

Allie dropped the fork she was holding and fixed her gaze on her aunt, who was smoothing a napkin around a fork and knife, not meeting her eyes.

"Yes, you do. How long?"

Mindy placed a wrapped set of cutlery on the counter and turned her head slowly. "Six months."

"Six *months*?" Anger churned in her belly. "And you waited that long to tell me?"

Mindy turned her full body toward her niece. "Allie, six months ago, it seemed like maybe you were at a crossroads. I wanted to hang on to see if you'd even *want* to take the café on. I wanted to give you a chance to explore other options if that's what you wanted to do."

"Wh-what do you mean?" Allie sputtered. Her life had been the same nearly every day for the last decade. She was 100 percent sure that she had not been "at a crossroads" six months ago, or at any other time.

"With your music. You were starting that project of yours. I was thinking maybe you'd start playing in a band again, even go on tour."

Allie recoiled. "That project is just for me. I missed playing music. I give the recordings to *George*, for fuck's sake. Did you think he was going to wrangle me a record deal at the seniors' center?"

"I didn't know what you were thinking." Mindy shrugged. "It was the first time I'd seen you playing music since you moved here. I thought you might be ready to make a change. But now I know you're not looking to get back into music, because, yes, I *know* you only give the recordings to George. And knowing that you're not going to be a musician made me think that you were ready to take over the café. You have a real future here. I wanted to make sure you were in a place to accept it."

Even though Allie had essentially just made the same point, hearing Mindy say that she wasn't going to be a musician was like a kick to the shin. The whoosh of panic was back, creating a white noise in her ears that blocked out whatever Mindy was saying.

"I need some air." Supporting herself with one hand on the counter, she moved past her aunt to the front of the café, her eyes locked on the door leading outside.

The door that was suddenly replaced by the hulking figure of Ryan Abernathy.

"Allie Jetski!" A smile split his face, and he held up one hand in an enthusiastic wave. She huffed out a heavy groan of frustration and clenched her hands into fists.

"Shut *up*."

She stormed past him, forcing him to jump out of her way. The last thing she needed right now was this weirdo talking to her.

"Hey!" Ryan shouted as she started up the sidewalk. She turned to see him loping along behind her. "Is everything okay?"

"No!" It felt good to shout, even at someone who probably didn't deserve it.

Ryan caught up to her and matched her pace. "You're fast for a short person." He was breathing heavily from the exertion. She noticed that the smooth skin of his cheeks above his beard had turned an attractive shade of pink. He yanked at the sleeves of the gray wool cardigan he wore over his button-down shirt, pulling it off and draping it over one arm. She slowed her speed slightly. To balance out this momentary softening, she glowered at him. He either didn't notice or didn't care.

"Anything I can do?"

"No."

"Do you want some company?"

She did, actually, but didn't particularly want to admit it. She was used to talking to Mindy at times like this, regaling her aunt with whatever injustice had occurred in her life. But now, with Mindy at the helm of this latest grievance, she had no one to talk to.

They walked side by side for two blocks, both silent. The street was clogged with end-of-day traffic. Taxis jockeyed for position with cyclists at each corner, and people wearing earbuds kept brushing past her, moving quickly toward their homes.

She reluctantly acknowledged that there was something comforting about Ryan's large, good-natured presence beside her. When they came to a stoplight, she paused and looked up at him. Was he ever not smiling?

"Hey, there. Feeling any better?"

"A bit." She did not smile back.

"Well, that's good, then. Would you like a soda?"

"Would I like . . . a *soda*?"

"Yeah." He gestured at the bodega on the corner beside them. "I'm thirsty, and I don't drink soda very often, but it appeals to me in times of crisis."

She squinted at him. "Are you having a crisis?"

"Are *you*?"

She didn't want to answer that question, so instead returned to his previous one. "Okay. I'll have a Coke."

Ryan disappeared into the store, leaving her alone in the waning light wondering just how exactly she got there. She didn't have long to contemplate. Ryan appeared quickly, holding two cans of Coke. He pressed one into her hand and opened the other with a satisfied murmur.

"Would you like to go sit somewhere?" He gestured west. "The park's just over there."

"I know where the park is."

Ryan laughed.

"What?"

"You're prickly."

She sighed. "Sometimes."

He smiled. "I like prickly." He held her gaze, and heat flooded her belly. She looked away.

"Well." She opened her can and took a long swig of the sweet, fizzy liquid. "You definitely came to the right city."

"Don't I know it."

The conversation faded into quiet. Allie watched a father trying to lock his bike without tipping his preschooler out of the child seat on the back. She started to feel silly for having had such a tantrum. She didn't like having the focus on her unruly emotions.

She glanced up at him. "So what show are you working on at Solidarity?"

"*Mixtape Universe.*"

"Oh!" Allie liked *Mixtape Universe*. The podcast had different guests every week and talked them through the creation of a playlist based on songs from significant times in their lives. She liked to listen to it during her early shifts. "That's a good one."

"I'll say! I was an actual fan before I even got the job. The job posting didn't say which show the position was for, but I will admit that I wouldn't have been nearly as excited if it was *Betty on the Left* or *Know Your Plants*. Music has always been my thing. And I majored in journalism at UA."

"Roll Tide." Allie couldn't resist cutting in with a smile. They'd had a barista for a few years who moved to the city after attending the University of Alabama. The school cheer was so catchy all the employees started saying it, which annoyed Mindy in a way that Allie found particularly entertaining.

Ryan shook his head and groaned. "Oh, don't you say that to me!"

"No?" She fixed her face into an innocent expression. "I thought it was a thing."

"You really think a fat music nerd on financial aid was a big college football fan?" He was still smiling, but she thought she saw a brief darkening of his expression.

"Point taken."

"Plus"—he returned to his previous jolly self—"I've been in New York for seven years. Haven't been back once. No tides rolling for me."

They entered the park and settled at a nearby picnic table. In spite of her foul mood, Allie admired the leaves on the trees turning colors and creating a crunchy layer across the expanse of grass. There was a yoga class happening in a large field west of them, a dozen spandex butts moving into the air in perfect unison.

"So, do you want to tell me what's going on?" Ryan was studying her face. She averted her eyes.

"No."

"Maybe you should, though."

"Why?"

"Sometimes it helps to talk to a friend."

"I don't have any friends."

It was weird to say it out loud, but it was true. She had coworkers. Acquaintances. Customers she chatted with. She'd had boyfriends, girlfriends, dates, occasional crushes. But no real *friends*. It was too hard to imagine what would happen if she lost her friends again.

"What? That's bananas. Everyone has friends."

"I don't."

"Since when?"

"Ten and a half years ago."

Ryan clearly wasn't expecting such a specific answer. He tilted his head to one side like a German shepherd confused by a rabbit on a TV screen. "How do you figure?"

She'd said it to shock him, but now she was regretting coming out with a statement that she'd inevitably have to explain. But it turned out that Ryan was quicker than she'd expected.

"Wait!" He smacked the top of the picnic table with his large, fleshy palm. "Was that when the Jetskis broke up?"

Slow talker, fast thinker.

It had been almost a decade since anyone had talked to her about her band, and now here was this guy who wouldn't shut up about it. It made her feel naked. And not in the sexy way.

But he *knew*. Here was a guy—sitting across from her, buying her soda, smiling at her as if she were the only person alive—who already knew. It was as though she'd lived two lives and now she was sitting at a picnic table with someone from her alternate reality. A sting of stress still pulsed behind her eyes but it was quickly changing into something like relief. She hadn't talked about it for so long. She seldom considered it safe to reveal herself to strangers, but Ryan's kind eyes and gentle manners were pulling her in, making her feel like a whole person again.

"Yes." She felt like a kid standing on the high dive at the community pool. Thrilled and terrified. "That was when the Jetskis broke up."

Ryan gave a low whistle, eyes wide. "So, y'all don't keep in touch?"

"That"—she took another sip of her soda—"is an understatement."

"Do you wanna elaborate?" Ryan fidgeted in his seat.

"Well, to make a long story short—"

"You don't have to."

She narrowed her eyes. "Oh, but I want to."

"Go ahead, then. Just please don't leave out anything important." He leaned forward, his elbows on the table.

"Jessi, Ayla and Mimi wanted the band to break up. I didn't. I was not a nice person about it. They all left our practice space after a big fight, and I haven't communicated with any of them since."

Ryan sat back, stunned. "What? Seriously? Like, not even on social media? You haven't sent them a Christmas card? You haven't run into one of them in the frozen food section of the grocery store?"

"Ayla and Mimi have some social media. They don't post much, though. Ayla lives here in the city somewhere, but I've never run into her. I tried to send her a message on Facebook once, but I don't think she uses her account anymore. Mimi moved to Portland, Oregon. She has an Instagram account, but it's private. And Jessi . . ."

This was the part that hurt. She swallowed the lump in her throat. "Jessi just . . . disappeared. She's not on social media or online at all, really. Not as Jessi Jetski or under her real name. She was always the one who wanted to keep our names and identities secret. I guess she kept on doing that. When I search for her online, all I find are old photos of us four from some zine or whatever."

She'd stopped searching. Every dead-end click and nostalgic band photo chipped away at her heart.

Ryan blew out a long exhale. "You must miss them. Especially Jessi."

It was a minute before Allie could speak.

"We were best friends. For a long time."

She couldn't look at Ryan. She stared past him at the people walking through the park and drained the dregs from her soda can.

Twilight was settling over them. She stood up. "I have to get back to work. There's some . . . stuff going on at the café."

Ryan nodded and rose as well. "I should go, too. I'm sure my dinner is waiting for me at home."

There was an involuntary churn of disappointment in her belly. But of course. A guy that nice had to have a partner. Not that she'd expected anything to come of these chance meetings. He was cute, *really* cute, but she wasn't looking for a boyfriend.

"Look." Ryan turned to her as they prepared to part ways on the sidewalk. "If you want to talk about whatever is going on with you, I'm always around. Can I give you my cell number?"

It was becoming clear to Allie that her own life was all she could handle at the moment. She had to get herself together. None of this waltzing around in her past or drinking soda with men in parks on a whim. Better to cut this off now. "I'm good. Have a good night. Thank you for the drink and the walk."

"My pleasure, Jetski."

He saluted her casually, two fingers bouncing off his temple beside those shining eyes.

Chapter Four

"Who's the guy?"

Ren was wiping the counter by the espresso machine when Allie walked in. Besides two tables with patrons tucked behind laptops, the café was empty. Mindy was organizing a pile of saucers that had just come out of the dishwasher, placing them in neat piles on the open shelves behind the cash register.

"No one." Allie moved past them and pressed the release button for the cash drawer with more force than necessary. She removed a stack of twenties and began counting them, smacking each one onto the countertop.

"Not no one." Ren leaned on the counter in front of her. "He knew your name. He chased you up the block."

"He chased you up the block?" Mindy echoed, abandoning the saucers and fixing Allie with an expectant look.

"He didn't *chase me up the block*." She looked down at her stack of cash, hoping they'd give up and stop staring at her. When she glanced back up, two pairs of eyes were still glued to her.

"His name is Ryan. He's a customer." She huffed. "He works at Solidarity. I met him the other day when I did that delivery. He's really annoying. Southern. Thinks everyone is his friend. It's not a big deal."

"I think you're protesting too much." Mindy poked Allie's shoulder and finally went back to the saucer stacking.

"He's cute." Ren tilted their head thoughtfully. "In a lives-at-the-top-of-a-beanstalk kind of way."

Allie swallowed a smile.

"Yes, and he certainly seems to like you." Mindy nodded. Indignance flared in Allie's chest.

"I'm not interested in him. Besides, I have *bigger problems* right now." She looked pointedly at her aunt, who took the hint and closed her mouth.

"Of course you're not interested in him." Ren shrugged. "You're immune to romance."

"What?" Allie shut the cash drawer and whirled around. That wasn't true at all. "I'm fine with romance."

Ren gave a disbelieving snort. "Allie, people come in here all the time checking you out and I have yet to see you go on one date. You hardly give them the time of day. Unless they're in their eighties and demanding Earl Grey."

"To be fair, you've only worked here for a few years. I can confirm that there was romance in the years before."

"That's true." Mindy chose to reenter the conversation from the other side of the room, where she was now busily sweeping up muffin crumbs with the good broom. "There was Jack in 2012. Until, what? 2014?"

"Something like that." Allie was now kicking herself for indulging this line of discussion.

"What was his deal?" Ren leaned on the counter.

"Alcoholic," Mindy and Allie responded in unison. Ren nodded.

Allie shrugged. "Nice guy. Too much trauma. And he just kept getting grumpier."

"Well, that's no good." Ren grinned. "You're grumpy enough on your own."

Allie rolled her eyes. "After him, there was Layla."

"Layla was nice. I liked her." Mindy nodded with enthusiasm.

"What happened with her?" Ren's pointed curiosity was starting to wear on Allie's nerves.

"We just weren't compatible."

Mindy laughed.

"What?"

"Don't you mean she wanted to actually get to know you and have something serious and you freaked out and got all weird and she got tired of it and broke up with you?"

Allie felt a tightness constricting her shoulders. She couldn't deny that what her aunt said was true. Layla kept saying that she wanted to *really connect*, and Allie could only dodge the emotional intimacy for so long. When they'd finally broken up on the platform at the Lexington Avenue station, amid a cloud of mysterious sewage stink and too-nosy onlookers, she'd decided that maybe she was better off staying single.

Ryan's smiling face surfaced in her mind. Yes, he was handsome. And she could admit that it felt good to have someone concerned about her. But that didn't have to mean anything.

"Anyway, Ryan isn't single, so no amount of you two bothering me is going to lead to anything."

"You never know." Mindy shrugged.

Ren nodded. "Guys don't chase girls down the street every day."

"He didn't—" Allie started to protest but gave up as Mindy and Ren dissolved into laughter.

"Oh, fuck this. I'm out of here. I'll be upstairs if you need anything." Allie had reached her limit with their irritating antics.

Her apartment was too hot after hours of the sun streaming through the closed windows, but at least it was empty of other humans. She opened both windows to let in the cool evening air, then collapsed backward onto her bed.

The day had overloaded her senses. She felt like a cartoon character who had always been black and white but was now suddenly colored in with bright-yellow highlighter. She had been so good at not think-ing or talking about her past for so many years, especially after Mindy's Café became her whole life. But now memories were filling her head, and she couldn't get them to leave.

Rolling onto her stomach, she scootched her body forward so she was hanging over the side of the bed. From underneath, she pulled a scrapbook, heavy and full.

She opened it to the first page. A note from Jessi, written in her achingly familiar scrawl, on a piece of notebook paper, fold lines still clearly visible. It had been shoved through the vents in Allie's locker one afternoon in the fall of their senior year.

Hey! Did you study for that stupid calculus test? I did NOT. Also, when are we going to start this band you've been talking about? My cousin knows a girl who drums. Meet me after the test and we can talk about it. My grandma said we could use the garage to practice. XO

That was the start of it all. The first piece of history in this sloppy scrapbook that she couldn't bring herself to throw away.

She flipped the page. Glued there was a photo of their first ever show, in Jessi's grandma's garage, with their setlist on the next page. They'd played three cover songs and one terrible original. Allie smiled. She couldn't remember much of that first song they'd written—they'd scrapped it quickly—but she did remember falling in love with the writing process. The four of them sitting on folding chairs in the garage, instruments plugged into the cheapest amps they could find, piecing together Allie's tentative lyrics and Jessi's lead guitar riffs, while Ayla and Mimi filled in the bass and drum parts.

Why does your grandma have a Jet Ski?

They always poked around the garage while they were taking breaks between practice sets. They never did find out why Jessi's grandma had a Jet Ski in her garage. But that mystery provided them with their band name (after a bitter fight when Ayla insisted that they should definitely be called the Esther Greenwoods after the lead character in a book she was obsessed with), and that same Jet Ski was on the cover of their first record. Allie flipped through another few pages of show posters and tour photos. She stopped on a review clipped from *Flipside* magazine, running her fingers over the tiny black-and-white album cover beside it.

> What the Jetskis lack in technical expertise they make up for in charming enthusiasm and clever songwriting. The poetic, political lyrics reminiscent of the Clash are skillfully shout-sung by lead vocalist Jessi Jetski and echoed in the soothing backing vocals of her complementary opposite, Allie Jetski. The band is poised to become a major player on the indie punk scene, with a fall tour already booked and interest from several reputable indie labels. Not bad for a bunch of teenage girls.

Not bad for a bunch of teenage girls, indeed. Allie closed the scrapbook quickly. At that time in their lives, everything felt possible. They had nothing to lose.

And then four years later, it all ended. She hadn't been ready.

She jammed the scrapbook back under her bed and pushed herself off in the direction of her guitar. She strummed a few exploratory chords before she clicked the spacebar to wake up her laptop. She could finish her recording of "We Belong" tonight if she just got the lead guitar parts right and then added the vocals. It wasn't as if she had anything else to do. And it would take her mind out of that scrapbook, drown out the whispers of her past. She clicked Record.

What did it mean, she wondered, to *belong to the light and the thunder*? Did Pat Benatar just mean that being with the right person made you feel as if you belonged to the whole universe? As if there was something larger than yourself keeping you safe? Allie had never had a relationship like that. Except for the one she'd had with Jessi, and that was a creative relationship, never romantic. She doubted she'd ever find anyone, friend or lover, who could compete with the sense of excitement and belonging that she'd had whenever she was with Jessi.

By midnight, the cover of "We Belong" was finished and burned to a CD for George. Allie was proud of this one. A perfect version of a song about belonging, recorded by someone who was suddenly unsure of where she belonged.

Chapter Five

"Mindy!" Allie called to her aunt as she kicked her way into the kitchen through the back door. "Mindy! You owe me! You owe me *huge!*"

No one was there. Assuming Mindy was in the office, she prattled on a little louder. "I got the knob for the stove. Boy was *that* an ordeal! But!" She dropped the heavy tote bags she'd been lugging. "I went to see Paolo at the market because, you know, I was already in the neighborhood, and he had these awesome pie pumpkins, and he gave me the best deal on them. At least I had extra bags with me, but I still looked bonkers riding my bike carrying ten pumpkins in bags hanging off of me everywhere!"

Still no answer or response of any kind to her monologue. She peered into the office. It was also empty.

"Mindy? She walked through to the front café space.

"Allie Jetsk-uhhh, Allie Andrews! Hello!"

Ryan Abernathy was in the café. Again.

"Hello, Allie!" It was George. Ryan was sitting across from George. In her spot. "Ryan and I were just talking about you!"

"I didn't know you were doing an '80s cover song project." Ryan leaned back in his chair and grinned at her. Goose bumps instantly covered her arms. She cursed her traitor of a body and shifted uncomfortably from one foot to the other.

She scowled. "That's because I didn't tell you. And what are you doing here anyway?" She looked past him at George, who had a wide smile on his face.

"Who made your tea, George?"

"I did." Ren appeared from behind Allie, carrying a bin of dirty dishes.

"Ren did just fine." George caught Allie's eye and shook his head briefly and stuck out his tongue.

"George, I saw that!" Ren rolled their eyes. "You're impossible. I do it exactly like Allie does."

"I guess Allie's just special." George nudged Ryan's arm. "Don't you think she's special?"

"Oh yes. There was never any doubt from me. *Very* special." He looked at her again, his eyes dancing around. He obviously grasped how uncomfortable this entire situation was making her. And for some reason, he found that hilarious.

"Where's Mindy?" Allie asked Ren, ignoring everyone else.

"She went to get some more pie pumpkins."

"Dammit!"

Feeling defeated, Allie slumped into the seat next to George. The old man patted her shoulder gently.

"Looks like you've had quite a day."

Allie shrugged and sighed deeply. Ryan slid his plate across the table to her. A very tempting chocolate chip cookie sat on the plate, untouched.

"Thank you." She slid it back toward him. "But I skipped lunch, and I'm so hungry that if I eat a cookie, my blood sugar will go bananas."

"You should come for dinner at my place." Ryan said this with a casual air that made her think it was common practice for him to invite near-strangers to his home for meals. Was this just normal for him? Was it weird that she thought it was weird? Ignoring her silence and furrowed brow, Ryan went on. "George! You should come, too!"

George waved his hand dismissively. "Thank you, my boy, but it's lasagna night at the residence. Can't miss it."

"I get that! Who doesn't love a good lasagna. Allie?"

"Yeah, lasagna's okay."

Ryan chuckled. The hearty sound made her cheeks warm, even though she knew he was laughing at *her*.

"I mean, do you want to come for dinner?"

"Oh. Uh . . ."

Not especially.

But she also didn't want to haul her uninspired self into the café kitchen to throw together yet another mediocre sandwich.

"Don't worry." Ryan leaned back in his chair and put both hands behind his head. His foot touched hers under the table, and she quickly tucked her legs under her chair. "I'm not cooking. I'm the cleanup guy. Anisha does all the cooking, and she's real good at it."

Anisha. Oh yes. The girlfriend. Maybe wife? Ryan didn't wear a ring, but that didn't always mean anything. Allie was starting to feel a little sick. She did not want to care whether he was married or not. She was about to refuse his invitation and start planning her evening of solitary sandwich eating when George spoke.

"Is Anisha your girlfriend?"

Ryan laughed at that. "Oh, no. Not that kind of thing. Roommate. Good friend as well. Not romantic."

He looked at Allie as he said the last sentence. She became very interested in a circular stain on the wooden tabletop.

George finished his tea and stood up shakily. "Ah! A single guy. Nothing wrong with that. I was once a hit with the ladies as well."

"Not hard to believe, in your case!" Ryan stood up and took the older man's elbow. "But I have to clarify that I am not now, nor have I ever been, a hit with the ladies."

George waved his hand as if he didn't believe this, and Ryan helped him navigate the closely packed tables and chairs on his way out.

When George had been safely delivered to the door, Ryan sat back down across from Allie.

"So, what about it? Dinner?"

"With you and your roommate?"

"My roommate who is a very good cook, yes. And she never minds if I bring home a friend to eat with us."

"I told you, I don't have friends."

"Do you have dinner companions?"

Allie stared at him. He held her gaze. How did a man have eyelashes that long, anyway? Her stomach rumbled.

She sighed. "Okay. Just this one time."

"Awesome!" He clapped his hands. "It's about a twenty-minute walk if you're up for that. Or we could take the train."

"Walking's fine."

She grabbed a sweater and her small hipsack full of essentials and said goodbye to Ren, ignoring their blatant stare as she and Ryan left the café together.

The setting sun cast a golden glow over the block as they walked west, making intricate patterns of light and shade around the fire escapes of the tall brick building on the corner. True to his overly friendly nature, Ryan stopped to pet a docile Great Dane, gray with black spots and a red kerchief, tethered to a bike rack. It occurred to Allie that they were both gentle giants.

When Ryan stood to walk again, he almost fell over a metal trash can. Instinctively, Allie reached out for his elbow and tugged him toward her, out of the way. They stopped walking for a second, and he looked down at her.

"Hey." His voice was soft. "Thanks for that."

They were standing so close together. And she was going to his apartment. How had she ended up here? She dropped his arm and took a step back.

"Be more careful. We can't have you falling and crushing people's dogs."

"Aw," Ryan looked back at the Dane. "BamBam can probably handle himself."

"BamBam?"

"Yeah, that's what his tag said."

Allie narrowed her eyes at him. "You pay an alarming amount of attention to very small details."

"It's one of my many alarming superpowers."

Allie laughed in spite of herself. Her shoulders started to relax as she allowed herself to enjoy Ryan's company and look forward to the free dinner on offer. An actual dinner made in a kitchen with multiple ingredients, served hot. She didn't know the last time she'd experienced that.

Ryan spent the rest of their walk chattering about the dishes his roommate liked to cook—ratatouille, tahdig, pad see ew—and then segueing to some minor gossip from the podcast studio about cohosts fighting over a new theme song.

"How about you?" Ryan asked as they rounded a corner, swerving around a riot of plastic flowers on display outside a Dollar Junction. "Any scandalous workplace gossip?"

The conversation she'd had with Mindy about her retirement echoed in her head. Did that count as drama? Allie's eyes followed a man on a bright-green Vespa whizzing by them, darting in and out of traffic.

"Nope," she finally responded. "Mindy is the most no-drama person there ever was. And that just sets the tone for everyone else. Ren's had crappy jobs before, and they are just always happy to be working in a place where they're respected and taken care of. We have a few other very part-time filler staff, but they're all students and just . . . chill."

"And Mindy is your aunt? Right?" he asked. "Is the whole family low-drama?"

This made Allie bark with bitter laughter. "Oh, no. No, no, no. But that's a story for another time. Or a longer walk. Definitely a few high-drama types in our family's past."

"Well, that's most families, I guess." Ryan shrugged.

Allie looked up at him in time to see a flicker in his usual cheery countenance. She was curious but didn't pry. They hardly knew each other.

A welcome and pleasant silence fell over them for the remainder of the walk. After they'd turned onto a quiet, leafy street, Ryan stopped at a well-maintained concrete stoop and nodded toward a security door made of decorative curving iron filigree.

"This is it." He unlocked the door and gestured for her to ascend the stairs. On the third floor, he stopped at apartment 306 and unlocked the door to reveal a tidy foyer opening into a large, warm space.

Ryan took her jacket and hung it on a hook by the door, alongside the most glamorous collection of coats Allie had ever seen. Every material, color and pattern she could think of were represented. Ryan saw her gawking.

"Ah yes, Anisha's wardrobe is one of a kind," he explained as he led her farther into the apartment.

Allie wasn't sure what she was expecting to find. A college bachelor pad, maybe? Broken IKEA furniture and dead plants? A man who remembered her from shows at a dirty Southern punk venue did not strike her as someone who would have invested a lot of money into home decor.

Whatever she was picturing, the room she found herself in was definitely not it.

The walls were the kind of exposed brick that Allie thought only appeared in the fake New York apartments seen on TV. She'd never actually been in a place that had them, but here they were. And the ceilings were so high; it was like a one-room museum. She was used to living in what was almost a crawl space. It suited her five-foot-two frame just fine, but someone like Ryan would barely fit in her bedroom. Not that Ryan would ever have a reason to be in her bedroom.

And the windows. Each tall window provided a generous view of Brooklyn's charming dusk. There was not a single broken piece of

IKEA furniture to be seen, just a collection of items that looked as if they were from one of Brooklyn's finer vintage furniture shops. And all the plants—there were a lot of plants—were clearly thriving. String of pearls and pothos draped their way down the tall shelves, and verdant spider plants hung in macramé hangers by each window. She followed Ryan into the large living area. Something smelled delicious. She detected rosemary. And garlic. And so many other things she couldn't identify but wanted to eat immediately.

"Holy shit." She spoke quietly, but Ryan still heard her.

"Yep." He nodded. "My apartment is fancier than me." He pointed at a closed door with an iron knob. "My room's over there. It's the smaller one. Bathroom's there, right past the entry. And Anisha's room is at the other end."

The large room where they stood had kitchen cabinets and appliances along the wall nearest to Anisha's room. Just in front of the kitchen space, a long rectangular wooden table sat surrounded by an array of mismatched chairs. Ryan flopped down on the long brown leather couch, its scuffed and weathered surface home to a pile of blankets and throw pillows of various shapes. "Have a seat! Dinner will probably be ready soon."

Allie perched on the edge of an Eames lounge chair that wobbled precariously. Seeing her startle and grip the armrest, Ryan sat up. "Oh yeah, that chair was Anisha's uncle's. It's more for show." He gestured to a nondescript armchair with a matching ottoman on the other side of the room. "That one is not as hip but way more comfortable."

Already feeling self-conscious, Allie considered staying in the wobbly lounger but gave up quickly and scurried over to the better option. Ryan was right. It was much more comfortable. She leaned back cautiously.

Just as she'd tentatively raised her feet up onto the ottoman, the door by the kitchen flew open and a gorgeous woman in a very dramatic, multicolored floor-length caftan burst into the room.

"Oh shit!" The woman—Anisha, Allie supposed—shouted as she went right for the stove and lifted the lid of a cast-iron Dutch oven that was steaming on top of it. "I had to get out of my jeans or I was going to die. But dinner is"—she bent to open the main oven, releasing more steam and a wave of the aroma that had greeted them, and then sang the rest of her sentence—"allllllmoooooost reeeeeeadyyyyyyy!"

Ryan grinned and called out across the room. "Anisha! I brought a guest!" He pointed one hand toward each of them. "Allie Andrews, meet Anisha Patel."

Anisha slammed the oven door and stood up abruptly, her gaze zeroing in on Allie, who raised one hand in an awkward wave.

"Allie with the band?" Anisha said, hustling toward them, wiping her hands on a tea towel as she went. Her accent softened the *w* into a smooth *v* sound.

Allie shot a withering look at big-mouthed Ryan and stood up to offer her hand to Anisha. "Allie from the *coffee shop*."

Anisha tilted her head to one side and looked questioningly at Ryan, who shrugged. Allie released Anisha's hand with a resigned sigh. "Okay, also from the band. But that was a long time ago."

"Well, if he was a mere boy of nineteen when he was watching you, it was definitely a long-ass time ago." Anisha flicked the tea towel at Ryan. An impressive snap rang through the air between them as the towel came in contact with his shoulder. He scowled but couldn't keep it up for very long before he broke into a grin.

"Must you always choose violence?"

"It's my favorite way of communicating, you know that."

It was rare for Allie to immediately warm to someone, but she couldn't help herself with Anisha. It was a magnetic draw that reminded her of when she first met Jessi in their freshman year when they were assigned lockers next to each other. Right from that moment, Allie would have done anything for the cool new friend with the half-shaved head and the engaging sneer.

"Allie?"

Allie's head snapped toward Ryan. "Sorry, what?"

"Do you want something to drink? Wine? Soda? Water?"

Allie wanted wine. She hesitated for a moment. Wine often made her overly talkative, and she wasn't sure she wanted to become Chatty Allie in front of two people who were essentially strangers. But her eye caught Anisha's kind expression and she uncharacteristically threw caution to the wind. "Wine would be great, thanks."

"Dinner's ready anyway, so we can move to the table." Anisha gently cuffed Ryan's head as she turned back toward the kitchen, messing up his neatly combed hair. He smoothed it back into place and caught Allie's eye.

"See?" He gestured at his head with his index finger. "Violence!"

Allie followed them to the table. She chose a wooden chair with aged white paint and a striped cushion on the seat. Ryan sat beside her, at a respectable distance. Anisha moved to the opposite side of the table, which was scattered with tealight candles that complemented the soft light from various lamps around the room. She insisted on serving them, ladling a silky orange soup into bright-blue bowls.

Allie closed her eyes and breathed in the scent, cumin and cinnamon and something else that she couldn't place. It put her usual sandwich-and-apple dinners to shame immediately.

"It's squash soup," Anisha said. "Nothing fancy, but then, I didn't know we were having company. And those are roasted potatoes. We have a little herb garden on our balcony, but most of the plants have given up and succumbed to autumn. Rosemary likes the cold, though, so I'm putting it in everything. Let me know if there's too much on those potatoes."

Everything was delicious, perfectly seasoned. Allie was suddenly overwhelmed by the whole experience of being there for dinner, watching Ryan and Anisha joke with each other in the light of the candles, steam from the soup floating up past the casual, happy expressions on their faces.

This must be normal for them.

Allie couldn't imagine it. Someone making dinner every night. A person across the table to recap the day with. She took a gulp of her wine.

"Do you cook every night?" She directed the question to Anisha, who was scooping seconds of potatoes onto her plate.

"Uh-huh." Anisha jerked her thumb in Ryan's direction. "He cleans up. It's way easier now that he has a more regular schedule and a job close to home. Our dinner schedule was ridiculous before he got the podcast job. He worked as an usher at two theaters in Manhattan. Totally different schedule every week. He either ate early or heated up leftovers late when he got home. We both like this better."

"It's nice." Allie drank more wine. "You're more than roommates, really."

Anisha nodded enthusiastically. "Platonic life partners. That's what I always tell him we are."

Ryan laughed. "I know, I'm spoiled, I shouldn't complain. But Jesus, more than once she's said that to a lady I brought home and scared them right away."

"You're exaggerating!" Anisha waved her hand at him and shook her head.

"Nuh-uh. What about Gemma? You freaked her out when you got me to do your laundry that time. Never saw her again after she found me folding your unmentionables."

"Are you sure she wasn't just put off by your irritating personality?" Anisha asked, with mock sweetness.

Allie wondered how many ladies Ryan brought home on a regular basis. She remembered what he'd said to George back at the café.

"He was just insisting that he is not a ladies' man," she said, smiling innocently and taking a sip from her glass.

"Ha!" Anisha grinned as she scooped more potatoes onto her plate. "He sure goes on a lot of dates for someone who isn't."

Ryan cleared his throat and crossed his arms over his chest. "First dates," he muttered.

"What was that?" Anisha held a hand up to her ear.

Ryan narrowed his eyes. "I said I go on a lot of first dates. Then, as you kindly put it, I apparently drive them away with my irritating personality."

Anisha's eyes softened, and she held Ryan's gaze. "Hey. I was joking. And anyway, you're usually the one that breaks it off before the girls do. I don't think those ladies get to know you enough to learn how truly irritating you are."

Ryan gestured toward Anisha and looked at Allie. "And there you have it, folks! My ever-loving platonic life partner! Who thinks I'm deeply irritating, apparently."

"I'm sure Allie thinks you're irritating, too." Anisha said, standing up. "You're lucky she's now met me. You may actually get to see her again. More wine, Allie?"

Allie smiled. The two of them were fascinating. She slid her glass forward.

"Sure. Why not?"

Chapter Six

"None of them?"

Two hours later, Allie, who had absolutely been planning to leave as soon as dinner was finished, was reclining comfortably in the non-tippy armchair, nursing her third glass of wine. Anisha and Ryan shared the couch, their various limbs sprawled over throw pillows.

"None of them," Allie confirmed.

"Not even Jessi?" Anisha could not believe that Allie had lost touch with all of her bandmates. "But you said she was your best friend!"

"She was." Something about being made to talk about the band for what felt like the fiftieth time that week had defeated Allie's defenses. Safely ensconced in this cozy apartment, with these two people who wanted her to talk, made her braver.

That and the wine.

"Okay, I admit that I'd never heard of your band until Ryan showed up excited about meeting you last week, but I'm all in now. What a story. You started touring when you were eighteen?"

"Yep. Right out of high school. My mom was kind of an asshole." Allie paused. "Not kind of. My mom was a huge asshole. Like, bitter that my dad died, and just lonely and sad and drunk and mean. And then she got sick." Allie swallowed. "And . . . she died. Cancer. But by the time that happened, I wasn't living there anymore. We weren't close. I was sad, but maybe not as sad as I should have been." It was more than she usually admitted. Even to Mindy, who knew full well what a rotten parent her own sister had been, Allie was always careful to make things seem not that bad. Her mom kept her fed and clothed. She worried that she'd seem like a brat if she complained that her mom just never seemed to *like* her.

"When the band started to gain momentum, I basically just moved out of my mom's apartment and into a tour van. I lived with Jessi during our downtime. And then after my mom died, I lived with Jessi all the time. Jessi's mom was an asshole, too, but she lived with her grandma, who was amazing. We'd show up in the middle of the night after driving for hours to get home at the end of a tour, and then we'd crash and wake up at noon the next day. Jessi's grandma would be waiting in the kitchen for us, and she'd have made us huge bowls of udon soup. After eating all the shitty food we ate on tour, I would drive all the way home thinking about that soup."

She could picture Jessi's grandma's kitchen, with its bamboo place-mats and bright-yellow curtains. The steam from the pots of broth and noodles fogging up the sliding doors that led to the peaceful garden out back. She and Jessi always sat in the same spots, across from each other at the shiny wooden dining table, grinning while Jessi's grandma scolded them for not eating enough. As if they were sisters who had been sitting there all their lives.

She dragged her mind back into the present. "Anyway, soup or no soup, I was always ready to be on the road again."

"And Jessi? Did she like being on the road, too?"

"At first." Allie ignored the voice in her head that always urged her to clam up when she got to this part of the story. It was hiding behind a thick curtain of red wine. "But later she met a girl— Jasmine, her name was—and fell in love, and then she didn't want to tour anymore."

Allie met Ryan's eyes. He hadn't asked any questions, but he was listening intently. The open affection in his expression caused a plume of adrenaline to rush through her. She looked away from him quickly.

"But I don't get it." Anisha sat forward, abandoning her nest of pillows for a moment. "Why are you not still friends?"

Allie exhaled with force and looked at the ceiling. Here it was. The part of the story that hurt the most.

"I fucked it up."

Allie looked at her new friends on the couch across from her. Anisha's feet were tucked up against Ryan's leg. They were both waiting for her to continue.

"I didn't think the relationship was serious, and I told her she was messing up everything we'd worked so hard for all because of some girl. I was jealous. Not because I was in love with Jessi, but because I guess I thought that we were, like . . . I don't know . . ."

"Platonic life partners?" Ryan offered.

Allie smiled at him. "Yeah. Something like that. Anyway . . ." She downed the last of her wine and put the glass gently on the coffee table. "I was awful to her. She was already getting tired of touring. She wanted to be at home near her grandma and have, like, a normal life, I guess. But I didn't listen to her. I just said all kinds of mean and dismissive things and then told her that if she chose her girlfriend over our band, then I didn't want to have anything else to do with her." She looked from Anisha to Ryan and back again. Neither of them seemed to be thinking that she was an irredeemable monster, so she continued.

"Mimi and Ayla didn't want to get in the middle of it, but they also didn't want to be in the band without Jessi. Plus, they saw how I was acting like a shithead, so they just bailed, too. So, since I had no friends left in Jersey, I packed up my one bag of stuff and moved to Brooklyn. Mindy gave me an apartment and a job. That was ten years ago, and nothing much has changed since."

Anisha collapsed back into her pile of pillows. "Shit, Allie. That's intense."

Allie nodded. "Yup."

"You must have really loved your band."

Allie froze. It wasn't the reaction she was expecting. She'd thought Ryan or Anisha would say something along the lines of *We all make mistakes* or *You were young*. The kinds of things Mindy used to say before she gave up asking Allie to talk about what had happened.

"I did. I did love my band." Allie's throat got thick, and her eyes burned. She coughed and straightened in her chair.

"I loved your band, too." Ryan stood up and walked toward a shelf between the two windows that held an impressive record collection as well as the record player itself and two large speakers. He flipped through some of the albums and then pulled out the first Jetskis record. The cover showed them all standing around the Jet Ski from Jessi's grandma's garage. They'd pushed it out into the street and taken the photo at sunset. The suburban Fort Lee neighborhood stretched out behind them. The streetlights had just come on, and the sky was orange.

Ryan pulled the album out of its sleeve and held it above the turntable. "Do you mind?"

Allie shrugged. "Go ahead, I guess."

Anisha sat forward, excited. "Amazing! Play it!"

Taking care not to touch the grooves, he laid it on the turntable, lowered the cover and pressed a button on the front. Allie heard a few seconds of static from the speakers, and then the first notes of her lead guitar riff for "You're So Strange" filled the room.

She hadn't heard their songs for years. Jessi's loud, aggressive vocals filled her with a fizzy excitement, and then, as her own melodic voice came in as the backing vocals, she felt instantly wistful for the way their voices worked in tandem. They hardly ever had to talk about it. The songs just *worked*.

Anisha looked at her with wide eyes. "You were *good*."

Ryan, who was still standing by the record player, nodded. "Damn straight they were good."

Allie didn't know what to say. She smiled and sat still, listening to the album for the first time in years. They'd only had enough money for one day in the studio, so they hadn't spent much time correcting takes unless an error had ruined a song. The tiny mistakes they made during the recording were now so familiar they seemed like intentional parts of the songs. The album was a time capsule, all of their emotion and excitement frozen on vinyl forever. She'd thought it would hurt more to hear it. But Anisha and Ryan were right, it was *good*. Listening was a sweet kind of pain, like a mouthful of sour candy.

They listened in silence for a few songs. Anisha offered more wine, and Allie declined, already feeling too buzzed from what she'd consumed.

"You know . . ." Anisha leaned forward to fill her own glass and then flopped back onto the couch and took a long sip. "Ryan's always wanted to be in a band."

"Yeah?" Allie looked at him, her eyes full of questions. "What do you play?"

"Nothing!" His strong, husky laugh filled the room. "But in my daydreams, I learn the drums."

"Because of 'Doctor Worm.'" Anisha nodded.

"'Doctor Worm'?" Allie looked from Ryan to Anisha. "What's that?"

"'Doctor Worm'!" Ryan seemed to think repetition would explain it. "You know the song by They Might Be Giants? About the worm who wants to play the drums?"

Allie laughed. "Wait, I might actually know that song. I think it was on one of the mixtapes we used to play in the van on tour. Doctor Worm isn't a real doctor, but he is a real worm?"

"That's it!" Ryan smiled. "*I'm* not a doctor or a worm. Or a drummer, for that matter."

"I'm sure you could learn if you wanted." He looked like a drummer. She could easily imagine him, brow furrowed, sticks in hand, cheeks pink from the exertion. His large, firm hands holding the sticks, muscles flexing in his forearms. Was she blushing?

Nope. This is not going to turn into a crush.

"Maybe someday." Ryan winked at her, and her insides turned to goo.

No.

She had enough problems.

When the album ended and she discovered with a shock that it was nearly 11 p.m., she collected her jacket and purse and said thank you and goodbye to Anisha.

"I can walk you home," Ryan said, reaching for his coat.

"No!" Allie protested quickly. "I mean, it's an easy walk, and the streets are still full of people. Not dangerous at all. And to be honest"— she held up her phone, headphone wires cascading down—"I kind of like to walk and listen to music after, uh, busy evenings."

Ryan nodded. "I get it. You need some introvert time. But just— Can I see your phone for a minute?" He held out his hand. Allie slowly placed her phone in his palm. He tapped on the screen and then typed something with his thumbs and handed it back.

"I know you said you didn't want my number, but I really do need you to text me to let me know you got home safe. Otherwise, I'll feel weird."

Allie felt a heat gather in her chest, and she bit back a smile. "I suppose that's okay."

"Good," he said. He put his hands in his pockets and rocked back and forth on his heels.

"Good." She bit her lip. "See you. I mean, maybe."

He smiled. "See you maybe."

The idea of Anisha and Ryan becoming her friends was less terrifying than she expected. They seemed to actually like her, even after she told them how awful she'd been to her bandmates. As she left the apartment, a wave of cautious happiness washed over her. Opening the music app on her phone, she searched "Jetskis" and clicked Play. The ghost of her past self filled her ears as she stepped out into the lively nighttime streets of Brooklyn.

Chapter Seven

"I'll do it. I'll take over the café."

Allie looked at herself in the mirror as she spoke. She was not convinced by her own declaration. She had approximately five minutes left on this brief respite from work before the produce order arrived. She huffed out a frustrated breath and tried again.

"Okay. I will take over the café. But I'm changing the name to Allie's Café."

That felt even more absurd. She didn't want to change the name of the café. She wasn't even sure she wanted to take it over. But maybe if she said it a few more times while watching her face in the mirror, she would start to feel as if it was true.

"Mindy, I've decided I will . . . Aw, fuck this." Allie shook her head and picked up her hairbrush from the ledge under her mirror. She brushed her hair back into a ponytail and smoothed her hands down her canary-yellow jumpsuit. She assessed the rest of her look—blue socks, red high-top sneakers and a new red bandanna that Ren had grabbed for her at a consignment shop—with pleasure. At least her outfit schedule remained reliable. As she left her apartment, she appreciated the beat of her sneakers hitting each of the back stairs in a comfortable and familiar rhythm. The delivery truck driver was knocking on the kitchen door as she arrived.

Once she and Ren had hauled in all the boxes of lettuce and tomatoes and whatever else had caught Mindy's eye on the weekly order
form, they both leaned up against the prep counter to gulp down large
glasses of ice water. The autumn weather was cooling, but it made no
difference when they had to carry a whole load of heavy boxes into the
kitchen while the ovens were on.

"Where is Mindy, anyway?" Allie asked, setting her empty glass in
the dishwasher.

"Dentist." Ren refilled their own glass. "Why? Do you need her?"

"Naw." Allie was relieved but kept her face neutral. "I'm good."

"That guy is here."

"What guy?"

"The tall one with the beard."

Allie went still. "Ryan?"

Ren nodded. "He got here right before the order arrived. Says he
wants to see you, but not to rush. He's trying the new cookies."

Besides cookies, what did Ryan want? She'd told him the story of
the band breaking up; she'd humored him by accepting his dinner
invitation, and now she had no idea why he was back at the café. Was
he just being . . . friendly?

I'm so out of practice when it comes to having friends.

Allie shook her head and tightened her ponytail, then made her
way out to the front on slightly shaky legs.

Ryan was seated at a table by the window, leaning back with his
long legs stretched out to one side. His face broke into an inviting
smile when he saw her, brown eyes crinkling at the corners.

Allie felt her stomach flip and then dug her nails into one palm to bring
herself back to reality. This was not the time for a crush. Not when she
could hardly sleep at night for worrying about her future at the café. Not
when everything she'd depended on for years was suddenly shaken up.

"Allie!" Ryan wiped his mouth with a napkin and gestured at the
empty chair across from him. "Do you have time to sit down?"

Ren was at the counter, and the café was quiet, so she nodded and sat down.

"Hi." He smiled at her.

"Hi."

"I think we need to find Jessi."

Allie physically recoiled. She squinted at him in confusion. The silence was filled with Carole King declaring that it was too late, baby—Mindy had been in charge of the playlist that morning.

"What?"

"Sorry, that was abrupt." He sat up a bit straighter. "How are you?"

"Ryan, I don't think you can backpedal from that statement into pleasantries."

He grinned. "As you wish. So . . . we need to find Jessi."

"Why?" Allie's heart was hammering at the thought.

"You never had any closure with her. I bet if you find her and talk to her, you'll feel better about the whole thing." He pushed his plate of two cookies toward her. "These raspberry oat ones are my favorite so far. Want one?"

Allie could not think of a thing to say. She leaned forward, broke a piece off and put it into her mouth. He watched her chew, staying quiet, while she thought through this harebrained idea.

"And then what?"

"What do you mean, and then what?" Now Ryan looked confused.

"And then what? So I feel better, so what?"

"Allie." Ryan looked at her with gentle eyes.

"Ryan." She mimicked his tone perfectly.

He laughed. "Okay, I might be wrong, but do you think that maybe you might . . . want to play music again? As in, write songs and play shows? I know you're recording covers for your project—which, by the way, I really want to hear sometime—but I'm talking about playing music the way you used to. Maybe you want to be in a band? It might help if you stopped feeling terrible every time you thought about what happened when you *used* to be in a band."

Allie sat back again. "Huh." The way he put it made it actually seem possible. She took another piece of his cookie, chewed and swallowed. "You might have a point. But I think you're underestimating Jessi's desire to not be found. It was her idea that we all use Jetski for our last names so we couldn't easily be identified. She wanted us to have that level of control over our own story. Totally dedicated to the DIY punk ethos. She's probably booking acts for a basement club somewhere, having to turn away bands in droves because everyone wants to play at her exclusive and rad place."

"And I think *you're* underestimating the punk scene, and frankly, I think you're underestimating lesbians."

Allie almost choked on the cookie. "You think I'm underestimating *lesbians?*"

Ryan ignored her question. "When you played in the band, didn't everyone know someone who knew someone you'd already met? Didn't each venue tell you who to find and who to watch out for at the next venue in the next town? Didn't everyone who had been in a band eventually join another band with someone from someone else's previous band?"

"Okay, sure, yeah. That makes sense. But . . . lesbians?"

"Look, I'm not personally a lesbian."

This time, Allie did choke on a crumb as she emitted a surprised laugh. Ryan waited while she retrieved a glass of water from the kitchen and sat back down. "As I was saying," he continued, "I'm no lesbian, but Anisha is queer, and what I know from her is that queer people work just like music people. Everybody knows everybody. The lady on the *L Word* show had a whole chart about it. And since Jessi is queer and a punk, and if you are pretty sure she's still in the scene, I don't see how we could *not* find her. It will just take some askin'."

Allie was compelled to agree with him on most of his points. She didn't think it was going to be quite as simple as he predicted, but she would never have thought of just *talking to people* to find Jessi.

Allie didn't keep in touch with anyone from her music days anymore. Even people she'd thought of as friends, the occasional club booker or music writer she'd gotten along with especially well, seemed to just fade away after she wasn't "the girl in the band" anymore. Fans and scenesters had short memories.

Except Ryan, but he is obviously a weirdo.

She was also paranoid, at least right after the split, that people had heard what a jerk she'd been and didn't want anything more to do with her. She really didn't try. Music had been her whole life, and she'd just let it go like a balloon on a string.

"I don't have any contacts or anything, if that's what you're thinking," she told Ryan. "With punks *or* with lesbians."

Ryan grinned his slow, confident grin that she was beginning to enjoy in spite of herself. He always looked right into her eyes. "Leave that to me."

"Yeah?"

He leaned forward and held her gaze. "Yeah. Anisha and I both want to help."

"Why?"

Ryan sat back again, his face contorted with confusion. "Why?"

"Yeah." Allie folded her hands on the tabletop. "Why do you want to do this?"

"Huh." Ryan looked off over Allie's shoulder. It didn't seem to have occurred to him that anyone might wonder why he was willing to insert himself into their business. "Well, I guess because we both like you, and we're both pretty intrigued by the story of your band. And, as far as my own reasons . . ." His gaze moved back to her. "I just want you to feel better and play music again. Selfish, really. I want to hear the music you make in the future."

Allie's mouth was dry. A buzzy, nervous excitement made its way through her body. The fact that someone other than George was enthusiastic about her potential future musical projects was overwhelming.

And yet Ryan didn't even seem to think it was a big deal. He'd been texting her daily since they'd exchanged numbers, acting as if they were already friends. As if it was just meant to be. It was almost too much. She stared at him, trying to decide whether she wanted to go farther down this rabbit hole of unexpected companionship. Finally, she nodded.

"Okay, let's do it."

Ryan pumped his fist in the air before the sentence was fully out of her mouth. She held out her hand, as if she were asking an overexcited puppy to lie down. "I have one condition."

"Okay, ma'am." The glow in Ryan's warm eyes did not dim. "What's your condition?"

"You start learning to play the drums."

Ryan's boisterous fidgeting stopped, and his mouth fell open. It was fun to shock him. His unflappable demeanor was an entertaining challenge for Allie.

"I start to what now?"

"The drums. You start learning to play the drums. Or something. Play a fucking xylophone, for all I care. If you are making me do something scary and potentially disastrous, you can do something slightly less scary and less potentially disastrous."

Ryan watched her curiously, and she locked eyes with him, making sure he knew she was deadly serious. Sunshine from the window, filtered through the orange and yellow leaves of the tree just outside the café, lit up his face and shoulders in a constantly moving pattern of light and shade.

"Okay." He brought the palm of his hand down on the table, with just enough force to make the dishes clink. "I'm in. If you're going to get some closure on the passions of your past, I can get a start on the passions of my future."

Allie looked at him, struggling to keep a straight face as her lips curled into a smile. "That was really cheesy."

Ryan laughed. "Tough crowd! You can take the girl out of the punk scene, but apparently, the attitude remains."

She felt a fizz of pleasure in her belly as he teased her, and the air between them suddenly seemed charged. She quickly looked away, out the window, adrenaline shooting through her system. She may not have dated anyone for a few years, but she knew that *look*.

He reached across the table and took her hand in his. She looked up at him as her heart pounded in her chest. She closed her eyes for what felt like an awkward amount of time, allowing the warm feeling to flood her body.

For a brief moment, she felt herself standing on an emotional ledge. She could take the leap, squeeze Ryan's hand and tell him *I like you*, and see what happened next. She was surprised by how tempting that option was. Tempting, but terrifying. Most of the people Allie had loved had left her. And now her aunt, the one person she thought would stick around forever out of familial obligation, was also leaving her. She could not handle another abandonment, especially from someone she was starting to like. A lot.

She jerked her hand back toward herself as though she'd just burned it on the stove.

Ryan's face fell. His smile seemed to deflate before her eyes. "Allie, I—"

"It's okay!" Her voice was louder than she meant it to be. "It's fine. I'm fine. It's good." She scrambled to get up out of her seat, which made him hastily stand as well. Their table was bumped by her hip or his knee or some other body part that was now flailing through the space between them. Ryan's coffee sloshed as the table wobbled, and when they both stopped moving, they found themselves staring at the liquid as it pooled on the wooden tabletop, overtaking the random cookie crumbs like the tide coming in to demolish sandcastles.

"I'll get a rag from the kitchen." Allie was eager to get out of the café space and retreat somewhere she could be alone. Unless some weird, hand-holding giant decided to follow her.

"Allie, can I just talk to you for a second?" Ryan stood in the entry-way to the kitchen, watching Allie rummage through a drawer of various well-used dish towels. She could feel her cheeks warming.

It felt nice.

She couldn't deny the spike of excitement that had shot through her when his hand gently slid over hers. It had felt *normal*, too, like any one of the tiny everyday actions that happen between people who care about each other. That was even more unsettling than any burgeoning feelings she might be fighting.

And yet. Here he was, standing in the kitchen doorway with a concerned expression that looked very sincere. He knew her history. She'd seen his home and met his best friend. He'd shown up at the café repeatedly, even when she was rude to him. He'd bought her a soda mere minutes after she'd shouted at him.

Maybe she could . . . count on him? If he liked her, really liked her, maybe this *wasn't* the worst time to fall for someone. Especially for someone who made her feel so much like her old self. She opened her mouth, intending to apologize. Her heart hammered as she tried to think of what to say. But Ryan spoke first.

"Look, I'm sorry about that back there. Grabbing your hand."

"Ryan, it's—"

"Please." He held out one hand. "Let me finish up before you talk. I don't want you to get the wrong idea."

Allie's heart slowed.

"I *know* you and I are just friends. I just grabbed your hand without thinking. It absolutely was not meant to be a come-on or anything. I shouldn't have done it. I don't want you to think I'm out here being all sweet on you, making it all weird between us. I'm really happy being your friend. That's all. I promise. Nothing more."

Nothing more.

Allie was dizzy. She blinked, trying to calm the rush of emotion that had come over her and then receded and then returned in a slightly different form, all in the space of a few minutes.

What had she been thinking? She didn't have the time or emotional stamina for any kind of romance. And Ryan clearly didn't even feel that way about her. Him speaking first had saved her from an unimaginable humiliation.

Friends. They would be *friends*. That was better. Her mind filled with images of future dinners at his apartment, adventures and inside jokes and music filling their time. Someone she could actually depend on to stay in her life without drama or upset.

"Allie?" Ryan's voice cut through the fog of her thoughts.

She smiled at him. "Thanks, Ryan. Thanks for clearing that up. I'm glad we're friends."

He grinned, looking relieved. "I thought you didn't have any friends."

"Well," she grabbed a dish towel and closed the drawer and smiled in spite of herself. "I guess I do now."

Chapter Eight

"There's no Jessi Jetski *or* Jessi Nakamura mentioned on any of my friends' friends lists on Facebook. Or on my friends' friends' friends lists." Anisha sat back and took her hands off the keyboard of her laptop. "And no accounts for either of those names on Instagram for people who look anything like your Jessi. Do you want me to just start asking people? I could post something just to see if anyone I know knows anything?"

Allie shook her head. "Let's keep looking on our own for a bit longer before we start announcing things to your entire social media following. I don't want Jessi to think I'm publicly stalking her and get all freaked out. I already feel weird about friending Mimi on Instagram."

Mimi had been fine with the request, of course. It turned out that her account was mostly just photos of her backyard garden and chicken coop. Allie had sent her a message asking whether she knew where Jessi was, wondering whether that would be all it took. Disappointingly, Mimi responded that they'd lost touch completely after she'd moved to Oregon. Allie hadn't had the heart to communicate much more after that. The chickens were cute, though. They all had the names of female rock musicians. Joan Jett bore a striking resemblance to her namesake.

She'd told Mindy that she wanted some time to think about taking over the café before she made a final decision, but didn't tell her about the search for Jessi. Mindy had been trying for years to convince her to do something to "get closure" for her feelings about her band. She didn't know how her aunt would react if she knew that she'd finally listened to that advice when it was coming from someone else's mouth. To be fair, though, Ryan was a lot more friendly about the whole thing than Mindy had ever been.

Seated on the floor of Ryan and Anisha's apartment, she absent-mindedly smoothed over the short, silky strands of the faded blue area rug with her left hand while scrolling through the results of Google searches with her right. On the coffee table, Anisha had laid out a "working breakfast." Yogurt, nuts, all manner of fresh fruit and some ridiculously delicious caramelized apple turnovers that she'd gotten up to bake before Allie arrived. Ryan had to be at work at ten, so they'd agreed to meet early. For his part he was very prepared, his small note-book filled with scrawled ideas and leads.

"You want more coffee, Allie?" Ryan eyed her empty cup as he stood up from where he'd been sitting on the couch. A whole hour of him searching New York/New Jersey punk Facebook groups had yielded not a single lead. Allie shook her head. The two cups of strong coffee she'd already inhaled were making her heart jump around as it was.

"Ryan, can you put that yogurt back in the fridge? It's been sitting out too long." Anisha waved her hand at the end of the table.

Ryan picked up the yogurt but stopped to shake his head at Anisha before taking it anywhere. "It can sit out. It's made for the desert."

"Hummus!" Anisha shouted at him, the unexpected outburst causing Allie to jump. "*Hummus* is made for the desert. You get that wrong every single time. Honestly, what would you do if you didn't live with me?"

"Die of food poisoning, apparently." Ryan headed toward the fridge.

Allie giggled at the two of them, and then took a moment to finish her yogurt, fruit and pistachios, and let the spoon clatter into the empty bowl. "Okay, I'm looking at this little punk club in South Orange. Ryan, did you see this one? The Top Drawer?" Ryan came back to the living area and sat on the couch behind her. The rough denim of his jeans rubbed against her bare elbow. She leaned into him slightly, relaxing her body toward him so her arm pressed against the length of his leg. He was leaning over her, looking intently at the screen on her laptop. Allie was hyperaware of every point of contact between her body and Ryan's. She breathed in his scent—eucalyptus and pine—and worked hard to keep her face neutral and her mind focused on the task at hand.

"See, right here under 'Bookings'?" She poked her finger at the lower left corner of her screen. "It just says 'Contact J,' but the email is JNTD@punkmail.com."

Ryan nodded. "Could be Jessi Nakamura, Top Drawer! Is that what you were thinking?"

"I mean . . ." Allie shrugged. "It's a long shot, and I still don't think she'd use her real name, but it's worth checking into, I guess? Jessi would be an awesome club booker. She was always the one who was the most interested in new music."

Allie and Jessi always sat in the two front seats of their tour van. Allie drove; she was the only one of all of them who had a license and was brave enough to drive the van on the highways. Mimi and Ayla often slept in the back during night drives, but Jessi stayed awake and kept Allie company, picking music from the overflowing box of mixtapes that they kept in the footwell. Jessi played DJ, changing tapes and selecting certain songs, sometimes coming up with her own particular theme for the trip—songs that matched up and flowed from one to the other. Allie would let the music wash over her as she stared straight ahead at the highway. Often, she'd be so lost in thought she wouldn't notice when one song ended and another began. It felt like meditating. In those moments, she was strangely at peace. The seemingly never-ending roads stretched out before her in the dark.

"I'll email that address and ask if it's Jessi," Ryan said, swiping his fingers across the screen of his phone.

They hadn't had any more promising leads yet, but Allie enjoyed these sessions with Anisha and Ryan, who were both now as invested as she was in the hunt for Jessi Jetski.

After another quiet half hour with all three of them chasing various dead-end leads, Allie was ready for a break. She picked up her empty water glass and walked a loop around the room, trying to loosen the tension in her shoulders. She stopped near the kitchen counter, staring at the cluttered bulletin board that hung high above the sink. It was crammed with photos of Ryan and Anisha and notes that one of them had written to the other. Inside jokes, photo booth strips, and crudely drawn cartoons depicting one or both of them, all pinned haphazardly over top of one another. Allie felt lucky that the two of them had muscled past her defenses and were now regularly in her life.

"Hey, Allie, come here. I've got something to show you," Ryan called to her. She turned around to see him disappearing through his open bedroom door.

Anisha sighed. "Allie's not going to fall for your rudimentary pickup lines. She's too smart for that, you ridiculous man."

Allie blushed a horrifying shade of red and was grateful that Anisha was still staring at her computer screen and Ryan was now out of view, deeper in his bedroom. She filled her glass quickly and drank from it, giving her face time to return to a normal color. Should she follow Ryan into his bedroom? Her feet felt frozen to the kitchen tile.

"Har har har," Ryan scoffed at Anisha as he resurfaced. "Not a line, obviously." He smiled at Allie. The word *obviously* made her heart sink. They stood staring at each other in silence for another moment before he snapped out of it and spoke.

"I wanted you to see this!"

In his large hand, he held a small xylophone. The kind children play with. Allie remembered having one as a child. Her father taught her to play "Twinkle, Twinkle, Little Star."

"Ah yes." Anisha nodded after looking up only briefly. "The xylophone that matches your maturity level."

Allie giggled, walking back into the living room. "It's, uh . . . nice?"

"I sense that you are underwhelmed. But hang on." He walked back over to the couch and moved the plate of pastries aside so he could set the instrument down. Taking a small wooden mallet from the breast pocket of his shirt, he knelt in front of the xylophone and cleared his throat theatrically. "Ready?"

Allie sat back down, laughing. "As I'll ever be."

Ryan took a deep breath and closed his eyes for a moment. Then he started playing a melody on the instrument. It was simple, but catchy.

"That sounds familiar," Anisha said. "What is that from?"

Allie knew right away.

"Play it again," she told him. She sat on the edge of her chair, facing him, her body leaning forward, eyes on the mallet and the rainbow-colored metal bars of the xylophone. Ryan played the melody again, perfectly, and it immediately brought the lyrics to Allie's mind. She started singing. Her timing was perfect. She knew the song as if it were her own heartbeat.

Ryan's voice joined her on the second line, and she automatically slid into harmony. He looked at her, his eyes wide.

Her arms were covered with goose bumps. Ryan winked before turning his focus back to the instrument. They sang the rest of the verse as he played and then fell into an awed silence, the final note of the xylophone ringing through the apartment.

"Was that . . . Madonna?" Anisha finally asked.

"'Borderline,'" Allie and Ryan said in unison. Both nodding.

"I didn't know you could sing!" Allie felt almost high with the excitement of musical collaboration, even for one verse of one song. She'd missed it.

Anisha helped herself to another pastry and leaned back into the pile of cushions on the sofa. "Ryan's a great singer! He thinks I can't hear him when he's in the shower, but I totally can."

"Why do you have to make literally everything weird?" Ryan asked, his cheeks coloring slightly. Anisha smiled and shrugged, unconcerned.

Allie felt as if firecrackers were exploding in her brain. "Ryan, we have to record that! It's perfect!"

Ryan smiled. "Not gonna lie, I *was* really hoping you'd let me join your one-woman show."

"Well, you just aced your unsolicited audition. I'll do some bed tracks, and then you can come over and we'll work on it."

Ryan stood up and hopped from foot to foot, grinning. "Just say the word and I'm there!"

It was all Allie could do to keep from swooning. The harmonies, the simple but poignant song lyrics, the endless possibilities of how she would record and mix the song. It was the perfect way to wind her project down, now that she was almost finished. She hadn't been this excited about anything in a long time. How had she been managing, living day by day, a few blocks from this apartment and these people, and just . . . not known? She was so grateful to have them in her life. So grateful that she couldn't help the whisper of a worry that they might somehow leave her.

She shook that worry out of her head and concentrated on the excitement of the present. "Oh! I keep forgetting to ask: do you two want to come to the café's Thanksgiving dinner? It's two weeks from now. Mindy does it every year, a few weeks before actual Thanksgiving. Free food for friends and family. We're technically closed, but Mindy invites the entire world, so it's always packed."

"Will I get to meet George?" Anisha asked. She'd started coming into the café periodically but had somehow always managed to miss George. "I'm starting to think he's Ryan's imaginary friend."

"George will definitely be there." Allie nodded. "I can seat you beside him. He will *love* you, that's for sure."

"Just don't steal him from me," Ryan said. "You're already trying to steal Allie from me, with all your *snacks* and *helping.*"

Allie's stomach flipped. She bit back her smile at the thought that she was his to steal.

Anisha stuck her tongue out at him. "Obviously you need to up your game if all your friends like me better."

Ryan laughed and headed back to his room with the xylophone.

Allie closed her computer and slid it into her tote bag, grabbing one more apple turnover to eat on her way home.

"Thanksgiving at Mindy's sounds fantastic. Do we bring anything?"

"Just booze," Allie answered. "And even then, everyone always brings extra, so it honestly doesn't matter. We handle all the food. Mindy, Ren and I go full-on for a few days, getting everything ready. It's actually one of my favorite weeks of the year."

"Any buyers for the café yet?"

Anisha's question stopped Allie, who had been on her way out the door. She'd told Anisha and Ryan about Mindy's plans to leave, but Anisha was the only one who seemed comfortable checking in with her about it.

Allie sighed. "Nothing yet. Mindy's willing to let me take my time to decide if I want it, as long as there's no other buyer offering. She's not aggressively trying to sell it, either. But I think her patience has an expiry date."

"I trust you'll figure it out." Anisha's words were always soothing to Allie. Somehow, talking with her about these big things made them less scary instead of more. But as someone who had spent ten years avoiding her own feelings, she still felt herself occasionally resisting it.

"Thanks."

Ryan reappeared. "Do you want me to walk you back, Allie?"

He always offered and she always refused. "Thanks. I'm good. I want to listen to 'Borderline,' like, twenty times on the way home."

"I support that. Let me know if you need anything else from me."

"I will."

She waved to both of them and let herself out, her steps light on the stairwell as she plugged in her headphones and pushed through the door out onto the cool, sunny street.

Chapter Nine

"We need more soup. Who knew people would be all over vegan cream of mushroom?"

It was late afternoon on October 31, and they were running out of everything. Halloween was traditionally a slower day at the café, but a new family-friendly party at an event space around the corner meant a tidal wave of parents and preschoolers arrived just when they least expected. Allie and Ren were in the kitchen, scrambling to bake more cookies, when Mindy entered with the news about the popular soup.

"It's because you roasted the shiitakes first." Allie pointed at her aunt with a wooden spoon. "Just like I read in that *Times* recipe."

"It's *because*," Mindy countered, "these parents are exhausted and hungry and don't have the time or the free hands to consume anything more complicated than a cup of soup."

"You're both right." Ren's voice lacked its usual jovial tone. "Parents are tired. Soup is good."

Mindy turned to where Ren was unloading the dishwasher, then looked back at Allie. "What's their problem?"

"Halloween."

"Halloween sucks." Ren's unenthusiastic voice could barely be heard over the clanking of the dishes.

"My friend Marcy always said that Halloween was Gay Christmas," Mindy mused, pulling more soup out of the fridge.

Ren stood up and stared at her, eyes flashing with irritation. "*Christmas* is the Gay Christmas."

Allie laughed and rolled her eyes.

Ren continued, "Halloween is just the Drunk Olympics. It's not subversive, it's just a bunch of dingdongs clogging up the streets in cheap costumes so they can make everything noisy and then barf on the sidewalks."

Mindy smirked. "By all means, Ren, stop beating around the bush and tell us how you really feel."

The joke was not appreciated by its target, but Allie giggled as she made her way out to the café space to check on things.

The crowd in the café was substantially less wild than the Halloween revelry Ren had been describing, but it was certainly bustling. Every table was crammed with parents and children. The kids were either wild-eyed with delight (and probably sugar) or wailing inconsolably. The parents all looked exhausted.

Allie pulled out a stack of small stainless steel cups from behind the counter and grabbed a pitcher of water with her other hand. She began to walk around the café, pouring cups of water for everyone, receiving thankful glances from the adults as she made her way from one table to the next. These kids probably needed water to mitigate the sugar the same way whoever stumbled in later would need water to stave off the inevitable next-day hangover. As Allie poured, she considered inviting Ren up to her place for snacks and a movie after work. It might help shake off a bit of the Halloween gloom, and Allie didn't like being home alone on holidays when everyone else seemed to be out partying. It was one instance when she felt dissatisfied with her usual pleasant solitude.

She was refilling her jug behind the counter when the bell on the door jangled and she glanced up to see Ryan standing there with a grin on his face.

"Happy Halloween, Jetski!" He glanced around the room. "Yikes! Busy day."

"You aren't kidding." Allie pulled out another sleeve of cups and handed it to him. "Make yourself useful."

Ryan fell into step behind her, carefully setting cups down on tables so she could fill them. Together, they worked their way around the café until all tables had been served. The kids all stared at Ryan, mesmerized by exactly what, Allie wasn't sure. His height? His smile? The way he hummed pleasantly under his breath as he worked?

"So." He followed her back to the counter. "Are you here all night? Is it going to be this busy?"

Allie shook her head. "Mindy is on tonight. Ren will be here for a bit. I started at six, so I'm finished soon."

"Y'all got any Halloween plans?"

"Nope. Ren hates it, and I don't really care one way or the other." She stopped to squint past him, lost in thought for a moment. "And actually, I've never been into costumes. They always make me feel self-conscious."

"Yeah, I'm not a costume guy, either." Ryan leaned his elbow on the counter, bringing his eyes level with hers. "But I'll tell you what I am."

Allie smiled at him. "What are you?"

"I am a Halloween karaoke guy."

Allie tried to look at him suspiciously but couldn't keep her expression serious. "What is Halloween karaoke, exactly?"

Ryan shrugged. "Regular karaoke. But on Halloween."

"I see."

"So?"

"So?"

"You wanna?"

"Wanna what?"

Ryan heaved an exasperated sigh. "Do you want to go to Halloween karaoke? With me."

He was standing so close to her. Allie swallowed and felt her cheeks burn. Was he finally asking her out? She had no idea what to say. Should she tell him the truth? That she really, like, *really,* liked him but that she was terrified of ruining their friendship?

Ryan's left forearm, exposed by his rolled-up sleeve, was touching her hand on the counter. He leaned farther forward and winked at her.

"And Anisha, of course."

Allie could have kicked herself. She jumped backward as if his arm touching her hand had burnt her.

Of course. Get a hold of yourself.

Allie opened and closed her mouth, which seemed suddenly very dry. "I don't know, Ryan."

She sucked in a deep breath and consciously dropped her shoulders, bidding herself to act normal. She had to become Friend Allie again. She had to get her shit together. And quickly, before he noticed and figured out what she'd been expecting.

"Come on, Jetski. I know you have the pipes. You'll probably murder at karaoke. What's your signature karaoke song?"

"You obviously do not know me at all if you think I have a *signature karaoke song.* Also, who walks around deciding on their signature karaoke song anyway?"

"I have a list." Ryan produced his phone from his pocket and clicked on the Notes app. He held the phone up for her to see. Allie leaned in and read the list on the screen.

"'Mr. Brightside.' 'Like a Prayer.' 'Hold On.' '*You Oughta Know*'? Really?"

"Oh yeah, I crush with that one."

Allie found that hard to believe. She looked at the rest of the list.

"'Since U Been Gone.' 'Come On Eileen.' 'Jessie's Girl.' '*Whose Bed Have Your Boots Been Under?*'"

"Why are you questioning all the songs by Canadians? You don't believe I can sing in Canadian?"

"What I don't believe"—Allie wiped the counter with a cloth—"is that anyone carries around this kind of detailed list of possible karaoke songs."

"Not *possible*. Tried and true. This list is the result of years of experimentation and occasional failure. It is a solid list."

"I'll take your word for it."

"You can use my list if you don't have a song of your own choosing."

Allie straightened her posture, indignant. "I don't need your song list charity. I am very capable of making my own list."

"Does that mean you're coming with us for Halloween karaoke?" Ryan tilted his head, an eager smile spreading across his face.

Allie weighed the options. A night alone with only the possibility of cranky Ren for company while everyone else in the city was having fun or . . . this.

Allie shrugged. "I guess I'm coming to Halloween karaoke."

—

The bar that Ryan and Anisha had chosen was dark, with sticky floors. Allie walked in hesitantly, Anisha holding the door. Looking around at the dank interior, she was surprised to see most tables full of costumed patrons. A small riser was set up at the far end of the long room, with a microphone ready for singers. A large mural painted on the wall beside the soundboard depicted a vintage convertible being driven by Dolly Parton. There was nothing fancy about the place, but it had what could only be described as *a good vibe*. It reminded her of some of the places the Jetskis had performed when they were touring. Unassuming, kind of grimy spots that would end up having generous bartenders and actual toilet paper in every stall. There was an excited buzz in the air as people flipped through songbooks and chatted.

Anisha skipped toward the bar and loudly demanded a whiskey from the bartender who was wearing an Alice in Wonderland costume, with bonus cleavage.

"No costumes for you folks?" she asked, setting Anisha's glass of whiskey down on the bar.

"Every day is a costume day." Anisha took a swig from her drink and winked. As if to support her point, Anisha was clothed in a leopard-print pencil skirt, a striped crop top and a fuzzy pink jacket that looked as if she'd skinned a dozen teddy bears to get it. Her boots were covered in embroidered flowers.

The bartender looked her up and down and slowly smiled. "Fair enough."

Ryan turned to Allie. "Can I get you a drink?"

"Vodka soda, I guess?" Allie was out of practice drinking in dive bars, but she did remember that mixed drinks led to fewer hangovers.

"Two vodka sodas, please." Ryan held out some cash to the bartender.

Their drinks were delivered quickly, and they found a table with a good view of the stage.

"I'm gonna go sign us up!" Ryan bounced up within moments of sitting down.

"What, already?"

"Come on, Jetski, you said you had a killer song list."

"I did not say that." Allie felt panic rising in her chest. "I said I didn't need *your* song list."

"Look." Anisha stood up, pausing to glance over at the stage, where a woman was in the middle of an off-key but enthusiastic rendition of "My Heart Will Go On." "Let's grab a songbook. You can look through it and pick some songs. Ryan, leave her alone."

"She started it," Ryan was muttering to Anisha as they moved toward the table where a tall, skinny guy was squinting down at a soundboard, adjusting knobs as though that would somehow make the singer onstage hit the right notes.

A minute later, they returned with a binder full of laminated pages that were as sticky as the floor. Allie began flipping through it, looking for something inspiring but not embarrassing.

"And coming next to the stage!" The sound guy's voice boomed out through the speakers. "We have Ryan and Anisha singing that B-52's classic 'Love Shack'! Give them a hand, everybody!"

Ryan stood and held out his hand to Anisha in an exaggerated gesture of politeness. She accepted the hand, and they took the stage together, accepting the microphones handed to them. They were both grinning, and Allie wondered how anyone could be that comfortable everywhere, all the time.

A sparse drumbeat, with barely audible accompanying hand claps, filled the room. The screen behind the stage displayed numbers counting down from three to one and then, without any hesitation, Ryan began shout-singing into the microphone. Anisha clapped her hands and then swooped in for the second few lines.

As the first minichorus arrived, they both leaned back and howled into their mics. "Loooooove shaaaaack!"

The crowd was instantly with them. People stood up from their seats and sang along, clapping their hands in the air and shaking their hips.

Allie took a big gulp of her drink and then stood up, caught up in her own amazement as she watched her new friends throwing themselves into what was objectively a ridiculous performance. Anisha was off-key, but it could not have mattered less. When Ryan was singing, she was dancing, coming back to the mic for her own turns totally out of breath but beaming. The audience whooped, and people began to flood the dance floor in front of the stage. In the space of their five-minute song, they'd managed to supercharge the atmosphere of the room. When they finished, panting and beaming, the whole bar applauded. People hooted and pumped fists in the air; random strangers shook their hands as they made their way back to the table.

Ryan collapsed into his chair and drained his drink. He pointed at Allie's empty glass. "Another?"

Allie nodded. "I'll need one if I'm going to compete with that performance."

Ryan laughed. "It's not a competition, Jetski. We're all just here to bring the fun."

He left her with that thought and took off toward the bar. Allie watched people in the crowd patting his back and giving him thumbs-up as he went.

She turned back to Anisha. "That was incredible."

"Duets are the best!" Anisha smiled. "Did you decide what you're going to do?"

"Not yet." Allie looked back down at the songs, now feeling pressure to *bring the fun*, despite what Ryan had said about it not being a competition.

After a few more minutes of flipping through the pages while ignoring the drunken college girls belting out "Like a Virgin" on the stage, Allie reached for a slip of paper from the pile in the center of the table. Ryan handed her a pen.

"What'll it be?" He grinned, leaning over to see what she wrote. She scribbled her song title and name on the paper and held it up to him. His eyes widened. "'Alone.' Heart? Bold choice, Jetski!"

"I can do it." She may not have confidence in the other aspects of this endeavor, but she knew she could sing. And, more specifically, she knew she could sing every word of every song on the *Bad Animals* album, which was sitting in the crate of her dad's old cassettes back at her apartment. She delivered the slip of paper to the sound guy and then returned to the table for a third vodka soda and a few minutes of preperformance jitters.

When her name was called, she took the stage. She'd been onstage hundreds of times in her life but never, she realized, alone. It made her song choice weirdly poignant. Ann and Nancy Wilson singing about how they couldn't live another moment without getting the object of their affection alone. And here she was, feeling thrown by the lack of bandmates.

The piano intro started, and the countdown flashed across the monitor. The last moment before the lyrics kicked in seemed to stretch into infinity. But then she opened her mouth and sang.

The first few lines of the song were easy; anyone could have done a passable job with them. But the thing Allie loved about Heart was that they never waited long to get to the real singing. It was what made them one of her favorite bands to sing in the shower or in the empty café after closing. She shut her eyes and took an expertly timed deep breath, then belted out the first line of the chorus.

She was so focused on hitting every note with the full power of her voice, she didn't notice that the bar had gone quiet until the song settled into the quiet of the next verse. Daring to open her eyes and look out at the crowd, she saw dozens of faces staring at her with rapt attention. It shook her confidence slightly, but she held fast, calling on all the muscle memory of years onstage. No one was throwing drinks at her, which meant that this wasn't going any worse than the worst of the Jetskis' shows.

When she hit the next few lines of belting, it was clear that the crowd was with her, not against her. Their stunned silence broke into cheers as the song built to its crescendo. She felt her heart fill up with nervous joy, and she quickly closed her eyes again.

Just after the two-minute point in the song, she felt a spike of dread as she remembered a guitar solo was coming. What the hell was she going to do with her awkward body during a freaking *guitar solo*? As a rule, she hated guitar solos, and this moment did nothing to recommend them.

She didn't need to worry. As soon as the first note of the solo hit, as soon as her confident singing posture shifted to an uncomfortable fidget, Ryan and Anisha appeared in front of the stage. With props. Anisha was holding her own boot like a guitar, and Ryan did the same with a large drink menu. They immediately stole the crowd's attention as they each mimed the most dramatically ridiculous guitar playing Allie had ever seen. As Ryan spun around in a circle, she caught his perfect "guitar face" and laughed in spite of herself. The crowd in the bar amped up their cheers, some of them miming their own solos that rivaled Ryan's and Anisha's. It all served to take the heat off of Allie for those brief but agonizing instrumental moments. When the solo was over, her friends vanished, back to their table in the darkened audience, and Allie was once again the star of her own small show. She finished the song, hitting every note, and found herself actually enjoying the applause for a minute before she fled the stage and collapsed back into her seat at the table.

"Allie, that was amazing!" Anisha leaned over to grab her arm. "Holy shit, you're a fucking powerhouse."

"Well, thank you both for saving my ass with your expert guitar work." Allie giggled, self-conscious suddenly, as though everyone had been secretly standing outside her shower. She shook off the nerves. "Especially you, Anisha. You probably have tuberculosis of the foot now, after taking your shoe off in here."

"You would have nailed it with or without us. No one cares about an awkward instrumental break when the person onstage can actually sing." Ryan patted her shoulder and beamed. "Now let's get more drinks. I'm up soon, and I need a bit more vodka in me before I tackle Wilson Phillips."

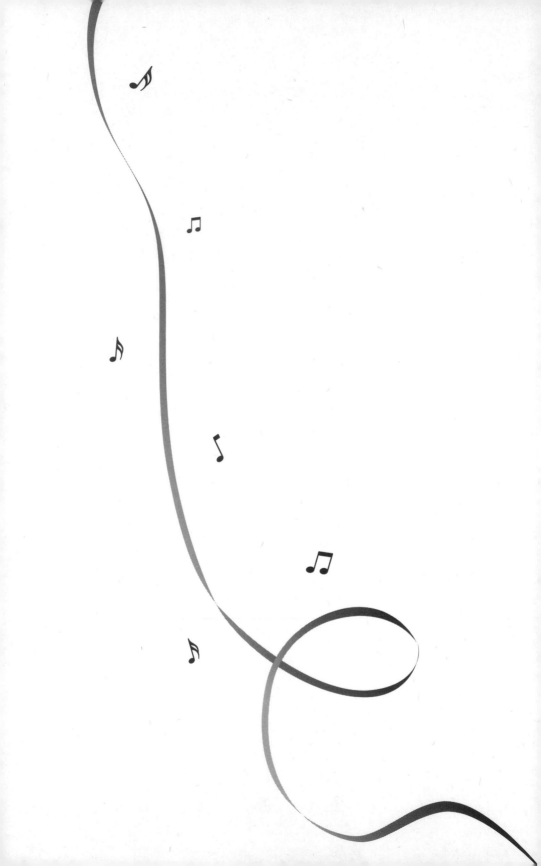

NOVEMBER

Borderline

Chapter Ten

"Why do we do this?" Allie moaned. She walked, hunched over, to the empty floor space in the middle of the café and threw herself down, collapsing with her arms and legs out like a starfish. "Why do I always remember Thanksgiving as being *fun*? It is completely *not fun*."

Ren wasn't far behind her, equally exhausted. They lay down beside her, and Allie ran her left hand over the stubble of their shaved head. It was the only motion her body had the energy to make.

"That feels nice. I am *broken*." Ren let out a groan as they shifted their weight to the side to look at Allie. "Why do we do this? Every year?"

"How do we always forget?" Allie moaned.

"What would Mindy do if we left?" Ren whispered, eyes wide. "We could crawl upstairs and hide in your apartment. Would she kill us?"

"Yes," Allie answered definitively. "She would. But I'd still try it if I was able to move, even a little bit."

Mindy entered the room, drying a muffin tin with a tea towel, as if she'd just woken up from a fortifying night of sleep, and not spent the past twelve hours immersed in grueling kitchen work. The community dinner may have been the best night of the year at the café, but the prep work was always a nightmare. "What's wrong with you two?" She gave them a disappointed glare.

"Mindy, are you a cyborg?" Ren rolled over and regarded their boss with suspicion. "Because there's no other explanation for the fact that you're still standing up."

Mindy huffed and shook her head. "I'm more than twice your age and about to retire. And I'm not the one lying on the floor like a deflated chicken."

"A . . . *deflated chicken*?" Allie asked.

"About to retire?" Ren said at the same time. They sat up abruptly.

Allie forgot about the chicken. Mindy's usually stoic face now betrayed an expression of momentary horror. Her body may have been unaffected by their hours of work, but clearly, her brain was getting sloppy.

Mindy and Allie had agreed not to tell Ren about the impending changes to the café until everything was settled. But neither of them had figured Mindy would blurt it out randomly after an intense day in the kitchen.

"Dammit." Mindy finally seemed tired, slumping down the wall until she was sitting with her feet out in front of her.

"What's going on, folks?" Ren asked, looking from Allie to Mindy and back to Allie again.

There was nothing to do but tell Ren the truth. Allie and Mindy looked at each other and had a short, silent argument with their eyebrows. Neither of them wanted to be the one to say it out loud.

"Folks?" Ren's voice held a hint of panic.

Mindy, for all her usual confident bluntness, was looking mortified. Allie sighed and began the explanation. When she finished, Ren looked at her, bottom lip wobbling, eyes wet.

Allie lunged at Ren and hugged them. "I'm sorry. We weren't going to tell you until it was all figured out."

"It's just"—Ren snuffled into Allie's shoulder—"this is the only job I've ever had with a decent boss and, like, *respect*. And I know when I come in that I'll be safe and it won't suck. You know what I mean. I can't imagine not working here."

"We'll make sure you're taken care of." Mindy sounded uncharacteristically shaken as she leaned toward them. "No one wants your life to suck. No one wants you to feel unsafe. Even if you're working for someone new."

"But I don't want to work for someone new!" Ren leaned back out of Allie's hug and collapsed onto the floor again. "What if the new owner is a jackass?"

"I'm not going to sell my café to a jackass," Mindy said with such certainty Allie wondered whether she'd already included a "no jackasses" clause in the deed of sale. She turned to Ren.

"And besides, it might be me! *I* might be the jackass you're working for!"

Ren laughed and clambered up to grab a napkin off the counter to wipe their nose with. "Well, obviously, that's the worst-case scenario . . ."

Allie laughed and slowly lifted her tired body off the floor. "Nothing is happening yet. We promise it will be okay. Now, I know Mindy's going to make us peel potatoes until our hands fall off, so let's get to it."

Mindy was just getting back to her feet when they heard banging on the door. "We're closed!" she yelled over her shoulder as she disappeared into the kitchen. Allie moved to follow her. It was Ren who actually looked at the person on the other side of the fogged-up glass.

"It's Ryan!"

Allie's head swung around. Sure enough, Ryan's frame filled the long window in the café door. He smiled when he saw them and waved. Ren unlocked and opened the door. "Get in here before someone sees you and demands a latte or something."

"Thanks, Ren." Ryan nodded. "Allie, are you busy, like . . . right now?"

"What? This is our prep night."

"I know, but something's come up."

Ren snorted and muttered something unintelligible as they walked back into the kitchen. Allie ignored them. She moved closer to Ryan. "What's going on?"

Ryan pulled his notebook from the back pocket of his jeans and opened it, frowned as he consulted some scrawled notes, then put it away again. "Okay, so I was looking at one of the message boards, and there's this show at the Royal tonight with a bunch of punk bands." He pulled out his phone and unlocked the screen, handing it to Allie. "One of the bands is called the Sophomores, and look what this show listing says!"

Allie scanned the text on the screen until she saw it.

New guitarist Jessi Sophomore will be playing her first show with the band. The much-anticipated addition will no doubt send the band's exploding popularity into overdrive.

She looked up at Ryan and handed his phone back. "You think it's my Jessi?"

"It could be. So, are we gonna go?"

"Go where?"

Ryan tilted his head and smirked. "To the show."

Allie laughed. "I can't go to a punk show! I have a million potatoes to peel. I've been in the kitchen since seven o'clock this morning. And also, I haven't been to a punk show in ten years. Never mind that Mindy and Ren would murder me."

"Mindy! Ren!" Ryan called.

Their heads appeared in the kitchen doorway. "Yeah?" They said it in unison, and Allie laughed.

"Do you mind if I borrow Allie for, like, two or three hours?"

Allie shook her head. "I already told him I need to stay here."

"Nonsense." Mindy waved her hand as though Allie had just been in the way for the last twelve hours. "We don't need you."

"Yeah!" Ren chimed in. "We only have the potatoes left, anyway."

Allie stared at both of them, her mouth open. "There are *seven bags* of potatoes to peel."

"We'll have it done in no time! Go with Ryan! We insist!" Mindy stepped closer to her and sniffed. "But change your clothes first. You smell like onions."

Allie sniffed the sleeve of her shirt and had to agree. She reeked.

"I won't be long!" She sprinted up the stairs to her apartment.

Allie knew if she thought too hard about what to wear, she'd end up standing in front of her clothes in a state of confusion for all eternity, so she reached quickly for a short-sleeved black cotton jumpsuit. It looked like the kind of thing a mechanic might wear. But *cute*. A cute mechanic.

She still had her Doc Martens from her band days. Her wallet and phone went into the jumpsuit's generous pockets. Even though it had been ten years since she'd been to a punk show, she knew not to bring a purse.

Smelling significantly less oniony, she raced downstairs and hustled Ryan out the door before Mindy and Ren could make any ridiculous comments about them going on a date. They were seated beside each other on the train before she had time to think the situation through to its possible conclusion.

"What if it *is* Jessi?" She turned to Ryan, wondering whether he could sense her rising panic.

"Well." He spoke slowly. "That's the point, isn't it?"

"I just—" A strange and surprising sadness washed over her. She tried hard to conceal a choking sob as the tears came.

"Oh!" Ryan frowned with concern. "Oh dang."

Allie, not normally a crier, was caught off guard by her own extreme reaction. Struggling to get herself under control, she dragged the back of her hand across her face and sucked in a deep breath. "I'm sorry. I'm worn out from work and still . . . digesting this whole thing."

Ryan, with distress in his expression mirroring her own, reached his soft, wide arms around her and pulled her to him in a tight hug. Her ear was pressed against his chest, and their thighs were tightly pressed up against each other. She felt, through her sadness, that syrupy, heart-melting feeling again. She took a deep breath and said the first thing that came to her mind. "You always smell *so good*."

A raspy laugh echoed in his chest, and she lifted her head to look at him. He met her eyes. "Well," he said, still holding her, "I was never one of those people who thought showering wasn't punk."

Allie laughed and caught herself admiring his eyelashes. They were silent for a beat, staring at each other, but then the train lurched to a stop and the spell—or whatever it was—between them was broken.

Ryan slowly let her go and put his hands in his lap. "Do you want me to take you home? We can get off this train and catch the other one. We can be back at the café in a few minutes."

Allie shook her head. "No. I want to go. I just had the thought all of a sudden that if it is Jessi, I'll have to see her there, playing music with new people I don't even know. And what if their band is great?"

"If their band is great"—Ryan smiled—"then we'll hit the dance floor. But only if you want."

"It would be weird." She'd stopped crying but could still hear the notes of misery in her own voice.

"I get that." Ryan put a friendly hand on her shoulder. "Like seeing your ex with a new girlfriend."

"Exactly," Allie muttered. "Except they're also onstage and everyone is cheering for them."

Ryan widened his eyes. "Yikes."

"Right?"

"Okay, yeah, that's much worse than going to a party and seeing someone you slept with a few times."

"Now you get it."

"Well, I stand by my offer for us to just turn around and go back to the café."

"Naw." Allie managed a small smile. "This is the first year I've ever gotten out of peeling the potatoes. It would be a shame to waste it."

—

The Jetskis had played at the Royal more times than Allie could count. It had always been one of the most reliable venues for shows in the city. She had very clear memories of loading their gear through the heavy stage door that opened into a very dank alley behind the club. Mimi had once hidden behind a trash can and jumped out when Allie and Jessi were carrying Jessi's giant amp, causing Allie to scream and Jessi to drop her side of the heavy cabinet on her own foot. Mimi was the one who had to carry all of Jessi's gear for the next several shows, as Jessi limped and glowered.

Walking in through the front doors as an audience member felt very weird. The club was dark but smelled cleaner than Allie remembered from a decade ago. It was what musicians considered a good room. There was plenty of space to stand in front of the stage, and the low ceilings made for excellent acoustics. The shows that her band had played there were always crammed with fans, wall-to-wall sweaty humans, singing along. For this show, there was a crowd, though not packed in so tightly that it was impossible to navigate. Some people seemed excited, but others looked bored as they sipped their drinks. The excitement of being whisked away from the café was starting to wear off. It had been so long since she'd been in a crowded room at a rock show. The heat of the bodies and the claustrophobia of the space made her stomach curl into a tense fist.

"Can I get you a drink?" Ryan leaned down to speak the words close to her ear. The piped-in music was loud. His soft voice and steady presence comforted her. Allie remembered that she used to bring earplugs to every gig she went to.

"I forgot earplugs!" she shouted at Ryan to be heard over the music. "I am so out of practice."

"Well, that makes one of us." Ryan pulled two packs of bright-orange earplugs out of the pocket of his coat. "I got you! Always trust your sound tech friends to look out for everyone's hearing."

Allie took one of the packets from him, feeling a zing through her nervous system when their fingers touched. She smiled at him. "Yes."

"Yes, what?"

"Yes, I would like a drink. A vodka soda, please."

Ryan nodded and disappeared through the crowd to the bar. Allie scanned the room for seats, but the few that existed were already taken. It would be a standing-up night. She looked at her boots gratefully, feeling as though she should apologize for ignoring them lately when they'd always supported her.

Ryan returned with her drink and an identical one for himself.

"You don't strike me as a vodka soda guy," she told him, taking a long sip.

"Ah. Well, that's something you should know about me. I always order the same drink as the person I'm with."

"You . . . what? Why?"

Ryan shrugged. "My family doesn't drink, and I just never really did, either, until I moved here. When I was first living in the city, everything was so overwhelming and confusing I didn't have the mental capacity to also figure out what my 'signature drink' was, or whatever. I got in the habit of ordering whatever the person I was with ordered. That habit just stuck. And now it just helps me match the vibe of whoever I'm hanging out with, so I always feel a bit more in sync with them."

"That's strangely charming."

Ryan laughed. "That will be the title of my autobiography. *Strangely Charming—The Ryan Abernathy Story*."

Allie giggled, starting to feel the alcohol taking its slow effect. Her drink was watery and weak, but it still helped calm the tension that was simmering inside her.

"You doing okay?" Ryan asked. "Your eyes are a bit, uh, *wild*."

"I'm okay." Allie sucked in a deep breath. "Let's just maybe talk about something other than the fact that maybe Jessi is going to appear at any moment and I'll have to decide what to say to her."

Ryan nodded and put a reassuring hand on her shoulder. He slid the hand down her arm and squeezed her elbow once before releasing it.

"Oh, here's something exciting." He leaned closer to her. "I got myself some drums!"

Allie's eyes widened. "You did?"

"Yep. Someone at the studio was selling a set. And I asked our apartment building manager if there was anywhere I could keep them, and he gave me a key to this very gross storage room in the basement, so now I have a very creepy practice space!"

"I'm happy for you and your scary drum room."

"I knew you'd approve." They clinked their glasses together. "I think I'm going to call it Doctor Worm's Drum Studio."

Allie laughed. Ryan's affection for the ridiculous song about a drumming worm was another thing she'd classify as *strangely charming*.

"Are the Sophomores on first?" She wondered how long she'd be able to stand there in the crowd without wanting to fall asleep.

"No, sorry. They're third. You gonna make it?"

"I'll try my best."

"Hang in there, Jetski." Ryan put one warm hand on her shoulder and squeezed twice before letting go. Allie felt a rush of heat in her cheeks again. Minutes later, the first band was onstage.

Having to watch two other mediocre bands drained Allie's energy, and she was hardly able to keep her eyes open by the time the second band was unplugging their guitars at the end of their set. She'd been leaning against Ryan's warm, steady shoulder for the last three songs.

"They're up next. You ready?" Ryan had been scanning the crowd diligently. Allie knew he was looking for Jessi. So far, nothing.

"I'm ready." The exhaustion had the unexpected side effect of calming her down. As though her brain didn't have enough energy to power the constant buzzing anxiety anymore. She stood on her tiptoes to see the stage and waited.

First, a man came onstage. A young guy with blond hair that fell over his eyes. He wore black skinny jeans and a hoodie. The crowd started to cheer.

"Hello, Brooklyn! I am Steve Sophomore, and we're going to play a few songs for you tonight."

A spotlight stayed on him, leaving the rest of the stage in darkness. Allie could see other bodies assembling behind him but couldn't make out the details of any one person.

"Can you see anything?" she asked Ryan, whose height gave him an automatically better view.

"Nope." He leaned from side to side, squinting at the stage. "Too dark. Hang on a minute. They'll light things up when they start playing.

Steve introduced their drummer, a guy named Davey, and then the bassist, someone whose name was apparently Garbage. Spotlights lit up the band members as their names were said. Allie held her breath.

"And last but certainly not least!" Allie's heart was pounding. "You know her from that other band!" The crowd roared. Allie's heartbeat quickened. "But I know her as my little sister! Jessi Sophomore!"

His . . . sister?

The spotlight hit the last band member, and Allie could see immediately that Jessi Sophomore was a small, blond white woman who looked to be in her teens or twenties. The crowd around them was going wild, but she and Ryan stood still.

"Who?" Ryan pulled out his phone and opened a search. Allie didn't care who the girl was or why everyone was so excited. All she could see was someone who was definitely not her Jessi.

"She was in a viral video." Ryan leaned down to shout over the music. "She had some band with her friends in high school, and they did a song that got popular on social media. I guess this band started to get more attention because that guy is her brother. Her joining the band now is *huge*. Her real name is Jessi Kaplansky. She only took on the name Jessi Sophomore when she joined this band."

Of course. Of course no one in this crowd would be this excited about someone from the Jetskis. Allie felt the sting of humiliation behind her eyes. No one cared about her band. No one even knew who they were anymore. They'd packed this room twelve years ago, and now they'd been replaced by this band and a million others. Other bands who managed to keep it together and keep going and get famous.

She leaned on Ryan's shoulder again, more exhausted than ever.

"Allie, I'm sorry." His voice was heavy with concern. "I should have done more googling or something, or checked some Facebook groups. I just got so excited . . ."

"Not your fault." Allie patted his arm and gave him a weak smile. "You were just trying to help." She meant it. Hanging out with Ryan was the only thing about this evening that hadn't disappointed her.

"You wanna go?" He took her empty cup from her hand and placed it on the nearby bar. She nodded.

"Yeah." She'd never been more eager to leave a show. "Let's get out of here."

Chapter Eleven

Allie was behind the counter when Anisha and Ryan walked into the busy café on the night of Mindy's Annual Friendsgiving. She watched as they both stuffed cash into the Native American Rights Fund box by the door. The dinner was always free for everyone, but every year, they asked for donations and, without fail, pulled in a pile of money. Those donations, and the whole community dinner in general, were things that made Allie actually take a pause and appreciate what Mindy had taken years to build. On these nights, with the café warm and packed full of smiling friends and favorite customers, she felt lucky to be a part of her makeshift Brooklyn family.

"Alllllllllllieeeeee!" Anisha spotted her first and called to her through the crowd. Her stunning vibrant-orange block-print dress had sleeves that widened dramatically at the elbows, and under it, she wore red tights and black boots with red leather lightning bolts at each heel. Her hair surrounded her head and shoulders in a cloud of perfect waves. As she made her way toward Allie, everyone she passed paused to look her up and down. Ryan trailed behind her, taking advantage of the path she'd made through the crush of people. Allie felt her heart skip when he looked at her and grinned. He was wearing a soft blue sweater that made her want to touch him. The crisp white collar of his button-down peeked out at the neck, and his hair was impeccably tidy. For a second, it felt as if they were the only two people in the room, but then someone close to him dropped a wineglass on the ground, and he quickly turned to help clean up the mess. Anisha, unperturbed by the dropping of dishes, continued toward the counter.

"You look amazing!" Allie stepped around the counter for the hug she knew was inevitable.

"Who's your friend?" Ren appeared from nowhere at Allie's side.

"Have you not met Anisha yet?" Allie turned to them, shocked. "She's Ryan's roommate."

"I've come in for coffee a few times." Anisha shook Ren's hand. "You've probably been too busy to notice me."

Ren grinned, still gripping Anisha's hand. "I'd say that's unlikely."

"Allie!" Mindy's voice, with a note of slight panic likely indetectable to anyone else, cut through the crowd from the kitchen.

"You'll have to excuse me," Allie said to Ren and Anisha, who seemed to only have eyes for each other. She squeezed through the crowd to the kitchen, where she found Mindy struggling to hold a giant baking tray full of individual pot pies that had just come out of the oven.

"It's heavier than I thought!" Mindy explained, as Allie quickly snatched an oven mitt from the counter and grabbed one side of the tray. They righted it, sliding the pies back from their precarious places at the edge, and set it carefully on the counter.

"Next time, come get me!" Allie scolded.

Mindy took off her own oven mitts and dabbed her brow with a handkerchief. "You're not the boss of me." She was already on her way over to the other side of the kitchen, where the large pots of mashed potatoes were waiting.

"I'm the closest thing there is, though."

Allie felt a tenderness for her aunt, watching her work the kitchen almost single-handedly. She'd been feeding dozens of people at this dinner every November for years and years. It had never occurred to her not to do it. Allie wanted to be the kind of person who knew what they wanted and went for it. The kind of person who didn't have to answer to anyone.

"Well, you can stop telling me what to do and go tell everyone that they should find their seats soon. We should be ready for service in about ten minutes."

"Okay, I'll do that now. Just have to check on Ren first."

"Is Ren okay?" Mindy and Allie had both been protective of their friend since the upset over Mindy's revealed retirement.

"Oh yeah, they're fine. But I suspect they are in Flirting Ren mode. To be fair, it's directed at Anisha, who is a babe."

"Have you warned her that Ren is a bit of a cad?"

"I think we say *player* now. And not yet, but I figured I'd monitor the situation and intervene if necessary."

"Good plan. Let me know if I have to spill soup in anyone's lap as a distraction. I love Ren, I want them to be happy, but I can't take any more heartbroken people showing up here crying in my lap at 6 a.m."

"If I hadn't been here all three times when that happened, I'd assume you were overreacting."

Allie left her aunt arranging pot pies on platters and went back out into the café space. They'd borrowed extra tables from a friend of Mindy's who was an event planner, so there was very little available space. She and Ren had spent part of their morning amassing bouquets of black-eyed Susans and yellow dahlias, arranging them in old canning jars and placing them at regular intervals along the tables. Some petals were already starting to fall, littering the white tablecloths in patterns that looked almost intentional. Places were set with plates and cutlery, as many as they could cram onto each table, and the bulb lights on strings that laced across the ceiling were all turned on, keeping the café softly glowing as the sun set outside.

The tears in her eyes surprised her. She wiped them away quickly. Every year, for ten years, she'd stood in this place, watching a variation of this group of people gather and hug and eat and stick cash in boxes for important causes. She'd served pot pies and roasted vegetables and desserts, and watched as people shared the bottles of wine they'd brought from home. Tonight was no different, except that it might be the last time.

It was Mindy who made this happen. Mindy was the one who knew every person in the room. With Mindy gone, would these people even want to come to the café anymore? All those years, Allie had been keeping her head down, not really befriending many customers, just working to make sure the logistics were taken care of. Had she robbed herself of the opportunity for an actual community? Not the community she was used to—one of enthusiastic punk fans spread out across the country, attending shows and writing zines and sending postcards—but a different kind of community. One centered here, in the present. People willing to gather and catch up with each other over an annual dinner. Had she missed her chance?

Ryan and Anisha interrupted her melancholy by charging through the crowd toward her. She quickly wiped the tears from her face and greeted them. Her forced smile loosened into a more natural expression as they got closer. Their good vibes were contagious.

"Look what George brought me!" Ryan held out five burned CDs like a hand of cards in front of her face. She recognized them instantly.

"Aw, he didn't need to do that! I could have sent the files to you by email."

"Yeah, he actually wanted me to know that he knew that. Seems he is very clear on how digital files work. He seems to know as much about them as I do, to be honest." Ryan shrugged and Allie laughed. Of course George did. "He wanted to make it very clear that he was not some outdated old man who thinks the kids still listen to 8-tracks. Anyway, he said he wasn't sure you'd have time to send them, so he was helping me along by bringing them for me directly."

Allie glanced across the room at George, who was standing by the front window, leaning on his wooden cane, chatting with a dancer from the New York City Ballet who shared his enthusiasm for tea. George caught her stare and raised his wineglass slightly, winking. She couldn't help grinning back at him. "That means he didn't trust me to actually give them to you. He's just being polite."

"Oh yes, I got that message loud and clear."

Allie turned to Anisha. "Did you get to meet him?"

Anisha had been looking over Allie's shoulder, uncharacteristically distracted. "Sorry, what? Who?"

Allie looked back at Ryan and raised her eyebrows. He smirked.

"George," Allie clarified. "Did you get to meet George?"

"Oh yes!" Anisha recovered her focus. "I did. He was very complimentary about my outfit and recommended Julia Child's memoir to me. I mean, everyone recommends Julia Child's memoir to me, but from him, I might actually take that recommendation seriously." Anisha scanned the room and switched gears abruptly, leaning in toward Allie. "What's the deal with your friend Ren? Are they seeing anyone?"

"Uhh." Allie fought the urge to flee the conversation immediately. "I'm not . . . sure?"

Anisha was not fooled. She grabbed the sleeve of Allie's dress and pulled her in closer, her other hand yanking Ryan in as well. "Okay. Spill it."

It was strangely cozy and pleasant, being pulled into a tiny group for gossip like this. It reminded Allie of being backstage with her band, all of them clustered together having whispered conversations before a show. "Okay." She kept her voice as low as she could in the noisy room. "Ren has a bit of a *reputation*. With the ladies. They're a wonderful person and a super reliable employee and friend. But they have a tendency to, uh, charm their way into ladies' . . . hearts?"

Anisha translated. "So they're dynamite in the sack. I get it. Continue."

Ryan laughed and rolled his eyes at Allie, who was looking at him pleadingly, as though he might be able to end this conversation before she was forced to say more. Anisha, however, was still holding Allie's sleeve and did not seem eager to go anywhere.

"Yeah, I mean, I assume so. But they haven't ever wanted, like, to settle down or anything. And that causes, uh, problems?"

"Allie." Anisha spoke firmly. "You are being hella sketchy, and we have limited time before I decide if I should go flirt my ass off, so just give it to me straight—so to speak. Should I go for Ren or not?"

"Oh god, I don't know! It depends." Allie fidgeted.

"Allie." Anisha's tone was mildly terrifying.

"Oh, okay, fine. *No*. Please don't. People come here crying. Ren is a total heartbreaker. I know you can handle yourself, but I'd hate to have something bad happen and then you're mad at us all and don't want to come to the café anymore. It could get messy."

Anisha released her grip and smiled warmly at Allie. "Thank you. You're a good friend."

Allie exhaled with relief. She needed to focus on dinner, not on horny friends. "Ryan, you're loud, can you let everyone know they should take their seats? I think we're almost ready to serve dinner. Just announce it. They'll quiet down."

Ryan did one better and lifted his fingers to his mouth to emit a piercing whistle that silenced the crowd instantly. "Hey, ya'll! Allie says sit down because she's fixin' to serve some dinner!"

Allie patted his chest. His sweater was, indeed, very soft. "Thanks, buddy."

He grinned down at her. "Anytime, friend."

—

The beer that Ryan handed her was so cold, and the room still so warm, condensation immediately dripped over her hand and into her lap. She didn't care. She'd never needed a beer more in her life.

"Oh god, thank you so much for this." She twisted the cap off the bottle and took an enormous swig.

"No worries." Ryan twisted the cap off his own bottle. "As if I was going to let you serve me after everything else you folks did tonight." He nodded in the direction of Mindy and Ren, who were halfway through their own beers at the other end of the table. George and Anisha were also at the table, not drinking but deep in conversation. Allie had never seen him out so late. It was almost midnight. As if he'd heard her thoughts, George caught her eye and smiled.

"Stop looking at me like that," George said.

"Like what?" Allie grinned as she took another long sip of her beer.

"Like I'm about to turn into a pumpkin."

This got him a laugh from everyone at the table. Allie shrugged. "Just making sure Mindy doesn't bake you into a pie."

"I'm never making another pie again as long as I live," Mindy proclaimed.

"You say that every year," Allie and Ren responded in unison.

The dinner, as always, had been a wild success. The food was perfect, the café was full of laughter and conversation, and even with all the extra work—and cleaning, so much cleaning—Allie felt as if her heart was full. A sleepy contentment washed over her as she sat at the table with both her new and old favorite people. She'd always considered managing the café to be work, but when she looked around the room, with its dim lights and candles flickering and warm laughter coming from around the table, she wondered whether it might be more than just a job. Maybe this was her calling, her purpose in life. All those things she'd thought music was supposed to be.

Her thoughts were interrupted by Ryan whispering into her ear. "Hey, can you come into the kitchen with me for a minute?"

Her heart beat like a kick drum in her chest for a moment. Then she reminded herself of his very emphatic insistence that they were *just friends.* She finished the last of her very welcome beer and set the bottle down on the table in front of her.

"Sure. Let's go."

Allie pretended that she didn't see Mindy's and Ren's curious eyes following the two of them into the kitchen. Ryan was oblivious. As soon as they were alone, he stood beside her and pulled out his phone.

"I got an email back from that club in Jersey. The Top Drawer?"

"You did?"

"Yeah. I mean, it's inconclusive and not very helpful, but it might be something?"

"Let me see." Allie tapped the screen of his phone impatiently. He put in his passcode and pulled up an email. Allie read it aloud.

"Jesse is away this week, so I'm doing bookings. But we don't book anyone we haven't met or talked to, so just come to the club some night if you want a gig. Alan."

"Alan is a man of few pleasantries, it seems." Ryan set his phone down on the counter in front of them and turned to look at Allie.

"And that's not how my Jessi spells her name."

"I did notice that. But then I thought, *How much faith do I have in Alan when it comes to spelling?* And the answer was, not much."

Allie laughed. "It's a long shot."

Ryan nodded. "A long shot. But a short drive."

"Are you saying you'd like us to go visit Alan?"

"That's precisely what I'm saying. I have Wednesday off. Can you take a vacation day?"

"Well, not without Mindy and Ren thinking we're stealing away for a secret sex romp."

She saw Ryan's cheeks redden. She couldn't help but tease him; the exhaustion and the beer were making her punchy. "Oh, sorry! Did that *embarrass* you? Do they not talk about sex in Alabama? Or— Oh no—" She leaned closer to him and looked up at his red, but smiling, face. "Are you a *virgin?*"

Ryan rolled his eyes and shoved her shoulder gently to move her away from him. "Not by a mile. Do you want to go to Jersey on Wednesday or not?"

Allie grinned, satisfied that she'd succeeded in bothering him, even though his implied assertion that he was well acquainted with sex had set off a crowd of butterflies in her stomach. "Yeah, why not? Let's go to Jersey and meet our new friend Alan."

Chapter Twelve

On Wednesday, Allie found herself sitting beside Ryan as he confidently maneuvered the car he'd borrowed from Anisha onto the Williamsburg Bridge, bound for New Jersey.

Mindy and Ren had openly gawked at them as she climbed into the car, amazed that Allie had asked for a day off and very eager to tease her about taking off with "a boy." She'd told them she was going to help Ryan pick up a chair he'd purchased from someone online.

It was warm in the car. The front seat gave them a forced proximity and intimacy that made Allie's nervous system buzz like a fluorescent light bulb. The periodic smiling sideways glances that Ryan was giving her didn't help. She forced herself to fill the heavy air with conversation.

"Been a while since I was in a car." She tried to remember the last time and failed.

"You must know how to drive, though. Because of touring." Ryan fiddled with the volume on the stereo, keeping his eyes on the road.

Allie looked out over the water and at the distant buildings of Manhattan. "I was the only one in our band with a license."

"Seriously?" He glanced quickly sideways again and met her eyes.

"You did all the driving? Did they, like, pay for your meals and worship you as a goddess?"

Allie laughed. "Not quite. Mimi and Ayla usually unloaded all our gear. And Jessi always sat on the passenger's side and played DJ. It was before there was streaming music, and the van only had a cassette player, so managing the music was basically a full-time job."

"Dang, most bands weren't even releasing cassettes anymore at that point. You must have gotten tired of albums pretty fast if you were always working with the same collection."

"Oh yeah, we did. Jessi had a tape player at home set up to dub music from her records, but still, we could only bring so many cassettes with us. There's one Sleater-Kinney album I can literally not bear to ever listen to again."

Ryan laughed and did a quick shoulder check as he merged with traffic at the end of the bridge.

"Eventually, we started asking people to make us mixtapes." Allie was warming to her tour stories, the nostalgia slowly building within her. "We would ask everyone we met on tour to make them for us, audiences, promoters, even other bands we befriended."

Ryan pressed the brake as they hit an unmoving section of traffic. He looked at her with an unreadable expression on his face. She looked back, wondering whether he was going to confess something scandalous, right in the middle of this benign conversation about cassettes. But he didn't. He just shrugged gently and turned his attention back to the cars in front of them before he spoke again.

"And did people make them for you?" he asked as the car started to move again. "I mean, this was well beyond the era of cassette decks. Even for most dedicated music nerds."

"That was the surprising thing. People *did*. There was kind of a cassette resurgence in the underground music scene at that time. I'm sure you remember." She snuck a glance over at Ryan. "People who loved cassettes really loved them. It was considered cool, I guess. Whatever it was, it sure helped us out. We would usually get a few new cassettes each tour stop. Jessi was always excited to play weird new music for me while I drove."

"I still can't believe you did *all* the driving. It must have been exhausting."

His obvious care for her made the back of her neck hot.

"I just got used to it, I guess. I liked touring. Oh, and don't worry if you want me to take a turn driving today. I'm not, like, burned out for life or anything. I might be a little rusty, though."

"Just as long as we don't listen to Sleater-Kinney?" He looked over at her quickly and winked.

"Most of their catalog is fine. But if you put on *All Hands on the Bad One*, I'll voluntarily fling myself from the vehicle."

He laughed. "Well, I like driving, too, so you're off the hook. Plus, this car is great. It handles so well. I'm lucky that Anisha lets me borrow it whenever."

"Hey, I've been meaning to ask you something." Allie watched out the window as Manhattan's crowded streets flowed by.

"Go for it. We have about an hour's drive ahead of us. If I can't answer your question, I'll at least have time to make up an entertaining lie."

"Oh, nothing that requires lying. It's just, I realized after the Thanksgiving dinner that I have no idea what Anisha does for a living, and I feel like it's way too late to ask her."

Ryan chuckled. "Well, that's an easy one. She doesn't do anything for a living."

"Is this the entertaining lie you were talking about?" Allie gently shoved his arm. She held her hand against the warm fabric of his shirt for a second longer than she needed to. "Because, really, it could be a *lot* more entertaining."

Ryan laughed. "Nope. I'm serious. She doesn't work."

"She doesn't work? And you are a podcast tech? And you live in the nicest apartment in Brooklyn? And she has the best clothes I've ever seen and also owns this completely nonjunky car?"

"I know. It sounds bizarre. And she doesn't really like to talk about it, but Anisha is loaded."

Allie leaned back against her seat and attempted to process this information. "What, did she, like, design an app or something? Did she win the Mega Millions?"

"Neither." Ryan checked his mirrors and steered the car into the passing lane before glancing back at Allie. "Nothing that exciting. Her family owns a bunch of factories in India. They sent her here for school but didn't think she'd want to stay. She did, and they freaked out a bit but ended up giving her a trust fund or something? I don't know how it works. She's technically estranged from them, but she has enough money in trust to just . . . live. And, of course, she hates telling anyone about it. I don't think she'd mind you knowing, but I can guarantee it's not something she'll want to chat about."

"Understood." Allie exhaled, feeling a bit bowled over by the unfamiliar concept of having money just sitting there whenever you needed it. "But she's always busy! She's always coming home and changing clothes after a long day!"

Ryan nodded. "Volunteer work. She literally does it every day of the week. Harlem Green, Brooklyn Book Bodega, Big Sisters . . . I can't even keep track. After she bought the apartment and the car, she basically put herself on an allowance, and she gives a bunch of money away each month and spends all her time volunteering. She's the weirdest rich person I've ever met. Not that I've met many."

"She *owns* your apartment?" Allie turned to him with wide eyes.

"Sure does. Lucky me, huh? Every once in a while, she suggests that I live there for free, but I'm not comfortable with that. My rent is cheap, though."

"She really *is* an excellent platonic life partner," Allie mused.

Ryan laughed. "Ain't that the truth."

Allie leaned back in her seat. "Do you worry about what happens if one of you meets someone that you really like?"

He stared straight ahead and drummed his hands on the steering wheel. He was quiet for long enough that she thought he hadn't heard her and was about to ask the question again when he cleared his throat and spoke.

"I don't think that's a real worry for either of us. Anisha dates around. She's never really talked about wanting anything serious. And I don't have much luck with long-term relationships. Ladies get tired of me pretty quick. I've never really been able to get someone to stick around."

Allie found that hard to believe, but she didn't want to pry, and he didn't seem to want to elaborate.

As the landscape out the window shifted gradually from city to suburbs, Allie recognized the opening bars of the next song on Ryan's playlist. "I Want You to Want Me." She leaned forward and turned the volume up, knocking Ryan with her shoulder as she settled back into her seat.

"Ooh, what's this? A front seat mosh pit?" Ryan nudged her with his elbow. Allie nudged him back and started singing along with the first verse. Ryan's voice joined her, and they both sang louder and louder as the chorus kicked in, Allie bopping up and down in her seat and bumping into Ryan as much as she could without causing him to steer the car off the road. Ryan, for his part, kept one hand solidly on the wheel and made emphatic gestures with his other fist in the air. Whenever he could, he leaned toward her and knocked her back with his arm. Allie was giggling so much as the song drew toward its final chorus, she could hardly sing the words. The thing was, she maybe did want him to want her. And she was starting to think that maybe he wanted her to want him, too.

"Best front seat mosh pit I've ever been in," Ryan said as the song ended. He was breathing heavily from the exertion of it all. He smoothed his hair back into place and ran his hand down over his beard. They were now completely surrounded by suburban homes, steering through quiet neighborhoods, so much closer to their destination.

It took less than an hour to get to the club. As she stepped out of the car, Allie realized she wasn't even sure she was ready for what could happen when she went inside. She hadn't spent any time in the car thinking about what she would do if Jessi *was* somewhere behind the heavy, rusted metal door under the rudimentary sign for the Top Drawer. It had seemed like a long shot, a weird adventure that was mostly about getting to spend an afternoon chatting and driving around with Ryan. But now it was real. Her heart was in her throat.

Ryan looked down at her, his brown eyes warm. "Are you ready?" She nodded, inhaling deeply through her nose as quietly as possible. He'd probably be disappointed if he knew she was considering running back to the car and diving into the back seat.

The Top Drawer was a name apparently chosen with an affection for irony, since the club was very much underground. When they pushed open the metal door, they were greeted by a stairwell that emitted a wave of odor.

"Oof." Ryan waved his hand in front of his face. "That is a *lot* of urine."

Allie laughed. "Feels kind of familiar. Though I don't think we ever played here. I would have remembered a club in our home state."

"Yeah, from what I read online, it seems like it opened just a few years ago."

"Well, we definitely played a lot of places like this. Piss-stink essential oil must come in the starter kit for every punk club in the country."

They followed arrows scrawled on the wall in thick black ink down two sets of staircases and found themselves faced with another door, with a more elaborate hand-painted sign letting them know they had arrived.

Ryan glanced at her quickly, and when she nodded, he pulled open the door.

It took a moment for their eyes to adjust in the darkness after the fluorescent lights of the stairwell. The club was small, just one room with a foot-high riser at one end and a short bar along the wall far-thest from them. A table and chair and an open, empty lockbox sat by the door, ready for someone to take money from patrons in exchange for stamped wrists as they arrived for whatever show would be happening later.

"We're closed. Come back at nine." The words came from a skinny guy who was sitting on one of the barstools, eating a burrito and star-ing at his phone screen. His lank bottle-black hair hung in greasy chunks over his eyes, and his T-shirt, which was more holes than fabric, featured gothic lettering that read Cult Leader Death Pact. Allie had been out of the scene for so long she didn't know whether it was a band or just a random statement.

"Hey, are you Alan?" Ryan's voice prompted the guy to actually look up at them.

"Who are you?"

"You can't answer a question with a question." Ryan smiled. "It's not polite."

"Huh?" Alan did not seem ready for a match of wits.

"I'm Ryan Abernathy. I sent you an email asking if we could talk to Jessi. You said to come by the club?"

"Oh, okay." Alan put his burrito down. He turned toward a door just beyond the bar and shouted, "Hey! Someone's here to see you!"

As the door opened, Allie felt briefly lightheaded. What if all this time, all she'd needed to do was take a forty-five minute trip to New Jersey and descend a urine-soaked staircase? Ten years of wondering what had happened to Jessi, to have her walk out of a badly painted door in the middle of a tiny punk club half an hour from the high school where they'd first met. It was wild. This might be it.

Of course, it wasn't.

Allie tried not to look mortified when a young white guy with a closely shaved head and friendly, alert eyes walked through the door and smiled at them. "Hey! You wanted to talk to me?"

"Jesse, this is Ryan." Alan waved his hand from one guy to the other, ignoring Allie entirely. "He wanted to talk about bookings . . . or something." Alan went back to his burrito. Jesse walked across the room toward Ryan and Allie. As Allie exhaled audibly, Ryan put a gentle hand on her shoulder. His touch fortified her. She resisted the urge to curl into him, seeking the soothing comfort of his body. Now they had to make nice with Jesse for at least a few minutes before they could bail.

"Hey, man, nice to meet you." Jesse shook Ryan's hand and nodded quickly at Allie. "What's your band called?"

"Oh." Ryan laughed, sounding more self-conscious than Allie had ever heard before. "I'm not in a band. We actually just came looking for someone who we thought might be you, but we were wrong. We're sorry to waste your time."

"Aw, really?" Jesse looked confused. The large Xs tattooed on his hands gave him away as a straight edge—no booze, no drugs. He seemed like a fine person. She had no interest in him at all.

Apparently, the feeling was mutual. Jesse continued talking to Ryan as though Allie didn't exist. "You just totally look like you'd have a band. You kind of look like that guy in Numbrain. Do you know that guy?"

"Naw, man." Ryan shook his head. "I'm not in the scene at all." He gestured to Allie. "But she used to be. It was actually her bandmate we were looking for. Jessi Jetski? Jessi with an *i*. You know, the Jetskis? They were on Ego Records?"

Jesse glanced at Allie briefly but turned his attention back to Ryan. "Ah, I'm Jesse with an *e*. Haven't heard of them. They still touring?"

"Nope, not anymore," Allie answered. Jesse's eyes didn't leave Ryan.

"Well, man, I'm sorry. I don't know what I can do for you."

"That's okay." Ryan looked at Allie.

She shrugged. "We'll get out of your hair."

"Okay. Cool. You should come see a show some night, though. It gets really wild in here! Lots of great hardcore coming out of Jersey these days."

"Thanks, man." Ryan extended his hand to shake Jesse's again. Jesse shook it and gave Allie a barely perceptible nod. They didn't bother bidding Alan farewell.

As they surfaced back into sunlight and fresh air, Allie heaved a sigh, glad the disappointing experience was over. She hadn't really been expecting them to find Jessi so easily and so soon. She felt slightly shaken up, but not devastated. Ryan's calm, steady presence at her side had helped.

"Well, that was infuriating!" Ryan proclaimed, letting the heavy door slam behind him. Allie turned in surprise.

"I mean, it was a long shot. We knew that. It's cool."

"No!" Ryan shook his head. "I mean how he ignored you."

"What? Oh, you mean Jesse?"

"Yeah!" Ryan was incredulous. "He talked to me and assumed I was the one in a band, and he didn't even shake your hand! It was like you didn't even exist."

Allie knew she shouldn't laugh at him. She managed to hold it in for approximately ten seconds. Ryan looked stunned as the laughter bubbled out of her.

Bless his heart.

"Ryan, that shit happens *all the time.* That guy not acknowledging me was the least surprising thing that happened today. It's almost a cliché. Our band had all the typical stuff happen to us when we were on the road. Club managers thought we were groupies. People asked if one of our dads was our manager. Interviewers assumed we didn't play our own instruments or write our own songs. I learned to just ignore it. And, apparently, I am still good at that, because I tuned Jesse's behavior out completely."

Ryan stared at her for a moment. His shoulders dropped slightly. "Man, that makes me so mad." He started walking for the car, and she walked beside him, affection surging inside her. She put her hand on his arm, and Ryan halted to look at her.

"It's nice that you're concerned. And the more you talk about it and call it out, the better. I think ladies are tired of being told we're making a big deal out of nothing. Jessi always used to point out that it actually makes more of a difference when dudes speak up. Which is *also* infuriating, but I have no solution to that problem."

They walked in silence back to the car and got in. Ryan was about to start the engine when he patted his pockets and then turned to her. "Shoot, I think I left my notebook in there. Hang on." He was out of the car before she noticed that the book was sitting beside the gear shift. She looked out the window and watched a lady wheeling a baby stroller up the sidewalk while attempting to walk an enthusiastic golden retriever at the same time.

Ryan returned quickly.

"Your notebook is right there." She pointed.

"What? Ah good. Thanks."

Ryan started the car and turned it back toward New York.

Fifteen minutes later, Allie's phone dinged. An email had come in. She clicked the icon. A message from JNTD@gmail.com.

Hey, Allie. I just wanted to apologize for not treating you with respect when you were in the club. Ryan told me I'd been rude, and I realized he was right. He also told me I should listen to your band, and I just did. You ladies were awesome. If you are in a new band, please HMU for a show sometime. I'm really sorry for acting like a shit today. Ryan's right, we should all try to do better. Cheers. Jesse.

She looked at Ryan, who smirked but didn't take his eyes off the road. "Did he apologize?"

"Yep." Allie locked her phone and dropped it back into her bag. "Says he acted like a shithead and that you told him that he should try to be better."

"That is accurate."

Allie laughed. The South Orange landscape flowed by her window. She'd thought the day would feel like a failure if they didn't find Jessi. But it didn't feel like a failure at all.

As they made their way across the bridge back into Brooklyn, Ryan turned to Allie.

"It's almost dinnertime. Do you want to just come to our place?"

"I'm not even going to pretend to think it over." Allie put one hand on her rumbling stomach. "I'm super hungry, and also, I want to tell Anisha about our adventures in Jersey."

Ryan grinned. "Nonadventures, more like."

"She'll get a kick out of Alan, though."

"That is the truth." Ryan steered the car over the bridge and into the streets of Williamsburg, stopping and starting as traffic ebbed and flowed.

He pulled the car into a parking space near the apartment. Allie was still fussing with her phone and sunglasses when he appeared at her door and opened it for her.

"Ma'am?" He gestured toward the sidewalk with his arm. "Care to accompany me to my apartment so my zany roommate can feed us yet again?"

Allie smiled at him and stepped out onto the curb. She mimicked his accent. "Why, yes, sir, I do think that would be delightful."

Ryan laughed. "You do a great Alabamian. Do you want to come home with me and pretend to be my churchgoing Southern wife so my family will stop thinking that New York is basically a stepping stone on the way to hell?"

Allie willed herself not to blush. Ryan locked the car, and they started up the stairs to the apartment.

"Is that what they think?" Allie asked over her shoulder. "That you're damning yourself to hell by living here?"

"Pretty much." Ryan shrugged. And then sighed and repeated himself. "Pretty much."

Allie sensed he didn't want to talk about it, but she was curious. "*All* of them?"

Ryan blew out a gust of air. "Well, I have five siblings, and I'm the oldest, so I think most of them just think I am this, I don't know, random weirdo? I just never fit in with the family, I guess. I tried. I do love them." He stopped on the landing between staircases. They were both breathing heavily from the exertion of the climb. "My sister Rachel is just two years younger than me. I think, of everyone, she's the most likely to be cool with me, at least in theory. I don't think she would come visit here or anything, but she'd probably answer a letter if I wrote her one. We used to slide letters under each other's bedroom doors when we were kids. And even if she blocked my email and phone number, she couldn't have blocked me via the USPS."

"Why don't you write her, then?"

Ryan paused, looking up at the ceiling. "I guess I worry about how I'd feel if she *didn't* write back. Things got . . . bad with my family before I moved here. The girl I was seeing, Molly, was a friend of Rachel's. When I told Molly I was starting to have doubts about God, church, all of it . . ." Ryan paused and sighed.

Allie's hand gripped the banister until her knuckles were white. She held her breath, not wanting to do anything that might break whatever spell he was under that was leading to him telling her all this.

"She told Rachel. And Rachel told the rest of my family. And then they did this weird intervention type thing, which was terrible. And when I wouldn't say what they wanted to hear, they all stopped speaking to me. Molly, too. I had been thinking about moving out already, and living in a house where people treated me like a ghost just solidified that decision. Rachel cried when I said goodbye. So I do think she actually thought she was helping me." He looked down at Allie, almost as though he had just remembered she was there, and gave her an empty smile. "Things are better now. It's fine." He started walking again, and Allie knew the conversation was over.

Chapter Thirteen

"New Jersey certainly made both of you hungry." Anisha looked from Ryan, who was on his third bowl of soup, over to Allie, who was just finishing her second.

Allie nodded. Her cheeks were warm from the soup and the general good feeling of being back in Ryan and Anisha's apartment after the long day. She was just about to suggest that they all move over to the living room and maybe play Scrabble or something when Ryan dropped his spoon into his empty bowl.

"Dang, that was good."

"It was," Allie agreed. "Anisha, I would bathe in that soup."

"Speaking of bathing . . ." Ryan stood up. "I'll do the dishes later, okay? I need to have a shower."

Allie laughed. "You feel that the Top Drawer left you with some uncleanliness you just can't shake?"

"Naw." Ryan's cheeks went slightly pink. "It's just, I have a date tonight."

Allie felt as if she'd been hit over the head with a blunt object. She stared straight ahead for a moment and then, with effort, regained her composure.

"A *date*. Cool."

Anisha waved her hand at him. "Don't worry about the dishes. Allie and I will manage it on our own this once."

Allie's brain felt like an engine struggling to turn over. Why shouldn't he have a date? He wasn't dating *her*. He didn't *want* to date her, obviously.

Say something. Something nice.

"So . . . where are you going?"

Better than *Who is she?*

Ryan looked at her, puzzled. "Everything okay? Your voice sounds all weird."

She cleared her throat in a way that could only be called *aggressive*. "I'm fine, sorry, just had a . . . throat thing."

"Ah." Ryan pushed in his chair. "We're going to see that new documentary about the Velvet Underground and then probably go get a drink or whatever. She's coming to pick me up at seven thirty. Chivalrous, huh?" He laughed.

"Velvet Underground." Allie nodded and put a Herculean effort into keeping her voice neutral. "That's supposed to be a good one."

"Yeah. Sheila's interning for the podcast for a few months. She wants to be a music journalist. She seems pretty cool. No idea why she agreed to go out with me."

She helped Anisha clear the table, and Ryan disappeared into the bathroom.

As Anisha scraped the dregs of food from the dishes, they heard Ryan start singing loudly in the shower. Allie had never heard him singing at full volume, without any music or accompanying voices. It allowed her to really appreciate the steady, warm tone of his voice.

"Damn, he's good." She looked at Anisha, who looked up from her soup to nod enthusiastically.

"That's what I always tell him."

Allie paused to listen more closely. "What's he singing, anyway?"

Anisha laughed. "Church songs. You can take the boy out of Alabama, but you can't take the church songs out of his repertoire."

Allie listened to Ryan sing about how Jesus's light was filling his soul until she heard the water, and the song, stop. Only then did her thoughts return to the reason why Ryan was cleaning up in the first place.

"He never tells me anything about dates. Does he talk to you about who he's seeing?" She tried to sound as if she was just making conversation.

Anisha nodded. "He tells me a little bit, but no real details. Honestly, no disrespect to these ladies he goes out with, they're all smart and nice and all that. But I'm not putting the mental energy into knowing anything about them until I think one of them is actually going to stick around."

Allie took a moment to mull this over. "Really? None of them last?"

Anisha shook her head. "I think he gets scared that any relationship he's in will end in him getting abandoned. He's developed this super destructive tendency to bail really quickly on any relationship that might be going well, just because he's trying to beat them to the inevitable end."

"Huh." Allie busied herself rinsing glasses under the tap.

"Anyway, as deep dark sexy secrets go, his is pretty benign." Anisha laughed. She turned down the burner under the soup pot. "I was actually worried that he might be trying to date you."

Allie's head snapped up, and she stared at Anisha. "Worried?" Her pulse pounded in her ears.

"I mean, because I like you hanging around!" Anisha quickly clarified. "I didn't want him to scare you off with his weird baggage."

Allie laughed, slightly louder than she meant to. "Well, no worries about that."

Before Anisha could say anything else, the bathroom door banged open, and Ryan walked out, his bulk concealed by a large purple bathrobe. His usual good smell was strong enough to compete with the waning fragrance of lemongrass and ginger that still hung in the air from their dinner.

Anisha whistled at him. "Is that what you're wearing on your date? I hope so."

Ryan rolled his eyes and didn't bother answering her as he entered his bedroom, closing the door behind him. A few minutes later, he walked back into the main room, looking slightly more put together than Allie was used to seeing him. His jeans were freshly washed and a blue so dark it was almost black. He wore a gray cardigan over his usual denim button-down, and his hair was neatly combed. Allie swallowed hard and averted her eyes.

"So, I finished the basic bed tracks for 'Borderline,'" Allie said, awkwardly grabbing at conversation topics as he laced up his boots and pulled on his jacket.

"Oh, awesome!" Ryan smiled. "I have a few days off coming up. We can get together sometime next week."

"Perfect."

"I mean, unless . . ." Ryan looked away. "Unless this date goes really well . . ." He looked back up at Allie and fixed her with a questioning look that she couldn't quite decipher.

Does he want me to be . . . upset?

Anisha joined them near the entryway, wiping her hands on a tea towel. Her lips pressed together in a thin line. "You're ditching Allie for a girl you haven't even been out with yet?"

"I'm not *ditching Allie*. Take it easy. I'm just being optimistic about my date."

Anisha looked away from him and shook her head. It was the first time Allie had seen any kind of conflict between them. She felt mild panic, like a second grader whose mom and dad were sniping at each other at parent-teacher night.

"Optimistic? Or ridiculous?" Anisha squinted at him, suspicious.

"Same difference." Ryan smiled at his roommate, and Allie felt the tension start to fizzle. He turned to her. "Allie, I give you my word that I will come record with you on Tuesday. Even if Sheila is begging me to take her to Bora Bora for a romantic getaway."

Anisha gave a loud snort and then started coughing. Ryan rolled his eyes again.

A knock on the door jolted Allie from her position leaning against the wall.

Ryan looked at them. "Could you two get out of here? Last thing I need is two nosy chaperones watching me leave with my date."

"Come on." Anisha hooked her arm through Allie's. "Let's go hide in my room. Wouldn't want to interfere with Mr. Romance."

Allie forced out a laugh and gratefully followed Anisha into her room.

Never had she been less eager to meet a person than she was to meet Intern Sheila.

Chapter Fourteen

True to his word, Ryan showed up to record with her the following Tuesday. Allie had predicted that he would be too tall for her apartment. She was correct.

He'd been there for all of five minutes before he attempted to stand to his full height from where he'd been leaning over her computer and his head collided with the ceiling. The thunk was alarming.

"*Sweet Fancy Moses!*"

Allie wasn't sure whether to express concern for his head or laugh at his exclamation.

"This apartment is for short people," Ryan grumbled. He bent his knees and waddled over to the chair by the window. Allie retrieved two cans of sparkling water from her tiny fridge, and he accepted one gratefully, pausing before opening it to press the cool metal against his sore head. "I mean, I also like it. It's nice. Very *you*."

"Oh?" Allie laughed. "I'm tiny and cold and not up to current structural standards?"

"Well, yes, all that," Ryan answered, not missing a beat. "But also, it's cute and welcoming and everything is tidy. I know how you like things to be kinda predictable."

She didn't miss that he'd just called her cute, but she tried to ignore it for the sake of her already jittery nervous system.

He was right about her liking a predictable life, though that life seemed like a distant memory at this point. Some days, she wondered what would have happened if she'd never gone on that coffee delivery to the studio and met Ryan. The idea of Ryan—and Anisha—not being in her life had quickly become unfathomable. But where her feelings were concerned, things were getting . . . complicated.

"I'm glad you were able to come over tonight," she told Ryan, making sure she was looking intently at her computer screen as she spoke.

"Yeah, I've been busy. I'm sorry." Ryan had been going on dates, which, when combined with his work schedule, left less free time for him to hang out. Allie hated it, but she'd tried to be cool.

"It's no problem. How's, uh, Sheila doing?"

"Well . . ." Ryan tilted his head from one side to the other. "I guess fine? I pumped the brakes on us for the time being."

"Oh?" Allie struggled to keep her voice neutral.

"Yeah. She's younger than me. We didn't really have enough in common. I don't really think I was her type. It's fine. I wasn't in love or anything."

Allie adjusted the microphone so that it pointed at the xylophone, which sat on the table in front of Ryan. He held the wooden mallet in his hand, ready.

Ryan is available.

Trying to ignore her own thoughts, she positioned her headphones over her ears. "Okay, play a few notes, and I'll check the levels."

Ryan tentatively played the opening notes of the "Borderline" melody, and Allie stared at the bars on her laptop screen, clicking on a few of them to get the sound to be exactly what she'd envisioned. She picked up her acoustic guitar and nodded at Ryan, who played the melody again while she tested out some muted chords with an emphasis on the bass line she'd been hearing in her head. Satisfied with the levels, she handed Ryan her extra set of headphones, and he put them on. She plugged his headphones into her tiny soundboard beside hers and started the backing track that she'd made so he could hear it.

"This is amazing!" Ryan's voice was louder to account for them both wearing headphones. "It's perfect."

Allie stopped the music and pulled her headphones off, resting them around her neck. Ryan did the same.

"It's actually just a rudimentary backing track, mostly so we have the click track of the drums to keep us on time. I'm going to record my guitar part first, then you do your xylophone, then we'll add the vocals. Good?"

Ryan nodded. "Whatever you say, boss!"

Allie smiled. She had always avoided being the boss in all aspects of her life. But something about the way Ryan said it, the way he seemed delighted and impressed that she was in charge, made her feel good about it.

—

Singing with Ryan was the best thing that had happened to her in years. It felt similar to singing with Jessi, but less *urgent*. In a good way. Writing songs with her band had been exhilarating, but with that kind of exhilaration always came stress. They would all write together, try things out, argue about stuff that others did or didn't like, and then eventually end up with this shiny diamond of a song, refined from carbon under the heat and pressure of four people's opinions.

With Ryan, she was in charge; the song was already written, and he had very little to prove. He played his xylophone riff over and over until she was satisfied, and then he sang, in his strong and steady voice, whenever she asked him to. He could hold a note while she added harmony. They sounded good together.

"I think I'm going to try to mix this right now." Allie leaned over her laptop, her mind whirring with ideas for the final recording. "But you don't have to stay. I know it's almost nine."

By that point, Ryan was stretched out on her bed, resting with his hands behind his head and his legs hanging over the side. He lifted his head to look at her. "No way! I want to hear our masterpiece in its final form."

Allie grinned. "Okay, but you may want food. Ren should be just finishing up downstairs if you want to go grab something."

Ryan stood up carefully. He'd already hit his head several more times. "Sure thing! I'll go say hi to Ren and bring us up some snacks."

As much as she'd enjoyed having Ryan in her apartment for the evening, Allie relished this moment alone. She closed her eyes and thought through the song and the way she wanted the final product to sound. Absentmindedly, she picked up Ryan's mallet and tapped a few notes on the xylophone. She was still tapping out this new melody when Ryan returned, holding a plate with two huge slices of pecan pie on it.

"Hey, that's pretty. What's that from?" He set the plate down on the table next to Allie and handed her a fork.

"Nothing, I don't think. I'm pretty sure I made it up." She played it again and hummed another melody over top of the notes.

"Well, I like it! Make some words!"

Allie laughed. "I don't have a wand that I wave to conjure lyrics."

"That's not how it works, huh?" He grinned at her.

"It kind of used to work that way, to be honest. When we were writing as a band, I just used to shout out these sentences, and Jessi would come up with alternate verses. We could write a song in a matter of hours. But also, we had the dumb confidence of teenagers. Now I'm too in my head. I haven't written a song for a decade. Every time I try, I just talk myself out of it."

"That why you're doing the cover song project?"

"It's part of it, yeah."

"What's the other part?" Ryan was halfway through his piece of pie, and Allie hadn't touched hers yet. She took a small bite and sighed. Without having to get up, she nudged the crate of cassette tapes toward Ryan with her foot.

He looked down at it, confused. "Are these the cassettes from your tour van? The ones fans made?"

Allie shook her head. "No. Jessi took those. These ones were my dad's."

Ryan met her eyes and then reached toward the crate. "May I?" She nodded.

Ryan slowly took out various cassettes, one after the other, looking at each and then making tiny stacks on the table.

"Cyndi Lauper. The Bangles. The Go-Go's. Your dad liked these bands?"

"So much." Allie picked up a Pat Benatar cassette and rubbed her finger over the warped and banged-up plastic of the cover. The plastic squeaked as she opened it. "I assume this was his favorite. It's definitely been handled the most." She pulled the tape out and carefully removed and unfolded the insert. Ryan leaned forward to look at it.

"These things always feel so fragile to me. Like you could listen to them three times and then they turn to dust."

"Yeah, I'm lucky to have all of these. My mom got rid of most of my dad's stuff when he died."

"How old were you?" Ryan's normal exuberant fidgeting had turned to stillness.

"I was seven." She reassembled the parts of the Pat Benatar cassette and laid it on the table. "Old enough to remember him. But just barely."

"And what was he like?"

"He was nice." She smiled. "My mom's family was always— Well, that's where I get my prickly side you like so much." She glanced at

Ryan and found herself fighting a blush in her cheeks. "I mean, you've met Mindy, so you probably already knew that. But my dad was sweet. Easygoing. Not perfect; he drank too much beer and played his music too loud late at night. But when it woke me up, I'd go to the top of the stairs and watch him, and if he saw me, he'd look so happy. Like he was *lucky* I was there. And he'd make me come down and dance with him for a while, and then he'd take me back up to bed."

"How did he die?"

Allie swallowed. "Car accident. He was drunk. Didn't hurt anyone else. Just himself."

"And your mom?"

"Cancer. When I was eighteen. Likely also aggravated by drinking and hating everything and everybody."

Ryan exhaled. "Wow. I'm so sorry."

This was the point where Allie usually brushed it off. She never wanted to dwell, to be seen as a victim of a bad childhood when there were so many other people who had it worse. But this time, she just looked into Ryan's eyes and nodded.

"Thank you. It was pretty shitty. My mom died when I was on my first tour with the band. It was just Mindy and me and a handful of randos at the funeral. I cleaned out the apartment, junked all of her crap and then officially moved in with Jessi at her grandma's place. Jessi's parents weren't great, either, but she'd been living with her grandma since she was in third grade. She had a lot more stability than I did, and I just—" Allie sighed. This was starting to feel more painful. "I just needed that so much. Her grandma had been so good to let me live with them whenever we weren't on tour. No questions asked. Anyway." She picked up three of the cassettes and absentmindedly assembled them into a small tower. "Things would have been easier with my dad around. He kind of kept my mom in check. She was a grouch, but he was always pretty happy."

"So the covers project, it's kind of for your dad?"

She nodded again. "Yeah. It's like I get to go back to that living room, to listen to those songs again with him. It's the next best thing to having him here to listen to these new versions with me. Music was such a big deal to him. Even when I was a kid, I wanted to be a part of that."

"I get it." Ryan started gently placing the tapes back in the crate. "Anisha teases me about singing church songs around the apartment, but I love those songs. They're my version of your dance party memories. My whole family and me, with my brothers and sisters all too young to know any different, standing in church to sing to the Lord together."

"Hallelujah," Allie said softly.

"Hallelujah, indeed." He held her gaze.

"Have you thought any more about writing that letter to Rachel?"

Ryan shook his head. "I kind of put it out of my mind right after we talked about it. Maybe she doesn't want anything to do with me, and I don't think I'm ready for that door to be completely closed."

"Wait a minute." Allie was distracted by a sudden thought. "Ryan, Rachel . . . Are all of you *R* names?"

Ryan laughed. "Ronnie, Rayann, Ripley, Robert, Rachel and Ryan. I guess they thought it would foster some kind of connection between us. Also, it was pretty common in our town, like a weird viral baby-naming trend."

"Oh wow." Allie's eyes widened. "Did people, like, make fun of you?"

"Not for that. But for *lots* of other things. Let's save my childhood disillusionment for another night, shall we? I'm going to get out of your way so you can edit our song and then play it for me." He stood up, taking care to slouch so as not to make contact with the ceiling, and moved back over to her bed.

Allie looked at him for a moment. "No." She shook her head. "Tell me."

Ryan shook his head and opened his mouth, as if he was about to dismiss the subject again.

"I want to know." Allie held his gaze. After a moment, his shoulders fell, and he stopped shaking his head.

"I'll tell you the short version."

She nodded.

Ryan let out a long, noisy breath. "Kids made fun of me for all the things you'd probably expect. For them, I was too fat, I was bad at sports, I was friends with girls instead of boys. I was arty. I cried once when we watched a documentary about veterans with PTSD getting dogs to help."

Allie smiled at him, tenderness welling up in her heart.

"And because I was the oldest, I didn't have anyone to defend me or watch out for me. I had all these siblings and all kinds of cousins and stuff in town, but I was the oldest out of everyone. No one ever really helped me out. I had to fight through it all on my own. And then I had to make sure it didn't happen to any of my siblings or little cousins. It was damn hard. It all sucked. One of the nice things about living here is not having to be responsible for all kinds of people who don't even really seem to care if I'm happy myself. My life was exhausting before I moved here. Trying to protect myself and everyone else. Here, I just get to be who I want to be."

Ryan, who always seemed so friendly and open, had never actually been that honest with her about his personal life. It felt special being there with him, as if the singing had opened some imaginary door she'd previously been unaware of.

"Allie?" Ryan's voice snapped her out of her fog of thoughts.

"Yes?"

"Can you edit the song now?" He wiggled his eyebrows up and down.

Allie worked quickly. She already had a vision for the song, and the parts they'd recorded were perfect. She put on her headphones and hunkered over her laptop. Within an hour, she had a finished version pieced together.

"Are you ready?" she asked. Ryan sat up from where he'd been lying on the bed, looking at his phone to pass the time.

"It's done?"

"I think so."

"Oh man, yes, play it! I can't wait!"

Allie hit Play and went to sit beside him on the bed. The first notes of the xylophone riff, recorded alone without any other vocals or instruments, poured from her small but powerful speakers. After a moment, her muted acoustic guitar joined in, then the drum loop and finally the vocals. She was pleased to note that she'd mixed their voice tracks perfectly. They sounded good. *Great*, even.

When her vocal track slid into a harmony, Ryan held out his bare forearm for her to see. "Goose bumps."

Allie nodded and held her arm up beside his, barely touching. "Me too."

When the song finished, Ryan collapsed back on the bed. "That was . . . amazing. How are we that good?"

Allie laughed with relief and collapsed back beside him. "I don't know! We're greater than the sum of our parts, I guess."

Ryan angled his body toward Allie and propped his head up on one arm. "Allie?"

"Hmm?" She took a deep breath and raised her head so her face was level with his.

They were definitely too close to one another. Or just close enough.

He swallowed, held her gaze for a moment and then averted his eyes. She could feel his breath when he exhaled before speaking.

"What you said about your dad, that he seemed like he felt lucky to have you around. He *was* lucky. We all are."

Allie was sure he could hear her heart beating. It felt like a panicked bird trapped in her chest. She took a deep breath, staring hard, watching his eyelashes flutter as he blinked. Oh boy, she loved those eyelashes. His lips were curved into a nervous smile.

Ryan moved his right hand to her shoulder, silently.

Allie's mind swirled with anticipation and anxiety. She could barely breathe as he slid the hand up to her neck and gently pressed to move her head toward his. As her face got closer, she closed her eyes.

The crash was huge, like a tray of dishes hitting the ground. It echoed up from the kitchen, directly below where they were sitting.

Her eyes flew open. They both sat up.

"What was that?"

"I don't know." She was on her feet. Ryan followed her to the door of the apartment, where they both stood still.

Ren would have gone home ages ago. Mindy never came in after hours. It wasn't a noise that would have come from a random dish shifting in the drying rack. There had to be someone there.

Shit.

Chapter Fifteen

"Should we go down there?" Allie didn't know why she was whispering.

"Are you sure it's an intruder? Should we call the police?" Ryan was also whispering.

"Maybe we just go check? What if Ren left a tray too close to the edge of the counter or something? I hate calling the cops, and I would extra-hate it if they showed up and told us the dangerous intruder was a mug that slipped."

"That noise was *not* from a mug that slipped."

"Let's just go see what it is. But, like, slowly. Quietly."

"Slow I can do. Not sure about quiet. Your stairs are creaky."

Allie nodded. "If you stay on the left side of each step, it's a bit better."

"Noted. So, are we doing this? Vigilante justice?" Ryan looked more concerned than she would have expected a giant man to be about a noise in a kitchen.

"Vigilante investigation, more accurately."

"Fine, Sherlock. I'll go first. That way, if they get me, you can escape. You have more valuable skills to offer the world."

She paused to smile at him. "I can't confirm that, but of the two of us, you're more likely to scare someone into running away without a fight. So, yes, you go first."

They left her apartment, stepping as softly as the old floors would allow, and crept slowly down the stairs, their feet as far left as possible on each step. Allie's heart was pounding for an entirely different reason than it had been a minute ago. At the bottom of the staircase, Ryan put his hand on the knob of the door to the kitchen and turned back to her. They could both hear movement on the other side.

"Ready?" Ryan whispered. He looked as unsure as she felt. Allie drew in a deep breath and nodded.

Ryan tensed his face into a nervous squint and turned back to the door. He pushed it open and froze.

"Oh dang!" He reeled backward into the stairwell with his palm over his eyes.

"What is it?" Allie shrieked, leaping up one stair to avoid being crushed between his body and the wall of the stairwell.

"Boobs!" Ryan yelled. "My roommate's boobs!"

Allie still wasn't sure what was happening, but it didn't sound unsafe. She wriggled around Ryan, who was still frozen with one hand covering his eyes.

The situation became clear when she took a tentative step forward into the kitchen and saw Anisha there, perched on the edge of the prep counter, naked from the waist up. A person, who was definitely Ren, was emerging from under her voluminous skirt. Anisha rolled her eyes and put one arm across her chest in a gesture of reluctant modesty.

"You're being very dramatic for someone who has already seen my boobs *plenty of times*!" she called to Ryan, who was still in the stairway with one hand over his eyes.

"Never while you've been in the middle of a *sex act*!" Ryan shouted back. "Walking to your room from the shower is a whole different thing, *Anisha*! And for the record, I have always advocated for bathrobes."

Allie finally remembered why they were there in the first place and walked around the counter to check for what had fallen. Sure enough, a large metal dishpan lay on the floor, cutlery littered around it. Definitely the source of the crash.

Fucking Ren.

It wasn't as though Ren had never had sex in the café before. There had been several times when Allie had heard unmistakable moans coming from the bathroom toward the end of an evening shift when they were working together. They had an unspoken understanding that she wouldn't rat Ren out to Mindy. But hearing muffled groans from a bathroom that Ren was in charge of cleaning anyway was very different from finding a half-naked lady on their food prep surface. A slow burn of frustration was spreading through her system. And, though she tried hard to stifle the emotion, a bit of . . . jealousy? She had been all excited about her G-rated almost-kiss with Ryan upstairs, when all the while there was a full NC-17 scene happening just below them.

"Well, at least you didn't break any dishes," Allie said to Ren, who had now fully emerged from Anisha's nether regions and was standing beside the counter, looking only mildly embarrassed by the whole situation.

"Yeah, sorry about all that. I'll wash those again."

"And do a *vigorous* wipe-down of the counter, too, please." Allie looked at where Anisha's butt was still perched on their food prep surface, the ruffles of her long skirt making a nest around her body.

Ren nodded.

"Look, I don't want to be a buzzkill or anything," Allie went on, "but for fuck's sake, *please* don't have sex in the café kitchen. You have your own kitchens. Go have sex in one of those."

"Not ours!" Ryan had finally entered the room.

Anisha pulled her shirt back on. She was rolling her eyes when her head emerged through the neckhole.

"After this lovely interaction, I'm not particularly in the mood to have sex in anyone's kitchen." Anisha hopped down from the counter and, with an amount of haughtiness that Allie found impressive, picked her discarded underpants up off the floor and tucked them into her purse. "Ryan? You heading home?"

Ryan sighed. "Yeah. Let's head out."

Allie was stunned. How could they just carry on with their relationship as normal after a scene like this? Wasn't Ryan mad? Wasn't Anisha annoyed? Apparently not anymore.

How can they forgive each other so fast? And how can Ryan just . . . leave? Now?

Anisha stopped to give Ren a lingering kiss as they headed toward the door. "I'll call you," she murmured.

Ren smiled wider than they usually did. "Not if I call you first."

Ryan made a theatrical gagging sound as they retreated from the room. Anisha swatted his arm. Allie could hear them bickering as the café door closed behind them. The café was once again dark and quiet.

She left Ren to rewash the cutlery and scrub down the counter, and went back up to her bedroom. Should she text Ryan? And say what? *Hey, remember how we almost kissed?* No, the moment had passed, and who knew what Ryan's intentions had been anyway— maybe she had it all wrong. She looked at herself in the mirror and took her hair out of its messy ponytail. She looked exhausted. And kind of pathetic. Maybe she wasn't made for romance. Music was so much easier. She hummed a Belinda Carlisle song to herself as she changed into her pajamas.

Even though it was late and she had to get up early, she listened to their recording of "Borderline" six times before she shut her laptop and turned out her light. Ryan's harmonies were still echoing in her head as she drifted into an exhausted sleep.

—

The next morning, almost-kiss almost forgotten, Allie was once again behind the counter, taking orders from a small group of people who had no business being as rude as they were.

"We wanted two cranberry scones." The middle-aged man with dark hair and pretentiously thick glasses frames was jabbing at the pastry case glass with his index finger. "But there's only one in here."

"That's the last one." Allie tried to smile and pretend that he wasn't now staring at her chest. The woman he was with flipped her very shiny hair over one shoulder and huffed.

"Are you sure? Can you ask your boss?" The man dragged his eyes up to Allie's face. She felt a stab of annoyance in her chest.

"I am sure," she responded with a tight smile. "But the pumpkin scones are also very good."

He sighed. "Pumpkin's pretty basic, isn't it, though?"

Allie decided not to address this. "Let me know when you decide."

As the opening notes of "Let It Snow" bounced out of the speakers, Allie took a moment away from her frustrating customer interaction to smile at the ceiling and then glance outside.

They had a rule. No Christmas music until December first or until it snowed, whichever came first. Ren would have started in August otherwise. Christmas was the only time of the year when Ren had strong opinions about the music they played in the café, leaving Mindy and Allie to argue about the relative merits of Joni Mitchell for the rest of the year.

Sure enough, large white flakes were drifting past the window. The normal buzz of the full café seemed to turn up its volume as people started noticing and pointing it out to their friends. The first snow.

When Allie finally provided the unpleasant man and his companion with their scones and oat milk cortados, she stuck her head back into the kitchen.

"How did you even see that it was snowing? You don't have any windows back here."

"They have a sixth sense," Mindy answered for Ren. "Out of nowhere, they went running over to open the back door, and there it was. Snow."

Ren laughed. "Yeah, a sixth sense. Otherwise known as *a weather app on my phone.*"

"Well, whatever it was, I'm grateful to be notified." Mindy took her apron off. "We ran out of whipped cream, and I need to get some more before we get the usual first-snow run on hot chocolate this afternoon. I'll be back in a few minutes."

When Mindy left, Ren came to stand with Allie behind the counter. The café was full, but everyone was happily chatting and eating, providing a momentary breather. Allie started tidying the sandwich station. Ren immediately moved beside her to help.

"Look, I'm sorry about last night, and thanks for not telling Mindy."

"You owe me for that one." Allie smiled, more able to laugh about the experience after a good sleep. Remembering Ryan shouting "Boobs!" had been making her giggle to herself all morning. "But honestly, she's never said as much, but I'd bet any amount of money she's had sex in that kitchen over the years."

"No doubt!" Ren laughed. "The way that guy from the hardware store stares at her when he comes in. No way there wasn't something happening there before he married that lady with the hair."

Allie snickered. She finished wiping crumbs and arranging the lettuce bin and turned to Ren. "Anyway, even though it was not great that you were getting it on in the kitchen, I apologize for interrupting you."

"Ah, don't worry about it. I was to blame for the interruption, anyway. It was me who knocked the cutlery bin off the counter. That stupid bin ruined what would have otherwise been a very pleasant evening."

Allie was torn between keeping her secret and her burning desire to talk about the situation with someone.

"You're not the only one. I thought Ryan was about to kiss me before all that noise interrupted."

Ren immediately stopped stacking tomatoes. "What? Really? Allie!"

Allie could feel herself blush. The regret was already seeping in. "But it wasn't really anything, I don't think. We'd been up late singing together, and that always makes people mushy. Plus, he broke it off with that girl, Sheila. He was probably just feeling lonely."

Ren shook their head emphatically. "Ryan is about the least lonely person I've ever met. He wasn't feeling lonely. Allie, he *likes* you. Why are you acting like you're in sixth grade and a boy has never liked you before?"

Allie bristled. "Because he was the one who was very clear that he's not interested. He accidentally held my hand once, and he could not offer up disclaimers fast enough."

"What do you mean, 'accidentally held your hand'? People don't *accidentally* hold other people's hands. If we lived in a world where random strangers were constantly grabbing people's hands, I'd never leave my house."

Allie chose to ignore that particular premise. "We'd just had a good conversation, and he was, I don't know, feeling extra friendly or something?"

"You know another way to say *feeling extra friendly*?" Ren smirked. "Feeling like *he has a crush on you*."

"Nope." Allie was now certain that bringing this up had been the wrong move. "Nothing like that. When I pulled my hand away, he fell all over himself explaining that it hadn't been a romantic thing and we were just friends and that was all he wanted."

"You pulled your hand away? Why?"

Allie was starting to feel queasy. "I don't know. It felt weird. It was sudden. I wasn't expecting it."

"But did you like it?"

Allie flashed back to the feeling of Ryan's warm, soft hand gripping hers. It made her mind wander to the memory of them lying side by side on her bed last night. She wondered what his hands would have felt like on her skin. What his breath would have felt like on her neck. It gave her goose bumps.

"What are you thinking about?" Ren's voice booted the fantasy from her head immediately.

"Nothing!" Allie's cheeks were burning. She looked around frantically for something to clean.

Ren laughed. "You were picturing him grabbing more than your hand, weren't you?"

"I, uh, need to pee." She was panicking. Ren was laughing harder. Their voice followed her as she speed-walked into the kitchen. "It's okay to like a boy, Allie!"

It wasn't okay to like *this* boy. She'd just managed to actually form a friendship for the first time in years. If she propositioned Ryan and he said no, she wasn't sure she'd be able to go on being his friend. She needed Ryan and Anisha in her life. They'd only been there a short while, but it felt as if she now couldn't manage without them.

Why did I tell Ren?

She put her head in her hands. Would Ren tell Anisha? She would have to ask them not to. And besides, none of Ren's relationships lasted longer than a week, anyway. Even though Anisha was definitely not the type to come crying to the café after Ren broke things off, Allie doubted they'd be seeing very much of her after Ren did their usual vanishing act.

She stood up and checked her hair in the mirror, pausing to tighten her ponytail.

Everything will be fine.

She could hear the strains of "Blue Christmas" from the kitchen speakers wafting into the bathroom. Glancing in the mirror one more time, she locked eyes with herself.

Don't fuck it all up this time.

She nodded emphatically at her reflection, turned off the lights and returned to the world.

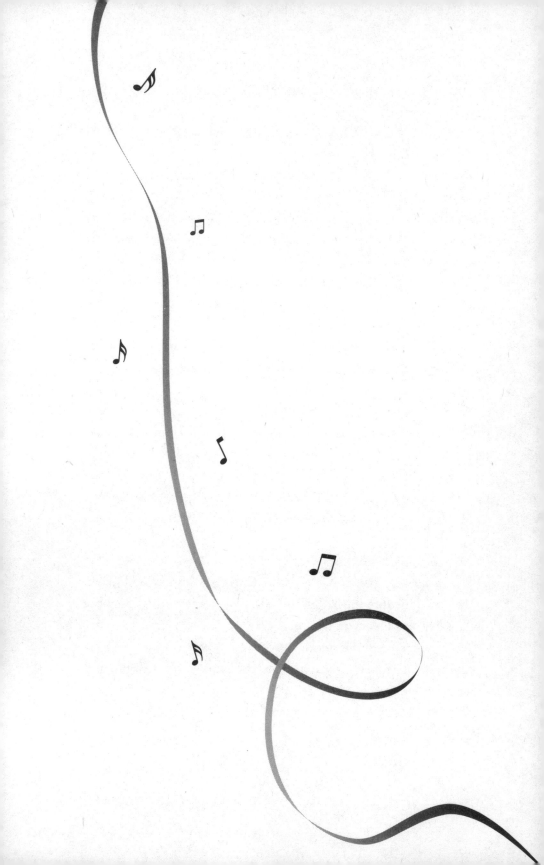

DECEMBER

Straight Up

Chapter Sixteen

The skies above Brooklyn seemed to know it was finally the first of December. They'd decided it was time to give it their all, snow-wise. A thick blanket of white covered everything, and the snow showed no signs of letting up.

The café was slammed all day long. People rushed to do their Christmas shopping when the weather and the calendar conspired to remind them. It was a day of mucky wet floors and patrons with over-whelming numbers of shopping bags. When Allie went out front to shovel the sidewalk, she looked back through the windows at Ren and Mindy smiling and laughing with customers, every table full, the windows fogging up with the breath and warmth of the inside. She took a moment to appreciate it. To love it from outside.

It reminded her of the day she'd arrived at the café. That day had also been snowy, though at that time, the weather felt oppressive and fore-boding, not joyful. She'd seen Mindy from the outside that day, too, and she could still remember the relief that coursed through her. At that time in her life, Mindy was the last person she had in the world who knew her and loved her. Seeing her steady, caring, no-nonsense aunt through the window as she arrived, unannounced, at the café, was the only thing that gave her even a shred of hope. She'd pushed through the café door, and when Mindy saw her there, eyes red from crying, suitcase in hand, everything felt instantly understood. She'd moved, rent-free, into the apartment above the café that night. Mindy had stayed up until 2 a.m. with her, getting the place into a livable condition. They'd barely talked, but Allie knew she was welcome and safe. She'd never left.

Now, with her shift over and the action of the day starting to wind down, she'd left Ren capably serving those evening customers who'd trickled in for hot chocolate or tea, and was comfortably ensconced in her own bed upstairs. Her apartment was always slightly colder than she wanted it, no matter how much she cranked the ancient radiators, but she was fine under blankets with her guitar in her lap.

She started strumming some chords, and it took her a few minutes to realize that she was playing a new song. Words started to come to her, and she scrambled for a notebook and pen to write them down.

She emerged from a creative fog half an hour later having written an actual song. Not someone else's song. Her own song. Lyrics about cassette tapes and road trips and the joys of being beside someone as a car moves along a highway, headed for something unknown.

She was just about to move over to her computer to record a rough version of the song when a snowball hit the middle of her window. It wasn't a hard smack, but it still seemed deliberate. She put her guitar down and went to the window, pulling a wool cardigan on over her pajamas as she went.

"Allie!"

Ryan was standing in the busy street, looking up at her, waving frantically. He wore a black knit cap pulled down over his ears and a rugged golden-brown coat with wide pockets and a corduroy collar. Beside him, easily a foot shorter than his six-foot-four frame, was a Christmas tree.

"I got you something!"

"I can't imagine what it could be!" She cranked open the window and leaned out to get a better look. The traffic light changed, and the street emptied of cars and trucks, providing a sudden moment of quiet. The snow was still coming down. Ryan's eyelashes and beard were caked with it.

"Can I bring it in the kitchen way?" He pointed up the alley toward the back of the café.

"Yes. I'll meet you there."

Allie moved back into her apartment and looked down at her rumpled pajamas with a tinge of regret. She hadn't planned for guests. Especially not handsome, snowy guests bearing trees.

Ren was letting Ryan in through the back door when Allie arrived in the kitchen. He stomped the caked snow from his boots onto the doormat, gripping the pointed top of the Christmas tree to keep it straight. It looked larger up close.

"Hey." Ryan's cheeks were flushed from the cold, and the snowflakes in his beard were quickly melting to droplets.

"Hey." She grinned back, fiddling with the buttons of her cardigan.

"So, how tall are the ceilings in your apartment?"

"Uh . . ." Allie had no idea. "About as tall as you, I guess, judging from how many times you've smashed your head."

"Right. Great." Ryan looked critically at the very top branch of the tree, which was level with his chin. "We should be good, then."

"Wait, is it for me? Not the café?"

"It's for you." He looked just as cheerful as usual, albeit slightly damp, and Allie fought the urge to place her warm hand on his cool skin.

Ren held open the door for Allie and Ryan as they carried the tree up to the apartment.

"You don't happen to have a tree stand, do you?" Ryan asked, as they set the tree on its side on the carpet.

"We must have one downstairs in the supply closet. We've had trees in the past that we put up in the café."

She left Ryan to doff his winter gear as she hustled down the creaking staircase to the supply closet. Sure enough, in a box marked *Christmas Is Over, Ren, Put It Away* she found the tree stand. She also nicked a string of white lights and some tinsel that were tucked away neatly with all of their other decorations, which hadn't been touched yet this year. Ren wasn't allowed to decorate until December, and the café had just been too busy to allow them time to do it.

Upstairs, Ryan was looking less like an arctic adventurer and more like a podcast tech. His coat and hat were hung neatly by the door, and he'd left his wet boots on the landing.

"I'm sorry. I didn't even ask if you wanted a tree. Do you want a tree? I'm fine if you don't. I can take it home with me instead. I just thought when I was here the other day that your apartment has that perfect corner by the window and how cool would it be to look up from the street on your way home and see a tree up there—"

"Ryan." Allie placed her hand on his arm to stop his nervous chatter. "I want the tree. Thank you for the tree. It smells fantastic."

She placed the stand under the window, and they carefully angled the fragrant tree into place, with Ryan holding it steady as she turned the screws of the stand until it was secure. When they were sure it was straight and steady, she wrapped a plaid wool blanket around the bottom of the trunk and wound the white lights around the branches. Ryan draped strands of tinsel while Allie searched for an extension cord so she could plug in the lights.

With the tree finally illuminated and minimally decorated, they stepped back and admired it. Ryan sat back on her bed, and Allie sat beside him, consciously leaving an appropriately friendly distance between them. She could not deal with the emotional roller coaster of another almost-kiss.

"It's a good one." She stared at the tree. "And you're right about how nice it will be to see it from the window when I'm coming home. I should steal more decorations from our box downstairs."

"Oh!" Ryan stood up suddenly. "I forgot!" He stepped toward the door, where his jacket hung, and reached into one of the front pockets. He pulled out a handful of small ornaments made from felt and string. "This is how they getcha, selling ornaments at the same spot as they sell trees. You know that lady who parks the little Airstream trailer and sells the trees in that alley off of Franklin? Anyway, turns out she also makes these things. She has a ton of them! I got all the music ones."

Ryan tossed them at her, one by one. A guitar, a drum, a page of sheet music with "Silent Night" embroidered at the top. A xylophone. She held that one extra tight in her hand.

Ryan was still rummaging through his pockets. "I can't find the best one. Hang on!" He dug one hand into each jacket pocket, feeling around frantically. "Oh yeah!" He stopped and reached into the smaller chest pocket. "I put it up there for safekeeping." He pulled out the last ornament and held it out to Allie. It was a tiny cassette tape.

"Oh, that's perfect." She stood up and took it from him, admiring the detail. On the label of the cassette, the words Christmas Mix were embroidered with tiny, perfect stitches.

"Okay, listen." Ryan hung the last of the ornaments on the tree. "I'm not here merely as an urban forester. I came to invite you to our holiday party. We do it every year. Everyone we know comes over, and there's drinks and food and a lot of embarrassing dancing."

"Oh! That sounds fun!" Allie grinned at him. She was clearly evolving into a new person if the thought of a party didn't make her want to hide under her bed. "When is it?"

"A week from Saturday. You don't need to bring anything. Tell Mindy and Ren they're invited as well. Though I imagine Anisha has already told Ren, if they've taken their mouths off each other long enough to speak an entire sentence."

Allie laughed. "Mindy won't come. She religiously goes to bed early in December because the café is bonkers busy every day."

"That's fair. At least you'll be there. I'm excited for you to meet some more of my workmates."

Allie worked hard not to think about meeting Intern Sheila and instead picked up her guitar and started strumming, then began picking out the melody of the song she'd written earlier.

Ryan turned his head to watch her play. When she let the music trail off, he spoke. "What was that? It didn't sound familiar."

"Oh, it's nothing." She put the guitar down beside her.

"By *nothing* you mean . . . something original that you wrote?"

"Yes." Allie smiled into her lap. "That is what I mean."

"Damn!" Ryan sat up. "Can I hear it?"

Allie hesitated. The song's lyrics weren't explicitly about Ryan. But she had to admit that the feeling of the song was the feeling she had for him. The slight regret of a connection that would not go as far as she'd originally thought. Deciding that there was no way he'd recognize himself in a nebulous lyrical theme, she picked up her guitar. "Sure."

She played the song once through, trying not to look at Ryan while she did it. Out of the corner of her eye, she could see that he was staring at her. When she finished, she resisted the urge to immediately tell him everything she wanted to change about it.

"That was amazing." Ryan's words finally drew her eyes to him. "I mean it. I knew you could write, obviously, and I knew you could play, but I didn't know you could write songs like *that*."

"What do you mean?" Allie tried to rein in her excitement. "Songs like what?"

"That was a classic songwriter song." Ryan sat up straight, warming to his topic. "That was a song that you could play by yourself on an acoustic guitar or play with a full band, and it would be just as great either way. It's a song that you could sell to a country singer or just keep playing at open mics in Brooklyn. Allie, you're so damn talented."

Allie didn't know what to say. She knew that she was good at what she did. She'd just been scared that no one else would care when she wasn't with Jessi and the rest of the band, with their great onstage chemistry.

"Have you thought about being in a band again? About touring? Even playing just by yourself anywhere?"

Allie nodded, hesitant. "I do think about it. A lot, actually. But now I've got the potential to take over the café, and I'm running out of reasons not to accept Mindy's offer. I know I could still play music if I did that, of course. But I couldn't have music as my career. Or even as a significant portion of my career."

"You couldn't prioritize it." Ryan clarified.

"Right. Exactly."

"Is that the biggest thing holding you back from taking the café?"

"Yeah. I love the café. I love working with Ren. I want Ren to feel safe in their job and not have to start over somewhere new. I want George to be able to see friendly faces every day, and I want the Thanksgiving dinner to still happen for all the people who love it."

"What do you want for yourself, though?" Ryan was looking at her steadily, his brown eyes locked to hers.

Allie sighed. "Mindy does a lot of spreadsheets. I don't want to do spreadsheets."

"Spreadsheets?"

"Yeah. I mean, I don't know what I want out of the rest of my life, but I know that I don't want it to include *more* spreadsheets."

"Well, I get that. I had to fill out a purchasing form for a new piece of studio equipment the other day, and it damn near made me want to die."

Allie smiled at him. "See? You get it."

The lights from the Christmas tree were casting a soft glow on his face. They sat together quietly, looking at the tree. She wanted him to stay longer, so she offered him a cup of tea, then retrieved two cups from the kitchen downstairs, ignoring Ren's salacious smirk.

When she arrived with the tea, he was hovering over the crate of her father's old tapes.

"I wanted to put one of these on, but I didn't want to do it without asking you first."

Her heart swelled. "Yeah, absolutely. Go ahead. I know you're careful."

He pulled a Paula Abdul cassette from the crate and held it up, raising his eyebrows.

"Compelling choice," Allie said. "I wouldn't have pegged you for an Abdul fan."

"I had a major crush on her during her *American Idol* years. Used to watch it at a friend's house because it was too secular for my parents' taste."

They listened to both sides of the cassette, chatting idly about nothing in particular. Allie pulled a pillow off her bed and lay on the floor with her head propped up high enough to look into his eyes. He leaned against her bed. It was wild to her that she could feel this comfortable around someone who had been an annoying stranger just a couple of months ago. They talked long after the cassette finished, and Allie felt a rush of disappointment when he stood up and said it was time for him to go. She hugged him tightly before he left and watched out the window as he disappeared into the dark and snowy streets, imagining an alternate reality where he was her boyfriend and he stayed all night.

She wondered, looking at the warmly lit tree he'd brought her, whether he ever thought about it, too.

Chapter Seventeen

The Saturday of Ryan and Anisha's party was a particularly gray one. The snow that had fallen during the first week of December had all since melted, leaving the sidewalks and streets wet and dirty. Allie looked out the café window at the icy rain and shivered.

She wasn't sure whether George would even make it in for his afternoon tea, but she set his favorite mug aside and kept her eye on the door. He hated the rain. But half an hour past his usual time of arrival, he appeared. She rushed to the door to help him in.

"It's a disaster out there." He was uncharacteristically gloomy as he wiped his feet on the mat at the door and handed Allie his umbrella. She stowed it away in the corner near his favorite table.

"Oh, I know. Been coming down all day. It makes for a slow day for us, which isn't entirely unwelcome, I admit."

George grinned at her as she took his elbow to walk him to his seat. "Oh? Shall I go, then?"

Allie laughed. "George, you are always welcome. You're barely a customer, anyway. You're one of us." She helped him into his seat and went back to fix his tea.

Ren appeared from the back. "Go sit with him." They put a hand on Allie's shoulder. "Have a break. You both look like you need some social interaction."

Allie carried the tea over and retrieved a glass of water for herself, then took a seat across the table from George.

"Any music for me?" George took a sip of his tea and regarded her with his watery blue eyes over the top of the mug.

"No, actually." Allie put her glass down. "Since Ryan and I recorded 'Borderline,' I haven't really been working on anything. I do want to get one more song, just to make it to thirteen total."

"Perhaps you need Ryan for the next one, too." George looked up at the ceiling in a bad imitation of innocence. "Perhaps you need Ryan for *many other things*."

Allie rolled her eyes. "Not you, too."

He turned his gaze back to her and winked. "I was talking to Mindy and Ren the other day when you were in the back. They've got a lot to say about you and Ryan."

"Well, don't listen to them. There's nothing between Ryan and me. We're just friends."

"Mindy and Ren don't think that's what either of you really want."

"Well, I can't speak to what Ryan wants." Allie sighed. "But, George. It's been years since I had friends. Actual *friends* who aren't coworkers or customers—no offense."

George shook his head and waved his hand, unoffended. She continued, "I thought I didn't miss it. But I did. I know that's ridiculous. Everyone needs friends."

George paused and stared past her, considering. "It's true. I always had a good group. School friends, then university friends, then archivist friends. Then, after Sheena died, I had a group of guys that I met for lunch once a week who'd all lost their wives. We called ourselves the Wednesday Widowers."

"George, that's the saddest, cutest thing I've ever heard."

George scoffed and waved his hand in the air again, dismissing her admiration. He went back to his tea and waited for her to continue.

"So, you get it, then. I finally have a friend—*two* friends, actually, because Anisha is my friend as well. I can't do anything that would risk that."

George was quiet. He seemed to be considering his words. "Sometimes *not* doing something is a bigger risk than doing it."

Allie patted George's hand and looked into his eyes. "Not this time."

"I really do just want to see you happy, Allie."

"I know you do. And I want that, too. I'd hate it if something happened to you and you'd never gotten a chance to stop worrying about me."

George huffed, his expression contracting in disgust. "Allie, I'm not going to up and *die* just to give you some meaning in your life. Get your own meaning."

Allie laughed. "Okay. Fair enough."

He nodded. "Back to my original topic. When will you have new music for me?"

"I swear I'll get back to it. I've started thinking about this new song. 'Straight Up,' it's called. You'll like it. It's catchy."

"Well, good. It will be hard to follow the xylophone and harmonies, though."

"I'll see if I can find another ridiculous children's instrument to add into this one, for you. How do you feel about the humble kazoo?"

—

When George was gone, Allie wiped down all the unoccupied tables and did a quick check of the clean dishes behind the counter and the cash in the cash drawer.

"I brought you my leopard pants." Ren looked up from where they were ladling muffin batter into trays. "They're in the office. They're cropped on me, so they should fit you just like regular pants."

"Thank you!" Allie was grateful to Ren for remembering. "I really have no clothes that are suitable for a party."

"That's because you have literally never been to a party as long as I have known you."

Allie considered this and found it to be accurate. "Sad, but true."

Ren wore the leopard-print pants often, sometimes with a selection of worn black concert shirts, and other times—date times—with a button-down black shirt.

"Thanks for loaning me your lucky pants." She grinned.

Ren groaned. "They're *not* my lucky pants. I've told you. I've never needed any luck in the pants department."

"Well, whatever they are, thanks for loaning them to me."

"No problem. Anisha and I were discussing what you would wear to the party, and honestly, if you hadn't asked me for the pants, she would have been forcing you into some of her clothes, which is probably not what you'd want."

Allie gulped. "Yeah, I'm sure I could *not* carry off whatever dramatic outfit Anisha would pull for me. Baby steps. Your leopard pants will be fine."

Allie had been thinking of Ren's lucky pants when she'd found a cropped black wrap shirt at a vintage store the previous week. It had sleeves that widened into voluminous bell shapes, and when she tried it on, she felt like a member of Aerosmith. In a good way. It was the kind of thing that she would have automatically ignored in the past, deeming it impractical for café work. No one needed a bell sleeve dragging through their soup, no matter how fabulous. But now? Now she had a party to go to.

"You're coming to the party after your shift, right?" she asked Ren.

"Yep." They nodded. "My party clothes are in the office, so I'll get changed quick and head straight there."

"Feel free to close up a bit early if it's slow."

"Oh, I was planning on it."

Allie rolled her eyes. "You know I'm technically your boss, right?"

"Actually, Mindy is my boss, and she already said I could close early."

"Of course she did."

"Unless?" Ren called after her as she started up the stairs to her apartment.

"Unless what?" Allie stepped back down and poked her head through the door.

"Unless this is your way of telling me that you've finally decided to take over?"

The hope on Ren's face made Allie's stomach clench.

"Sorry." She shook her head. Ren's face fell. "I still haven't decided."

"Well, a person can dream." Ren perked up almost immediately. "Now get going! You've got an actual human party to attend!"

Allie let the door close behind her and made her way up to her quiet, welcoming apartment. The Christmas tree's lights were plugged in, providing the only light in the room when she arrived. She stood for a minute, admiring the scene. The tree made the apartment feel less lonely, she realized. She hadn't known it felt lonely until it started not to.

After a moment of reverie, she turned on the overhead light and started to transform Café Worker Allie into Hip Christmas Party Allie. The task felt daunting. She pulled a Go-Go's cassette from the crate that held her dad's collection. Those girls liked to party. They could be her musical guardian angels.

She knew Ryan wouldn't care; all he ever wore was some version of a denim button-down and black jeans. But Anisha had specifically told her that if she showed up in "coveralls and clogs," she would be turned away at the door.

Allie rummaged through her dusty basket of makeup and tried to call up the skills she'd had when she used to get done up for shows with her band. She lifted a liner pen to her eye and—after having to wipe off one disastrous attempt with soapy tissues—was happy to see that her muscle memory had engaged. With thick lines above each eye, she decided to quit while she was ahead. Her hair had been washed that morning and wound up in a topknot wrapped in a bandanna. When she took it down, it waved over her shoulders. Low-maintenance hair. A random genetic gift from her dad.

The thought made her pause and glance over at the crate of cassettes sitting on the floor by her stereo. Paula Abdul was on top, the case so scuffed she could hardly see the singer's face beneath it. Despite her assertion to George, Allie was starting to lose interest in her covers project, and she was glad the end was in sight. She still loved the songs, and she had been listening to "Straight Up" a lot. But the lyrical narrator, wondering whether the object of their affections was going to love them forever or whether they were just . . . having fun? It was hitting a bit too close to home. There was nothing fun about trying to tamp down her crush on Ryan, but she just needed some time to get over it.

Had Paula ever figured it out? Allie laughed at herself for wondering, assuming the pop star probably had more important things to worry about.

Allie gave herself a once-over in the mirror before she left. She was surprised by the somewhat fashionable person who looked back at her. Ren's leopard-print pants were fitted and slightly tapered. She'd rolled the hems once to get them to stop right where her Doc Martens began. These boots were getting more wear this season than they had in the last decade. The black wrap top worked perfectly with the pants, just as she'd hoped. It tied around her midriff with two long sashes of fabric, and she'd tied the excess in a knot at her lower back. A thin line of exposed skin circled her body where the shirt ended just above the waistline of the pants. She felt sexy. It was weird.

She *liked* it.

She grabbed her coat and breezed through the kitchen, pausing to show Ren her outfit and getting a "Hubba-hubba!" for her troubles.

She had just called goodbye and was stepping out onto the street when Mindy appeared in front of her.

"Oh shit!" Allie put her hand on her heart and slowed her pace. "You scared me! I was just leaving."

"For Ryan's party?"

Mindy looked odd. Allie felt the fizzy excitement that had been bubbling within her start to drain away.

What now?

"Yeah. Is everything okay?"

Mindy nodded, hugging her oversized boiled-wool winter coat closer around her body. "Yes. But I need to talk to you. Can I walk you there?"

Allie nodded. They started up the block in silence. Allie noticed her aunt's navy-blue knit cap poking out from the pocket of her coat and yanked it out, handing it to Mindy.

"Here, put your hat on. It's freezing."

Mindy smiled and took the hat, pulling it over her long white braids. "Thanks."

They walked up the rest of the block. Allie tightened her scarf around her neck and then shoved her hands deep into her pockets. Mindy didn't say anything, and Allie was quickly frustrated by the silence.

"Okay, out with it." She stopped walking and turned to her aunt. "What's happening?"

Mindy turned to face her, blinking her eyes as a cold wind blew around them. "I've had an offer."

"An offer?"

"To buy the café?"

Allie blinked. "At *Christmas*?"

Mindy nodded. "I was surprised, too. I assumed I wouldn't hear a thing until the new year. But apparently, this person has been wanting something in the neighborhood for a while and is very motivated. They want to move here from Sweden. No, wait. Denmark? One of those countries with socialized medicine and stuff."

Allie had a lump in her throat. "Are they . . . Do they . . . Will it still be a café? What about Ren?"

"I don't know." Mindy looked down at the dark, wet sidewalk. "I don't know yet."

Allie looked down as well, watching the toe of Mindy's boot trace over a crack in the concrete.

Mindy continued, "I wanted to talk to you before I even start nego-tiations. It's still yours if you want it. But it wouldn't be fair to the potential buyer if I start talking to them and then have to tell them it's not actually for sale."

Allie nodded, the lump still in her throat. "How long do I have?"

"Well, I told them it was a busy time with the café and Christmas, but they want to hear from me by the twenty-seventh."

"Like in two weeks?"

"Yes."

Allie drew in a sharp breath and looked up at the ominous cloudy sky before she exhaled.

"Look, I know you're on your way to a party and this is about the shittiest time in the world to spring this on you."

"Yes!" Allie nodded vigorously. "This *is* the shittiest time in the world for this."

"Allie." Mindy's voice was firm. "This is a real thing that is happening and could affect the rest of your life. I wanted you to have as much time as possible to think about it. Go to your party. Think about what you want to be doing a year from now. Give yourself a mental Scrooge tour of your past, present and future. Your life has already changed so much in the past few months. Now you need to decide which direction it's going to go in from here."

Allie opened her mouth to protest, but Mindy held up a hand to stop her.

"Christmas isn't just good for people like Ren who want to throw tinsel at everything and listen to that infernal She & Him Christmas album forty times a day. It's a yearly mile marker. It will help you zero in on what you want to be doing next year at this time. And the year after that. And the year after—"

"I get it," Allie cut in. Her ears were starting to get cold. She hadn't worn a hat for fear of messing up her party hair. "Christmas will guide me. Or something."

Mindy smiled. "Or something."

Mindy wasn't a hugger, but she put one steady hand on Allie's arm, and even that small physical touch through Allie's thick coat was somehow reassuring. "Just go and have a good night. You'll figure it out."

"I've got no choice!" Allie called out as she started walking away from Mindy. She heard her aunt's laughter and turned to watch her retreat up the snowy street, back toward the café. She stood there for a few moments, even when she couldn't see Mindy anymore. Her first urge was to go home and get back into bed, but she shook it off. It was time to party.

Chapter Eighteen

Ryan and Anisha's apartment was already crowded with revelers when Allie arrived. There was no use knocking; she could hear a Dua Lipa song blasting and the loud chatter of people trying to talk over it. A hand lettered sign taped to the door warned partygoers to take their shoes off, or else.

She stepped into the apartment cautiously, seeing only strangers. After bending to untie her boots, she placed them with the sea of other footwear, all crammed in the corner of the entryway. When she stood up again, she was relieved to see Ryan weaving through the crowd toward her.

"Allllllllie!" His cheeks were red, and his smile was wide. "I'm so glad you made it! Here, I'll take your coat and put it in my room with the others."

She handed the coat to him and followed him through the crowd of people until they were at the door of his room. He pushed it open, and she followed, watching him place her coat carefully on his pillows, separate from the mound of other people's winter wear that was heaped in the middle of the bed. He stood up and looked at her. They were alone in the room, his large, comfortable bed between them.

"Uh . . . hi." She chewed on her bottom lip, suddenly feeling weird. She saw his eyes flick quickly up and down her body before settling on hers.

"Wow! You look *great*."

"Thank you." Her voice came out more breathy than intended. She cleared her throat and made an effort to smile. "I mean, Anisha *did* threaten me."

"Oh yeah, I was there. No coveralls. No clogs. You understood the assignment." Ryan nodded. They stared at each other in silence. The thrum of the music and voices outside the door seemed to recede for a moment. Finally, Ryan laughed awkwardly. "Well, you didn't come to this party to stand around in my room." He walked to the foot of the bed and offered his elbow to her. She stepped closer to him and looped her arm through his, chastely, like a character from a Jane Austen novel preparing to take a turn around the room. Allie wondered whether Jane Austen's demure female characters were always struggling to keep a lid on their lustful thoughts the way she was.

Ryan led her out into the apartment's main space. Anisha was behind the kitchen counter, wearing a dress that was essentially a giant red triangle constructed of ruffles that somehow looked amazingly cool and sexy on her. She wore black lace fingerless gloves with it, and her long hair was wound up on top of her head in a gravity-defying beehive.

"Wow." Allie spoke involuntarily, catching sight of her.

"I know." Ryan laughed. "I told her the outfit was a lot, and she said a lot was exactly what she was going for, so here we are."

Allie was wondering how long was too long to hold on to Ryan's arm when a thin woman in a sequined dress and fishnets crashed into them. Ryan yelped and jumped, letting go of Allie's arm in the process.

"Sorry! Sorry!" The woman's wild bleached curls temporarily covered her eyes as she righted herself and raked her hand through her hair to tame it. "I was looking for Deepak, and you all came out of nowhere!"

"Allie, this is Patti. She works on *This Ain't No Podcast*. Which, somewhat ironically, is our most popular Solidarity podcast." Ryan and Patti laughed, and Allie smiled at them both.

She'd listened to a few episodes of that podcast but didn't like it as much as *Mixtape Universe*. The long-form interviews were sometimes interesting, but without music being a part of them, she found her mind wandering.

"Hi, Allie, good to meet you!"

"Is Jonah here, too?" Ryan asked. Jonah was the host of *This Ain't No Podcast*. From what Allie knew, he was a bit of a big deal around the studio. Everyone seemed to think he was poised for whatever the highest level of fame was that podcasters aspired to. She immediately began searching her memory for anything she'd heard on the few episodes of the show she'd listened to. Something that would allow her to have a conversation without looking like a weirdo.

"Yep! He and Flora are over there in the kitchen."

"Oh, cool." Ryan clapped Patti on her shoulder. "We'll go say hi."

He held out his hand to Allie. "Want me to pull you through the crowd?" She nodded, already overwhelmed by the crush of humans in the apartment. Ryan took Allie's hand in his and moved them both through the crowd until they reached the kitchen. Allie willed herself not to sweat. She concentrated on releasing his hand as soon as they'd stopped moving, resisting the urge to hold on tight.

A dark-haired man, who Allie guessed was Jonah, saw them and smiled. He had one arm around the shoulders of a beaming blond woman with short hair and friendly eyes. He reached out his free hand to shake Ryan's.

"Ryan! Thanks so much for having us."

Jonah shot his partner an admiring gaze that caused a twinge of irrational envy to shoot through Allie's core. She wanted what they had.

"This is Ryan. He's the tech on *Mixtape Universe* that I've been telling you about."

"Oh yeah! I've heard a lot about your great work!" Flora extended her hand to Ryan.

"All one hundred percent true." Ryan grinned. "And it certainly wasn't me who shattered the best mic we had, a week into my triumphant employment."

Allie felt her cheeks redden at that memory. The first time they'd met. *I should have been nicer.*

"And this is Allie." Ryan put his hand on her back for a too-brief moment. "It was her fault I dropped the microphone."

Allie turned her horrified gaze toward him, and he raised his eyebrows. She knew he was asking whether he could tell the story, whether she was cool with being outed as a member of a now-irrelevant punk band. She nodded.

"She surprised me." Ryan winked at her. "Because I recognized her from this band she used to be in."

"He's a total weirdo," Allie cut in. "The band was not well known at all."

"What were you called?" Flora asked, seeming legitimately interested.

"The Jetskis!" Ryan now sounded giddy. Allie couldn't help but laugh at him. "I've got their record right h—"

"Wait, the Jetskis? My friend Ayla was in the Jetskis." Flora's smile widened as a look of delighted surprise crossed her face.

Allie felt like something had sucked all the air out of her lungs. "*Ayla?*" she croaked. "Ayla Darwish?"

"Yes!" Flora rocked back and forth on her heels.

Jonah tilted his head to one side and frowned. "Your ex-girlfriend Ayla? She was in a band?"

"Yeah!" Flora nodded enthusiastically. "I mean, it was years ago. She doesn't talk about it much now. You were all pretty young, right?"

Allie was still stunned. Ryan put his hand on her shoulder. The solid heaviness of his touch kept her grounded as the memories swirled.

"Yeah, we were. Wow. I mean, what a weird coincidence."

"Hey, you don't happen to have her number, do you? We're trying to track down another one of their bandmates." Ryan sounded so happy and casual. Allie's heart was hammering.

Maybe this is it . . .

She wasn't sure how to feel. She concentrated on remaining upright with a neutral facial expression while Flora scrolled through her phone for Ayla's number. Watching Ryan type it into his own phone and then immediately text it to Allie made her even more appreciative of his steady, calm presence within the chaos of this so far very weird evening.

George's words from earlier, about how not doing something can sometimes be a greater risk than doing it, echoed in her head, along with Mindy's advice to Scrooge herself.

Do I really want to be standing here across from Ryan at next year's Christmas party, as his friend, watching him chat with other people? Hoping he'll touch my arm again? Hoping no one else flirts with him?

She did not.

She snuck a look at Ryan as he listened to Flora and Jonah talk about a documentary they'd just seen. His hair was combed neatly, and his button-down was gray, not denim, but still paired with his usual tapered black jeans. He looked good. She couldn't help imagining what it would be like to touch his soft hair and undo those buttons on his shirt. Her mental "just friends" dam had burst, and now she couldn't stop her brain from supplying her with an IV drip of lust.

Fuck.

She was saved from her own thoughts by the arrival of Anisha, who had a tray of bubbling champagne in a variety of glasses and was offering it to everyone she passed. Allie took one and drank it quickly.

"Hey!" Ryan said, looking over Allie's head. "Ren's here!"

Anisha looked up and scanned the room, her face breaking into a wide smile when she caught sight of Ren, in a very cool black velvet suit, making their way through the crowd. Anisha placed her tray of champagne down on the kitchen counter and started weaving toward them, unable to wait for Ren to reach her. When she and Ren found each other, they immediately started slow dancing, unperturbed by the throngs around them.

"I've never seen her like this." Ryan had shuffled over toward Allie and was leaning over to speak into her ear. "It's a whole new thing."

"Yeah." Allie considered her experiences with Ren over the past few weeks. "Ren is acting weird, too. Different, I mean. Usually, by now, they're asking me to answer their phone and tell whoever is calling they have a migraine and can't hang out."

"Ren does not look like they have a migraine."

The couple was now making out, their bodies still poised for dancing, but their feet unmoving.

"Nope." Allie grinned. "Ren seems just fine."

"Do you want to join them?" Ryan asked.

Allie felt as if the floor had suddenly dropped away beneath her. "What?"

"Dancing, I mean." Ryan's cheeks turned red.

"Oh yeah!" Allie exhaled, steadying herself. "Absolutely."

One song faded out, and the opening strains of the next one began. "She's a Rainbow" by the Stones. Ryan and Anisha had been fighting over the party playlist for weeks.

"Was this one of your choices?" Allie asked as Ryan took her into his arms.

"Actually, we both liked this one. But I liked it especially because it made me think of you."

"Of me?" Allie looked up at him.

"Yeah." He smiled down at her. "All those jumpsuits you wear and the dresses in bright colors. Your work clothes. Ren and Mindy are always wearing black. The café is all white and gray and brown. So I can always see you right away when I come in."

Allie wasn't sure whether being told that she stood out at work was the level of romantic she was hoping for, but at least he hadn't said the song reminded him of another lady.

"Oh shit. *Sheila.*"

Ryan's grip tightened on her hand as he stared over her head toward the door.

"Sheila?"

"Yeah, remember I dated that girl? Well, she's here."

Allie turned slightly so she could look. It was useless. She was shorter than 90 percent of the people at the party.

"She worked at Solidarity, right? Everyone else from the studio is here. You can't be that surprised."

Ryan still hadn't met her eyes. He was staring over her, looking across the room. After a moment, he shook his head slightly, as if to dislodge whatever had overtaken him. "You're right. Of course she's here. Everyone is here. I just am not super excited about having to talk to her, that's all."

"I thought it ended fine?" Allie was working hard to sound cool. The climbing piano riff of "She's a Rainbow" made her heartbeat accelerate again.

"Oh, it did." Ryan finally turned his face back to her. "I just don't really have anything to say to her." He shrugged and spun them around so he was no longer facing the door. "And now I have to come up with some small talk, just to be polite."

Before Allie could decide what to say in response, Anisha and Ren danced up beside them. Anisha pushed Ren toward Allie and grabbed Ryan's hand. "Let's switch for a moment! Ryan and I have to discuss whether we need to move the couch now that everyone is dancing."

Allie accepted the hand that Ren held out to her and allowed herself to be twirled. Anisha was right, the mobs of people in the room were starting to pair off, turning the wide space into a dance floor. Allie had never seen anything like it. She temporarily forgot her angst over Ryan as the Stones song ended and a Talking Heads song began. She and Ren released each other but stayed close, dancing and laughing as the crowd moved around them.

Allie could hear multiple voices singing along even over the loud, exuberant music, which had just been turned up. The crowd parted as Ryan and Anisha pushed their couch and coffee table to one side. She felt the music filling the room and adding an extra level of magic to the whole scene. It was wild to be here, in a place with people she cared about, raising her arms above her head as the chorus of "Life During Wartime" escalated. It was perfect. How had she gone so long without this feeling?

Ren grabbed for her hand and pulled her into another twirl, ending with them close enough to hear each other over the music.

"Allie." Ren spoke urgently. "I think Anisha is *the one*."

Allie stopped dancing. "You . . . what?"

Ren nudged her. "Keep dancing, you look weird. I think she's the one. *The one for me.* I mean, as much as anyone can be the one for anyone . . ."

"I understand the concept of *the one*." Allie struggled to keep her feet moving while her thoughts churned. "I'm just . . . surprised to hear *you* say it."

Ren recoiled slightly but then seemed resigned. "Ouch. But yeah, okay, I see where you're coming from. But you know Anisha. How could anyone not love her?"

"You *love* her?" Allie stopped moving again. Ren did, too. They stared at each other.

Ren gulped and nodded. "I love her."

"Holy shit." Allie stared for a moment longer and then noticed people around them starting to look over, curious. She grabbed Ren's hand and prompted them to start dancing again.

"Yeah, I wasn't counting on it, either. But sometimes life gives you weird surprises."

The song ended, and Allie grabbed Ren in a tight hug, feeling nervous for them.

"Congratulations?"

"Thanks."

"Have you told her yet?"

Ren shook their head. "Not yet. Probably tonight. It's just sitting there in my head, you know? Once you think it, it's really hard to stop thinking it. And now I'm worried that whenever I open my mouth, I'm going to shout it."

"Well, probably don't shout it." Allie smirked. "That would be weird."

"Thanks for the hot romance tip." Ren rolled their eyes. "I hear you're an expert."

"Okay, uncalled for." Allie swatted them. "Leave me out of this."

Anisha and Ryan, finished with the furniture moving, appeared again beside them, and Allie watched Ren and Anisha move back through the crowded room, with eyes only for each other.

"They're goners!" Ryan shouted over the music. "Good for them."

"Yep." The butterflies in Allie's stomach were returning. It was going to be a long night. "*Good for them.*"

Chapter Nineteen

Allie couldn't remember the last time she'd been awake until 4 a.m.

She was routinely awake *at* four—after a good night's sleep, her alarm rousing her so she could shower before starting the early baking at the café—but never *until* four.

The last party guests had left half an hour earlier, and she'd collapsed on the sofa with Ren and Anisha. Ryan had flopped down into the good armchair, and they all sipped periodically from the large glasses of cold water that Anisha had retrieved from the kitchen before she sat down.

Party detritus was everywhere. Beer cans, wine bottles, ashtrays full of the stubs of joints, someone's forgotten cardigan, an inexplicably abandoned sock. The furniture was still pushed up against the wall, and the music still played, but the apartment was like the site of a carnival that had just been packed and towed away. Only memories and garbage remained.

"That was fun. I think I'm drunk." Ren's voice was muffled by Anisha's shoulder.

"Honey, you were drunk and then sober and then drunk again." Anisha patted Ren's head tenderly. "Drink your water. And I'll make sure you take some Advil before bed."

"Bed?" Ren raised their head slightly. Allie saw a glint in their eyes and laughed.

"Why don't you two head to bed, and Ryan and I will clean up?"

"Are you sure?" Anisha asked, but she was already standing and pulling Ren up by their arms. "We could stay up and help . . ." Her words were interrupted by Ren, now with some kind of lustful second wind, pulling her toward her bedroom door.

Ryan pushed himself out of the chair with a groan. "We got it, kids. You head off. We'll even leave the music on so we don't hear . . . *things*. Our gift to you."

As Ren and Anisha retreated, giggling, Allie was reminded of how happy she was not to have a roommate. Not that she was ever worried about anyone overhearing the loud sex she wasn't having. Her brain once again called up unwanted images of Ryan in her bed. She was working so hard to dislodge the thoughts, she jumped when Ryan touched her shoulder.

"Sorry!" He chuckled. "You asleep on your feet?"

"No." She laughed awkwardly. It sounded like a bad Woody Woodpecker impression. "I'm fine. Let's get this done."

Ryan retrieved two garbage bags from under the kitchen sink, and they went to work, sweeping cans into one and trash into the other. Ryan stacked the wine bottles in a cardboard box by the door, and Allie swept the dirty floor, singing along with Ella Fitzgerald, who was wondering what someone was doing New Year's Eve.

"Ah!" Ryan called from across the room. "This is the Christmas section of the playlist. I had to beg Anisha to let me put some holiday songs on there. She had a strict "no Jesus songs" rule, but I managed to sneak some in."

"Do you stay in the city for Christmas?" Allie stooped to sweep a mound of dirt into the dustpan.

"Yep." Ryan stopped moving and looked off into the glittery Brooklyn night beyond the big windows. "I've never really had enough cash to go on vacation or anything. And I'm not really welcome back home, of course. My family thinks I'm out here fixin' to hand out abortions and vegan cupcakes every day."

"The horror!" Allie giggled.

"Yeah, well, I'm living in New York and not going to church. It's all the same thing to them."

Allie could hear the sadness behind his words. She caught his eye from across the room. "I'm sorry. That sounds rough."

Ryan shrugged. "Well, I usually say it is what it is, but you're right. Thank you. It is rough."

They continued their cleaning. The bags filled up quickly, and the apartment began to look normal again. When Allie had cleared the last of the plates and cups from the living room and rinsed them in the sink, she stood for a moment, observing the room with her hands on her hips.

"Should we move the furniture back?"

Ryan was about to answer when one song on the playlist faded into another, and he looked over at the speakers with reverence. "Oh, here we go. Mahalia Jackson."

Allie leaned back against the kitchen counter as the first verse of "Go Tell It on the Mountain" poured into the room like honey. Ryan walked toward her.

"One more dance? Before this night is officially over?"

Allie bit her lip and nodded.

He wrapped his left arm around her waist and, with his other hand, took hers gently and folded their arms against his chest. Ryan sang happily along with the music, and she smiled at him. All of the tension about the temporary mess and uncertainty in her life receded. Ryan's closeness and enthusiasm for this one Jesus-y Christmas hymn allowed her to be in the moment.

And she fucking *loved* the moment. He smelled so good, even after hours of partying. His hair was slightly mussed; the first two buttons of his shirt were undone. His strong arm around her waist held her warm body against his.

"Oh!" Ryan spoke suddenly, pulling her out of her fog of contentment. "That Ayla thing! We didn't even get to talk about it!"

Allie looked at his chest and imagined laying her head down against him, listening for his heartbeat.

"I mean, come on!" Ryan continued. "What a break! We can call Ayla and— What?" He stopped talking, focusing on Allie's face. "Are you okay?"

"Yes," Allie said firmly. "I am okay."

"Did you want to talk about Ayla?" As the words left his mouth, Ryan seemed to realize that maybe she did *not* want to talk about Ayla. Allie shook her head.

Ryan moved closer to her. It was a barely perceptible move, a shuffle of approximately half an inch, a tightening of his hand around her waist, but Allie felt it. She slid her hand farther along his shoulder, closer to his neck.

"What *do* you want, Allie?" Ryan's voice was quieter suddenly. Allie was sure he could hear her heart beating over Mahalia Jackson's soulful wail.

Well, here goes nothing.

She looked up at him. His eyes dipped down and rested on her lips.

Fuck it.

"I kind of want to kiss you."

What a ridiculous way to say it.

She looked away, desperate to travel three minutes back in time.

Ryan's warm hands moved from her body and gently turned her face toward him. He was smiling.

"Should we . . . talk about—I mean . . . is it—I . . . Oh forget it."

He kissed her. And she kissed him back.

His soft lips were gentle against hers at first, but the urgency quickly built. His hands moved from her head to her neck, then down the sides of her body.

Ryan removed his lips from hers for a moment but left his forehead touching hers. He traced one finger along the ribbon of bare skin between her shirt and pants. "This inch of your skin has been driving me wild all night."

Allie trembled.

He leaned down farther so he could kiss her neck, gripping his body closer to hers. She wasn't sure how to process all of this, but luckily, her mind was occupied with other jobs, like sending pulses of heat to her low belly. She was so turned on she could hardly stand up.

She could feel Ryan's hardness against her as his hands moved around her waist and pulled her closer to him. His tongue tentatively moved between her lips, and she opened her mouth, wanting as much of him as she could get in that moment.

"*Sweet Jesus's ghost.*" He murmured the words into her mouth and moved his hands back up to her face, kissing her with decided passion. She usually laughed when his Southern expressions came out, but she felt no urge to laugh at this moment. She just wanted to keep kissing him. If things could happen exactly according to her wishes at that moment, it would be the two of them, naked, immediately.

The song ended and another one began. Allie registered the change only vaguely. At the front of her mind was how Ryan's hands were now moving down her body. She gasped as his right hand slid across her breast over the thin fabric of her shirt.

"Is this okay?" His whisper made her stomach lurch. She could hardly choke out an affirmation. He went back to kissing her hungrily. Her knees trembled.

"Let's go to your room," she whispered.

"Yeah?" He drew back slightly and looked into her eyes. She nodded and took his hand, trying to control the urgency with which she pulled him toward his bedroom door. She stood by his bed, momentarily awkward, as he quietly shut the door. The click of the lock was the most erotic sound Allie had ever heard. She could not wait for whatever was about to happen in this room, on that bed.

Ryan was by her side again quickly, turning her slightly so her back was against the wall. His hand was back at her breast, and the other wrapped around her waist. Her body was on fire. She grabbed handfuls of his shirt in her fists, pulling his body into hers. She could not get him close enough. Pushing harder against her, he bent and gently bit the tender flesh of her neck. She moaned.

"Can I take your top off?" His voice sounded strangled, as if he could barely control it.

"Yes, please." Allie's words were heavy with desperation. Ryan slid his hands around her back and began loosening the knot of her wrap shirt.

"This knot back here is infuriating," he whispered in her ear. "It's the only thing keeping me from putting my hands on you."

Allie felt her knees grow even weaker. Ryan made short work of the knot and soon was pulling her blouse down over her shoulders. She was wearing a bra that barely qualified as one, a thin lace thing that was the only one she had with a V deep enough to not show under the shirt.

Ryan moaned as he looked at her. "Should we . . . lie down?" His voice was warm against her ear.

"Oh yes."

He turned her around, and she finally let her knees buckle as Ryan lowered her down onto his wide bed. His blankets were warm and soft. She pushed herself up toward his pillows, and he joined her, hovering over her on his hands and knees. He leaned his face down and took her breast in his mouth, licking and sucking through the thin lace. Her eyes rolled back. She whimpered.

"Take your clothes off." She could barely get the words out.

Ryan's voice was close to her ear again. She could feel his beard against the sensitive skin of her neck. "You're good with that?"

She nodded and opened her eyes to watch him unbutton his shirt and pull off the T-shirt he wore underneath. As he pushed his jeans down over his legs, she held her breath in anticipation.

"You're staring at me." He stopped, a hint of nervousness crossing his face for a fleeting moment. He was wearing only a pair of black boxer briefs, his stomach hanging over the waistband. He had a tattoo of a tree running up one arm. Allie stared at it, amazed that she got to see him like this.

Ryan saw her staring at his tattoo and looked down at it himself. "It's a longleaf pine."

"It's really beautiful. You—" She felt suddenly shy, now that they weren't all over each other. "You look great."

Ryan's eyes softened, and his cheeks went red. Then he seemed to remember why they were in his bedroom in the first place, as his eyes wandered over her body stretched out on his bed. "I'd like to see much more of you right now, if that's okay."

"That is more than okay."

Their passion returned the minute he touched her, tracing his hand down her belly to the button of her pants. He pulled them over her hips, taking her underwear with them, and then returned quickly to her bra, which he unclasped and tossed over his shoulder in a way that she found almost unbearably hot.

He pressed his body onto hers, and she could feel him holding himself up slightly, worrying about crushing her. He didn't need to worry. She was dying to feel his full body pressing into every part of hers. She moved one hand down and pushed past the waistband of his underwear, wrapping her fingers around him. His sharp intake of breath made her blush. He let himself relax into the bed, just to one side of her, as much of his body touching hers as possible as she moved her hand slowly.

"Is that okay?" she asked him.

"I like it." He moaned and moved his own hand down her belly and slid one finger into her soaking sex. "How about this?"

"Mmm-hmmmm." She could only moan her affirmation.

"You're so wet." His fingers circled.

Her eyes fluttered closed. "Oh . . ."

Ryan's breath was warm as he spoke into her ear.

"Allie, you are just so beautiful. And sexy." He kissed her face softly, his fingers moving faster. "Can I put my mouth on you?"

"Fuuuuuck, yes." She struggled to speak. She took her hand off him, mentally resolving to return to that later, and let him gently slide her body to the edge of the bed. He knelt on the floor, positioning himself so his hot breath warmed her thighs.

He moved her legs farther apart slowly and then he paused, his eyes wandering all over her body. Just as Allie thought she was going to have to start begging, he pressed his mouth against her, holding her hips with his large hands.

His tongue parted her and took its time, gently and then more forcefully. She could no longer speak. He took one hand off her hip and slid his fingers inside her, holding her body firmly as he continued to make her feel as if she was going to explode. It didn't take long. She was so wound up from their heated makeout—and from the months of wanting him—her orgasm arrived swiftly, coursing through her body. As she moaned and twisted, her body buzzing with waves of climax, she opened her eyes briefly and saw he was watching her. His eyes were tender.

He likes me. The thought cut through the pleasure clouding her brain. *Maybe he has liked me this whole time.*

As Allie recovered her ability to breathe, she was struck by how much time they'd wasted. Even though it was only a few months, why had they not spent them doing exactly what they were doing right now?

Grasping Ryan's hand, she pulled him up toward her and started pulling his underwear down.

"You don't need a rest?" He smiled, pressing his body against hers again.

She shook her head emphatically. "Do you have a condom?"

"Yes." Ryan leaped off the bed and pulled open the bottom drawer of his dresser. He returned to the bed with the condom and a hard-on. Allie took the package from him and carefully ripped it open. He kneeled above her as she rolled the condom onto him.

He groaned and put one hand on her hip as though to steady himself. "You should be on top, if that's okay. I don't want to crush you."

"Lie down, then." She stared at him. He did as he was told. She climbed onto him, and he exhaled, eyes closing, hands running down her body and ending with a firm grip on her hips. He moved her, gently, back and forth on top of him. It lit up her body again, having him inside her. She tilted her head back and moved with him. She could feel her hair sweeping across her naked back as she rolled her hips.

"You look amazing," Ryan murmured. He was breathing hard. "Can I touch you again?"

She moaned and nodded. "Uh-huh."

Keeping one hand on her hip, he moved the other one to touch her exactly where his tongue had been. Allie's breath came out in short gasps, and they found a rhythm together, moving slowly and then speeding up, together. Ryan's eyes were closed, his head tipped back. She noticed the fair hair on his chest and arms and the map of freckles across his shoulders. He was gorgeous. And right now, he was hers.

His circling fingers sped up. She felt herself clenching.

"Allie, I . . ." Ryan panted. "Allie, I don't think I can hang on for much longer. You feel so good. I want to make you come again."

His words lit a fire in her, and the wave of intensity she was riding peaked. She closed her eyes and felt herself tighten around him. Tilting her head back, she cried out, her body writhing with a second, deeper rush of pleasure. She shouted his name. Probably more than once. She moved her hands to Ryan's chest so she didn't collapse.

"Good?" Ryan was breathless, staring into her eyes. She couldn't speak, so she nodded. He closed his eyes, tipping his head back and pushing into her with a yelp.

"Allie. Oh god, Allie. Oh, please . . . don't . . . stop." He moaned. He grabbed her weakened, sweaty body and held her close to him, one hand on her back, one hand tangled in her hair. "Oh, *Allie*."

And then it was over. And then they were just themselves again, the veil of lust slowly lifting. Allie collapsed beside him on the bed, breathing hard, suddenly noticing the silence of the room. For the first time since they'd kissed, she found herself remembering that he was her *friend* Ryan. Maybe this had all been a careless mistake. Maybe he didn't really want this.

As if to answer her thoughts, Ryan reached for her, pulling their sweaty bodies back together.

"Hot damn, Allie," he murmured into her ear. "*Hot damn.* That was amazing."

She could be nervous tomorrow. For now, she just wanted to sleep.

Chapter Twenty

"Well, here we go."

Allie was poised at the door of Ryan's bedroom, hand on the door-knob. She could hear Ren and Anisha laughing in the kitchen. It was 2 p.m., the day after the party. The day after . . . She looked down.

She was wearing a T-shirt of Ryan's that came almost to her knees. She'd also borrowed a pair of woolly socks. They covered the bottom half of her legs. Though the sheer size of his clothes provided automatic modesty, it would still be very clear to their friends what had happened last night. And this morning. And then almost again just a few minutes ago, until they both decided they were too hungry to do it again.

"You ready? They're going to bug us." Ryan smirked at her.

"Yeah. Of course they are."

"And it's absurd because we're the ones who caught *them* having sex in the café. We should not be embarrassed. I mean, no one should be embarrassed. But if anyone should, it's them."

It occurred to Allie that his babbling might be an indicator of nervousness. "You okay?"

Ryan stood up straight and tightened the belt of the purple terry cloth bathrobe he was wearing. "Yes. I'm fine. Sorry, I get weird like this sometimes. Puritanical holdover, thinking I'm somehow going to get in trouble for having sex."

"Has that actually happened to you?"

"Once. Sort of. That was more getting in trouble for coming home at three in the morning, but I think my parents knew that I wasn't at a particularly exciting Bible study session."

Allie giggled. She tightened her grip on the doorknob. "We can do this. We are consenting adults."

"Very consenting," Ryan said, his hand wrapping around her waist. "If I remember correctly, we both consented *several* times . . ."

Allie closed her eyes and willed herself to resist him. If only in the interest of breakfast. "We agreed." She removed his hand from her body. "We need to eat."

"You're right." He held both hands up in a gesture of surrender. "Let's get this done."

When they emerged from the room, Ren and Anisha abruptly stopped their own conversation and openly stared. It didn't take long to cross the living room to the kitchen, but on this particular occasion, it felt like an epic journey.

"Well, then!" Anisha's smile took up most of her face. "How was your night, *friends*?"

Allie squinted and rubbed her palm over her face. "Is that coffee?"

"Oh, this?" Ren asked, holding the coffee pot just out of Allie's reach. "This here? This is coffee, yes. Coffee for people who admit that all their friends were right that they should *totally bone the podcast guy.*"

"Is that me?" Ryan reached over Allie's head and easily extracted the coffee pot from Ren's hand. "Am I the podcast guy you were supposed to bone?" He poured coffee into a mug, added cream and handed it to Allie.

"Well, mission accomplished," she muttered into the cup as she drank, unable to hide her smile.

He knows how I take my coffee.

Anisha and Ren whooped.

"Okay, folks." Ryan poured a cup for himself. "We're all adults here."

"*Yeah*, we are." Anisha managed to make this sound wildly salacious, and Ren laughed. They high-fived.

Ryan rolled his eyes and headed for the fridge. "Let us know when you're done."

"We're done." Anisha boosted herself up to sit on the counter and looked at Ren. "Are we done?"

"I guess so." Ren sounded unconvinced.

"Oh, by the way, I told Ren about the Jessi search. They want to help."

"Yeah, I figured that would happen." Allie shrugged. "Just don't tell Mindy."

"Wow." Ren leaned back against the counter beside Anisha. "One night of good sex and you're totally chill?"

Allie accepted the bowl of yogurt and fruit that Ryan was handing her. "I guess that was all it took."

Ryan caught her eye and leaned against the counter with his own bowl of yogurt. "We actually had a breakthrough in the search for Jessi last night."

"That's right!" Allie had somehow forgotten. The events between the conversation with Jonah and Flora and the present moment had overwhelmed her memory. "We did!"

Ryan explained the discovery of Ayla to a rapt Anisha and Ren. Allie listened and considered what to do next.

"And then Flora gave us Ayla's number, so we can call her and see if she knows where Jessi is. We're so close. I feel like she's right there, waiting for us." He turned to Allie, putting his arm around her shoulders. "We should call her today! Dang, I'm excited for this one. I wonder if I'll eventually get to meet all the Jetskis? What a great couple of days." He winked at her.

"Actually," she said, "I was thinking I would call her myself? And maybe see if she wants to have coffee with me?"

Why am I talking in questions?

Her palms were sweating as she worried about offending Ryan, but she couldn't change direction now. "I don't want us to freak her out. And I should probably . . . apologize? It's weird, I know. Just something that I should do by myself this time."

She saw something flicker in Ryan's eyes. A flash of hurt that he quickly worked to conceal. He removed his arm from her shoulders. "Oh yeah, sure. Of course. She's *your* friend. I get it." He set his empty bowl down gently on the counter. "I'm gonna go have a shower." He kissed Allie's head as he walked by her. Anisha watched him go and leaped off the counter as soon as the bathroom door shut behind him.

"Allie, don't let him get weird."

"Get weird?" Allie was overwhelmed by Anisha's intense attention.

Anisha clapped her hand to her forehead and groaned. "He's having a freak-out right now because he thinks you don't want him around."

"It's not that!" Allie could hear the panic rising in her own voice. "I just . . . want to apologize. It might be too much for two of us to show up!"

"I know." Anisha nodded and held Allie's arm. "It's totally a reasonable request. That's why you can't let him spiral. It's just like I told you! He'll do this. He'll convince himself that you don't really like him, that this was some kind of mistake on his part. This is what he does. He gets all in his feelings really quick, and I never say anything if it's just some girl I don't care about, but I like you, and I can't deal with the idea that he might fuck this up."

Allie looked at Ren, who was nodding solemnly. Her heart plummeted. This was exactly why she'd spent so long convincing herself to never make a play for Ryan. She was standing in this perfect kitchen, with her perfect friends—the first she'd had in years—and she was one wrong move away from losing everything.

Again.

Losing everything again.

Anisha grimaced. "He will seriously try to abandon you before you can abandon him."

Allie's mind wandered back to Sheila's arrival at the party. Would the same thing happen to her? Was she now destined to be some girl that Ryan felt he had to invite to the party but didn't actually want to talk to?

Her stomach lurched.

This was all a mistake.

When Ryan came out of the shower, she followed him back into his bedroom, feeling awkward about it, but not sure where else to go.

"I wasn't sure if you'd still be here." Ryan was smiling but not looking into her eyes.

"Uh, did you want me to go?"

"Only if you wanted to."

She sat down on his bed, anxiety flowing through her. Ryan dressed quickly. She wanted to look at him but, somehow, now felt embarrassed. Instead, she flipped through a music magazine from his bedside table.

Ryan finished buttoning his shirt and turned to her, taking a deep breath.

"I want us to be friends."

Allie looked up at him. She'd never felt relieved and destroyed in exactly the same moment. But here she was, those two contradictory emotions coursing through her as she fought to keep her voice steady. She nodded and swallowed. "Me too."

Ryan's eyes widened. "You . . . too?"

What had he expected her to say?

Does he want me to fight with him about it?

"Yes. I value our friendship, and I don't want to lose it." She sounded like a robot.

Ryan looked at her and was silent for longer than she expected. Her stomach clenched. She bit her lip and steeled her resolve.

It only takes one fight to ruin everything forever. Don't ruin this forever.

Ryan took a deep breath. "Yes. Same. I don't want to screw up our friendship with, you know, all those expectations that come with, uh, romance."

Until several minutes ago, Allie had been thinking that adding all those expectations to their existing relationship was a great idea, but now the thought of losing Ryan and, by association, Anisha had pushed that opinion out of her mind. Her fears of being just another Sheila were stronger than her desire to see Ryan naked, even though her desire to see him naked was achingly strong. She let her eyes rest on his handsome face. He was looking at her with a strange expression. Was it pity? She did not need to be pitied.

"It's fine, Ryan. I get it. I agree with you."

Ryan blinked at her and then gave a sharp laugh. "Right? Just because we had great sex doesn't mean we need to try to have a *relationship*, you know? I'm kind of bad at relationships, anyway. But we could be friends, like, *forever*. I mean, if you wanted to. I don't think that we'd be doing each other any favors by trying to make this more than it is."

It felt like more to me.

Allie squashed the thought as soon as it entered her mind. She would get over that feeling. That feeling of *more*. She and Ryan could both get over their attraction to each other for the sake of their friendship.

And besides, maybe Ryan wasn't being weird, maybe Anisha was wrong. Maybe he was the one who was being honest.

He doesn't like me. Not the way I like him.

She stood up. She needed to get out of that room. "I've got to . . . uh . . . get going."

She scanned the room for her discarded clothing, not wanting to stay there for any longer than absolutely necessary. Getting over their night together was going to take some hard work, but she would force herself to do it.

She was suddenly desperate to be alone.

Chapter Twenty-One

When Allie said she wanted to walk home by herself, for the first time, Ryan didn't offer to walk with her. It was a relief. She absolutely could not handle him being nice to her at that moment. If she was going to effectively salvage their friendship, she needed time and space to reset her brain.

Anisha loaned her a black sweater that was nicer than anything Allie had ever owned. With Ren's leopard-print pants back on, it almost felt like a fresh outfit. She bundled into her winter coat and boots, and left the warm apartment for the cold streets, trying to forget about the worried looks Anisha and Ren were giving her as she closed the door.

Technically, she and Ren both had the day off, but Allie knew if she checked in at the café, there would be plenty for her to do. She was still avoiding thoughts about Mindy and the potential café sale. Usually, she found herself daydreaming about Ryan when she wanted to avoid thoughts of the future of Mindy's. But now she wanted to avoid thoughts of him as well.

What the fuck is happening to my life?

She took a sharp detour to avoid the café and, instead, found herself standing under a tree beside a bookstore, pulling out her phone.

She selected Ayla's number, took a deep breath and hit Call. Her heart beat faster as the phone started to ring.

"*Hey, hey, you've reached Ayla! I'm screening your call. Leave a message.*"

"Hey, um, Ayla? It's Allie. Allie Andrews, like, from the band. I got your number from a friend of a friend, and I was wondering if we could get together sometime. Call me back. If you want. If not, I get that, too. Uh . . . bye."

She put her phone back in the pocket of her coat and kept walking, looking for somewhere to get a coffee that wasn't the place she'd worked at for a decade.

Just as the barista at the poorly named Bean There Done That Coffee handed her an admittedly delicious-looking latte, Allie felt her phone vibrate. Instantly flustered, she fled the café, juggling her take-out cup as she attempted to answer her phone. She stepped over to one side of the sidewalk and leaned her shoulder against a building.

"Hello?"

"Allie? Is this Allie?"

Ayla's unmistakable cackle rang through the phone.

"Ayla! I'm so glad you called me!"

"Allie! Oh my god, it really is you. Girl! I can't believe it! Where are you right now?"

Allie squinted at a street sign and gave Ayla her approximate location. "I just got a coffee at this place called Bean There Done That." She wasn't sure why she was offering Ayla that information. She had no idea what to say now that they were actually talking to each other after so long. It felt like a dream sequence or a weird play.

"Oh, I'm not far from you! Stay there! I'll be there in about half an hour. Does that work?"

After Ayla hung up, Allie stood awkwardly on the sidewalk, wondering how to react. She felt like crying, kind of. Also like laughing. She zeroed in on the café she'd just left and walked back in and sat down, as if she'd always been intending to step out for a moment to answer the phone.

True to her word, Ayla crashed through the café door twenty-seven minutes later. Allie recognized her immediately.

Ayla's hair was still long and dark and curly. Her glasses were still the black square-framed Ray-Bans she'd always worn. Her lipstick was still a dark-plum color. Her clothes were still all black. Allie wasn't prepared for how comforting it was to see her friend after such a long period of time. A jittery warmth poured through her.

"Allie!" Ayla shrieked upon spotting her, causing everyone in the café to look at them. Allie didn't care. She opened her arms and accepted Ayla's hug, squeezing her friend with a ferocity that felt long overdue.

When they parted, Allie saw that Ayla had tears in her eyes. Both of them were smiling and sniffling.

"Oh my god." Ayla pulled a chair out from the table where Allie had been sitting. They both collapsed into their seats and stared at each other, periodically giggling. "You look so good, Allie! Holy shit."

Allie ran her hand over her head self-consciously. "Oh no, I don't! I've been up all night."

A quick memory of what she'd been doing to keep herself up passed through her head, and she could feel herself blushing. She tried to shake it off. "My friends had a party, and it went really late. I haven't even been home yet to change. I feel greasy." She was babbling. Her time with Ayla felt limited. She couldn't figure out why. Then it dawned on her.

I'm waiting for her to remember that she hates me.

"You look great, too! You look exactly the same!"

Ayla grinned and rolled her eyes behind her thick glasses. "Oh, thanks!"

"It's a compliment!" Allie laughed. "A total compliment."

"I'm going to get a coffee." Ayla stood up again. "You good?"

"I'm good." Allie held up the coffee she already had.

Ayla was back quickly, her hands wrapped around a cup of unadorned black coffee. She sat down, leaned back in her seat and smiled at Allie.

"So, I'm super curious, not only about why you called but also about who gave you my number in the first place."

"It was a woman named Flora. Her boyfriend is Jonah Dale. From that podcast? He works with my . . ." Allie's mind was again involuntarily full of an image of Ryan's naked body under hers. "My friend Ryan. Jonah and Flora were at this party last night, and Ryan mentioned that I was in the Jetskis and"—she watched as Ayla started nodding—"turns out she knew you. What are the odds?"

"The weird small-town Brooklyn phenomenon." Ayla was smiling. She looked past Allie for a moment. "It's wild that she's dating that guy."

"He seemed to really like her."

"She is very, very likable." Ayla sighed heavily but then laughed. "Anyway, enough about my weird romantic failures. How did you end up hanging out with a bunch of podcasters? Do you have a podcast now?"

"Oh no, not at all!" Allie found this thought unfathomable. "I work in a café. My aunt Mindy owns it. I deliver coffee to the podcast studio sometimes."

"You work in a café?" Ayla leaned forward, brow furrowed. "How's that?"

"It's uh . . . kind of weird right now, actually." Allie took a deep breath and gave Ayla a brief explanation of the situation with Mindy and the offer on the café.

"And do you think you want it? The café? Do you want to be the owner?"

Allie shrugged. "I guess I do? I can't really think of anything else that I would do at this point. I've been working at the café for ten years. Ever since—" She stopped, unwilling to bring up the last time she and Ayla had seen each other.

Ayla finished the sentence. "Since the band broke up."

Allie nodded. "Yeah. Since then."

Ayla leaned back and took a sip of her coffee. "I'm pretty surprised, I gotta admit. If you'd asked me *What do you think Allie is doing?* I definitely wouldn't have said *Managing a café in Brooklyn.*"

"Really?"

Ayla looked at her with disbelief in her eyes. "Yeah, Allie. Of all of us, it's you who I always thought would actually be a musician."

Allie felt as if she'd been hit over the head with a blunt object. "A musician?"

Ayla looked at her with a disbelieving squint. "Yeah, of course! You were the only one of us who was serious about it. And you had the most talent and wrote the best songs. I used to look you up online every few years just to see if you had an album out yet. I wanted to be able to say I'd been in a band with you when you were first starting out." Ayla laughed. She held Allie's gaze as she raised her coffee cup to her lips. "So, what about music? Are you playing music now? Like, even for fun?"

"Kind of." Allie felt a whoosh of shame. The idea that Ayla had been looking her up, expecting her to have actually been successful with music made her feel as if she'd let everyone down. "I mean, I've been working on this little project, just for me, doing covers of songs from the '80s. From all these tapes that my dad and I used to listen to."

"That sounds . . . cool?" The way Ayla said it betrayed her belief that it was actually not particularly cool. "What about writing, though? You were such a good songwriter."

"Uh, a little bit." Allie definitely did not want to tell Ayla that she had written exactly half a song in the past ten years, and that it was a song about a guy she was currently very confused about. "So, wait, what about you? We're only talking about me. What do you do now?"

Ayla smirked and struck an exaggerated glamour pose. "Senior Librarian, New York Public Library."

"Wow!" Allie was legitimately impressed. "All those hours of reading novels in the van really paid off."

"Well, that and the master's of library and information studies I got after the band broke up." Ayla nodded. "It's really my calling. It sounds dorky, but I fucking love being a librarian."

Allie could tell from the expression on Ayla's face that she was being sincere. It was nice to see someone who loved their job that much.

"That's amazing. I'm so happy for you!"

"Thanks, Allie." Ayla drained the last sips of her coffee and set the mug down gently on the table. "It's so good to see you. I can't believe we haven't found each other before now."

"I actually sent you a Facebook message a while ago, but you never answered."

Ayla looked at Allie, eyes soft with regret. "Aw, damn. I never check my Facebook. I don't even know if I have the password anymore. I'm on LinkedIn, though."

Allie grinned. "How profesh!" It was a silly abbreviation left over from their band days. The clubs they played at and the places where they stayed were always such shitholes, any sign of comfort or organization was always a total surprise. *That club actually had a mirror in the ladies room*, Allie could hear Jessi saying. *How profesh!*

Ayla giggled. "Yeah, well, I guess fancy library careers don't build themselves. Please don't disown me for joining the mainstream. Anyway, you still haven't told me why you wanted to see me. Why now? I'm so happy to see you, but I'm also really curious."

Allie took a moment to look over Ayla's shoulder out the large front window of the café. Outside, she could see a lady who was walking her dog reach down and pick up the tiny creature, tucking it under her arm before continuing up the street.

Maybe I should get a dog. Humans seem to be making everything into a giant, awkward mess.

Allie took a deep breath. "I guess the short answer is that I'm trying to find Jessi."

"Trying to find Jessi?" Ayla's echo was incredulous. "Why?"

"Uh." Allie laughed nervously. "Not one hundred percent sure on that one, but something like . . . *closure,* I guess?"

"You two really haven't talked? Since . . . that day?"

Allie nodded. "And my, uh, *friend* thought that if I saw Jessi again, we could maybe talk about it, or something? Then I might feel less bad about starting to do music again."

"Ah, so you do want to play music again."

Allie looked at Ayla. "I never stopped wanting to play music."

Ayla smiled in a way that made Allie feel uncomfortably pitied. "Allie, people join new bands after their old bands break up. Even if the circumstances of the first breakup were bad. And lots of people do better in their second—or third or fourth—band. It's not, like, a sin to want to keep playing music. You could be the Jetskis' Dave Grohl."

Allie snorted with laughter at that and relaxed slightly in her chair. "I didn't think I could do it without you all. Without Jessi."

Ayla put her hand over Allie's hand on the table. "Allie, I'm not sure what you're remembering, but I can confirm that the Jetskis was never going to be a career for any of us. Jessi didn't want to be in a touring band. She wanted to get married and live in New Jersey."

"She never told me that."

"She wouldn't have! You were so serious about the band. None of us wanted to tell you when we were tired of it. But we should have. That was on us. I'm sure that's why we had that big fight. We'd all been keeping it in instead of being honest with you."

Allie could hardly breathe. "None of you wanted to be in the band?"

"We did at first!" Ayla rushed to console her. "We absolutely did! I loved making that first record, and our first tour was a blast. But we were just ridiculous teenagers. Once the band became an actual job that we had to, like, keep showing up for, we lost our enthusiasm. It's rare that people get a job when they're eighteen and it turns out to be a job they love and want to keep doing."

"I thought we were *lucky*." Allie was unsure how to process this.

Ayla nodded again. "I know. And we were. But not in a way that the rest of us wanted to be."

Allie exhaled. "Wow."

"I always felt bad about it. We wrecked this thing that was so important to you, and then we all just disappeared."

"So, you don't see them anymore, either? Jessi and Mimi?"

Ayla shrugged. "Not really, no. I think we all just felt kind of worn out and guilty after the band was done. I didn't want to see anyone who was going to remind me about this cool thing I'd given up on. I just threw myself into library school, and that turned out to be the right thing for me."

"Mimi's doing well in Portland, though."

Ayla smiled, her eyes tender. "Is she? I haven't heard from her in years."

Allie pulled out her phone to show Ayla the Instagram chicken photos.

Ayla, confessing that she'd never really understood the appeal of Instagram, nonetheless studied the photos in Mimi's feed with immense interest.

When she'd scrolled through a few posts, she set the phone down in front of Allie.

"It's great that we all used to tease her about being a secret hippie, like that was the worst thing anyone could ever be. And now there she is sewing her own clothes and raising happy chickens and having this great life. Why was being a hippie so bad, again? Man, for a bunch of people who considered ourselves nonconformists, we sure wanted everyone to be exactly the same. Remember when Jessi drew peace signs on Mimi's backpack, and we all thought it was such a burn?"

Allie smiled. Her heart beat faster as she drummed up the courage to ask the question she was really wondering about.

"Do you know where Jessi is? What she's doing?"

Ayla shrugged. "Got married and lives in New Jersey."

Allie was stunned. She opened and closed her mouth twice before she was able to push some sound out.

"What?"

"Yep. Like I said. That was what she wanted. She and Jasmine have a bunch of kids. I ran into them once in Central Park, probably two years ago."

Allie's eyes widened.

"She married *Jasmine*?"

Ayla laughed. "I know, right? As if she met the actual love of her life when she was a twenty-two-year-old punk singer."

Allie sat still, staring down at the tabletop. She had an urge to bid Ayla a quick goodbye and flee. She forced herself to take a deep breath and act as normal as possible.

"Wow. All of this is . . . a lot." Suddenly, Ayla's mention of the meeting in Central Park sank in. "So, you aren't in contact with Jessi anymore?"

Ayla shook her head. "Naw. You know how she is. No social media, no online activity. She isn't sending anyone any Christmas cards. Looks like she's doing great, though. They all looked really happy when I ran into them in the park that time. She said they were living in Jersey. It was kind of hard to talk—the kids were just crawling all over her. And I was in a rush. Sorry I can't really help you find her."

"No, you've been helpful, for sure! I was running around thinking she was booking bands for a club or playing in some group that was about to get super famous."

"Naw." Ayla shook her head. "She's not doing any of that. She never wanted to."

They sat for a bit longer, drinking their coffees and getting caught up on the less dramatic details of their lives. When her cup was empty, Ayla reached for her coat and said she needed to get home.

"Thanks, Ayla. It was really good to see you."

"It was good to see you, too. Give me the name of your café, and I'll come in sometime." She smiled warmly. "I bet it's great."

"It is great." Allie opened her phone and texted a link to Ayla. "I'd love it if you came."

"And you and this guy who you keep calling your *friend* in a weird way should totally come to my New Year's party."

Allie should have remembered that Ayla rarely missed any kind of conversational subtlety. She blushed. "Thanks. I'm not really sure what's going on there, but it's a whole other story. We're not at the New Year's party stage, anyway."

Allie stood to hug Ayla again before they parted ways, and held on a little longer than she usually would have.

Chapter Twenty-Two

After her conversation with Ayla, Allie felt suddenly desperate for the warm, predictable atmosphere of her tiny apartment. Snow was starting to fall as she made her way home, the early winter dusk teasing the city, threatening to plunge it into darkness before everyone was ready for it.

Allie arrived in the café to find it bustling. One of their occasional part-time staff was in the kitchen while Mindy worked alone at the cash. She was blasting the Linda Ronstadt album that she knew Allie and Ren both hated and singing along over the loud hissing of the milk frother.

"Allie!" She waved.

Allie lifted her hand in return. "Everything good here?"

"Absolutely. It's been a while since you and Ren have been off on the same day. I almost forgot how good I am at this." She laughed, more animated than Allie had seen her in a while. She smiled in spite of her own cloud of miserable uncertainty.

"I'll be upstairs if you need me."

Mindy waved her off as she slid a cappuccino across the counter to a customer and picked up the tongs to move a pastry onto a plate. "I'm fine. Go have a shower. You look like you haven't slept in a year."

"Thanks for that." Allie made her way upstairs, the thrum of Linda Ronstadt's bass notes reverberating through the floorboards.

She turned on the shower and stripped off Ren's pants and Anisha's sweater. How appropriate that she was dressed in other people's clothes on a day when everything about the last twenty-four hours had left her wondering who she was. Was she a person who would be happy running a café or someone who would only be fulfilled by a music career? Was she someone Ryan actually cared about or just a friend that he had accidentally slept with? Was she the girl who had alienated her whole band by being a bitch or someone who could be—and had been—forgiven? It was a relief to be alone under the warm rushing water. She washed her hair and covered herself with soap, remembering Ryan touching her less than a day ago.

Maybe this is his thing. Maybe he befriends women, sleeps with them, and then that's it. Anisha seemed to think he fucked things up because he was scared, but what if he was just a manipulative asshole?

It was a long con if that was his intention with Allie. Surely there were easier ways to get into someone's pants than helping them conduct an extensive search for their ex-bandmate.

And buying them a Christmas tree.

Her tree was waiting for her in the corner of her room, lights shining in the winter darkness. She lay down on her bed, facing the tree and the windows, which were giving her a pleasant view of the city lights outside.

I could stay here. I like it here.

The shower had helped. Sweatpants and her Blondie T-shirt and her warm bed also healed a small part of the pain in her heart. But she still felt broken as she lay there. After a few minutes, she got up and shuffled over to her crate of her dad's old cassettes. Paula Abdul was still on the top of the pile. That album was much too perky for how Allie was feeling. She dug into the crate and pulled out a Bangles cassette instead, longing to hear their version of "Hazy Shade of Winter."

The foreboding, cynical lyrics, sung in driving harmony, would help her feel less alone.

With the cassette spinning slowly in her boombox, Allie slunk back to her bed and covered herself with blankets. She felt as if she hadn't exhaled in two days.

Maybe this was too much action for her. Too much excitement after years of days that were so similar she couldn't remember what happened week to week. She would go back to her small life, forget about romance with Ryan, forget about writing new songs, maybe even forget about finding Jessi. That would make her feel better.

She threw the covers off herself and stood, jamming her feet into her slippers. She could hear Mindy singing along to "Poor Poor Pitiful Me" as she descended the stairs.

Her aunt was just leaving the kitchen to head back out front, so Allie joined her. Mindy looked her up and down critically. "I'm glad you cleaned up, but you can't come to work in those clothes."

Allie rolled her eyes. "I didn't come down to work. I came down to talk to you."

There was only one customer left in the café, a man staring at his laptop, wearing headphones. He had a full cup of tea and a lemon tart sitting beside him. The part-timer had gone home. Mindy was alone.

"Okay." Mindy nodded. "We can talk in the kitchen for a minute. That guy seems occupied."

They walked back into the kitchen and stood on opposite sides of the counter.

"I wanted to tell you that I've decided I will take over the café. And the building. And everything."

She'd expected Mindy to be happy, at least as happy as her reserved aunt ever got. But Mindy regarded her with a suspicious gaze. "Are you sure? Why now?"

"What do you mean, why now? You just told me yesterday that you had an offer! Now seems like a reasonable time."

"But yesterday, you weren't even close to knowing what you wanted to do. And to be honest, I thought you were ready to refuse and were just trying to spare my feelings. You've been out partying and god knows what else for twenty-four hours. When have you even had time to think this through?"

"Believe it or not, I am able to have thoughts while doing other stuff. It's an actual human quality that I happen to possess."

Mindy did not laugh. Her already squinty eyes got smaller. "Is this about Ryan? Did something happen with Ryan?"

Allie broke eye contact and hated herself for it. "No. Nothing happened with Ryan." She fidgeted.

"Okay," Mindy said, leaning forward. "So, something happened with Ryan. That's established."

"Oh, fuck off," Allie muttered.

"Look, Allie." Mindy laid both palms flat on the prep counter. "Please do not agree to take on a business and a building and an entirely new set of responsibilities just because a boy made you feel sad."

"That's not what this is." Allie looked back up and matched her aunt's stare. "He didn't make me feel sad, and that's unrelated to the café, anyway."

"I don't believe you."

"Well, then, I don't know what to say to you." Allie threw up her hands and struggled to keep her voice at a reasonable volume. "You asked me to take over the café, and then you gave me a hard deadline because of this offer, and now I'm telling you I want to do it, and you won't even accept it. What the fuck am I supposed to say, Mindy? Do I beg for this thing that you've already offered me?"

"I just don't want you to do it for the wrong reasons."

"This isn't an episode of *The Bachelorette*! There are no right or wrong reasons! There are only *reasons*!"

Mindy was silent. Allie wondered whether her aunt had ever seen an episode of *The Bachelorette*.

"So, what are your reasons, then?" Mindy asked quietly.

Allie sighed. "I like it here. I feel safe here. I'm good at managing the café. I'd hate to see everything you've built over all these years end up destroyed. I can't picture any future for myself other than one where this place is a huge part of my life."

Mindy looked to the left, sniffed once and turned back, a small smile playing at the corners of her mouth. Allie slowly smiled back.

"Satisfied?"

Her aunt nodded, shaking her head once and arranging her features back into her usual frown.

The bell on the café door jangled, and they both looked back toward the main space. "I have to go back out there." Mindy smoothed her hands down the front of her apron and then put one hand on Allie's arm and squeezed. "I'll decline the other offer tomorrow morning."

Allie left her aunt to serve the new customers and went back up to her apartment. Invigorated, she opened her laptop to her recording program, grabbed her guitar and headphones and positioned her microphone in front of her. Without overthinking, she started playing the chords to "Straight Up," keeping the arrangement much simpler than the Paula Abdul original and slowing down the '80s pop tempo so it became an almost sultry, yearning version.

As she opened her mouth to sing, she felt every one of her tangled emotions pouring out with her voice. She did three takes of the song and then slammed the laptop shut, leaving the mixing and editing for the next day. Suddenly, she was beautifully calm, as if singing the song had relieved her of all the stresses of the past few weeks. She was finally back in charge of her own life.

She fell asleep on top of her covers in her sweatpants. It had been months since she'd slept so well.

Chapter Twenty-Three

Ren was singing.

There had been a lot of singing in the café lately, and Allie hoped they weren't scaring off any customers. Today, it was a heartfelt and dramatic rendition of "It's the Most Wonderful Time of the Year."

Ren gestured theatrically to Allie as they sang, throwing their arms apart and then moving one hand over their heart.

"You are loopy." Allie laughed, stooping to unload a tray of steaming dishes from the dishwasher. She'd told Ren a week ago that she'd agreed to take over the café. Ever since then, her normally cool coworker had turned into a gyrating joy machine.

"I'm just happy!" Ren countered, retrieving a tray of mugs to bring out to the front. "My job is safe. My girlfriend is a hot, horny genius. My outfit looks great. It's almost Christmas. Everything's coming up Ren!"

Allie shook her head but couldn't hide her smile. Ren's reaction had so far been one of the best things about her decision to take over. Seeing them so happy and secure just confirmed her decision.

"But you didn't tell anyone yet, right? Even Anisha?" Allie's voice was firm.

"On my honor, I did not!" Ren said. "It's been hard. But every time

I feel like talking about it, I just make out with her instead. It's working pretty well, I gotta say."

"Because she's a hot, horny genius?"

"You got it!" Unaffected by Allie's mockery, Ren moved smoothly back out to the front, holding the tray of mugs on one hand and singing, as though they were a waiter in a musical review.

A moment later, Ren popped their head back into the kitchen. "Ryan's here."

"He is?" Allie's voice was higher than usual.

Ren regarded her with a squint of suspicion. "Yeah. Are you . . . surprised? You folks are still boning, right?"

"Uh." Allie laced her fingers together and twisted her hands. "No, we decided we're better off as friends." Her words sounded unconvincing, even to her.

"Oh boy." Ren shook their head. "I do not want to be in the middle of whatever is going on there. Come out and talk to him yourself."

"Excuse me?" she shouted after Ren as she bent to unload more dishes. "What if Mindy and I hadn't wanted to be *in the middle of whatever was going on* when that very pretty lady named Alice cried all over Mindy and then me and then Mindy again while you hid in the bathroom for an hour and a half? Huh, Ren?"

"Hey, Jetski!"

Allie's body snapped back up into a standing posture.

He was smiling wide, looking like his normal self, no trace of the awkward, confusing Ryan from the day after the party. Her heart leaped. She forced herself to stay calm.

"Hey."

Still handsome. He was wearing his winter jacket, the tan chore coat that Allie thought particularly suited him, with a bright-red beanie. And now that she knew how good he was in bed, it was hard to be in the same room with him without wanting to grab him and drag him up to her apartment.

"I have good news." He slid his large frame into the kitchen and kept his back against the wall.

As far away from me as he can get.

Allie sighed, still working hard to act normal. "Yeah? What kind of good news?"

"So, our podcast is hosting a night at the Brooklyn Arts Fest. They're calling it *Mixtape Universe Live*. It's going to be, like, a bunch of musicians playing one song each, and I got you on the gig."

"You . . . what?"

"I got you on the gig!"

"Like . . . to cater it?"

"No!" Ryan tilted his head and looked at her. "To play."

"Ryan." Allie furrowed her brow. "I can't *play* at a festival."

"Why not?"

"I have written exactly one half of a song in the last ten years. No one even knows who I am. I've never played live without a band."

"That's the beauty of this exact situation!" Ryan was buoyant. "You only need to play one song. Everyone is playing one song. Like a live mixtape. Get it? And there are so many artists of varying degrees of fame, no one will blink about an emerging artist like you, especially if we introduce you as *from the seminal underground punk band the Jetskis.*"

"Ryan, I—"

"And you won't have to do it alone. I'll play with you."

"You?"

"I've gotten really good on the drums. I mean, I can handle criticism, but I think I'm capable of holding it down for one song that we play together. It's gonna be great!"

Allie stared at him. What was going on in that big, ridiculous head of his?

She rubbed her eyes with her fists, hoping that when she put her hands down and looked again, he would have vanished and she would not have to deal with this situation. It didn't work. Ryan's Labrador retriever expression was still there, looking at her expectantly. She felt her insides twist with frustration.

"Ryan, I'm not playing your show!"

"What? Why not!" He tilted his head more dramatically.

"Because I'm not this person!"

"What person?"

"This person who just takes chances and tries new stuff and plays a fucking show when she's been irrelevant for a decade! And . . . has casual sex. I am not that kind of person!"

"Allie—"

"No! Listen to me! This is all on your terms! You added me to your—I don't know—*harem*? Of random ladies you've slept with and it didn't mean anything to you, and now you're pushing this gig on me because you think it would be cool or whatever, and you're not think-ing about me. *I don't want this.* I don't want hookups and random, unpredictable performances. That's you. It's not me. Stop pushing your shit onto me and cramming me into some hole in your life that needs filling. *It's hurting my feelings.*"

She gasped for air after the words were out.

Ryan was staring at her. His eyes were wet. She felt a twinge of regret but tried to shake it off.

Don't feel bad for telling the truth.

But she *did* feel bad. She hated fights.

"I—" Ryan raked his hand through his tidy hair. "I must have really messed this up."

He looked at Allie as if he was waiting for her to respond. She stayed silent. He exhaled, looking at the floor. "Well, first of all, that sex wasn't, uh, *casual* for me. It wasn't a random hookup. It made me, like, ludicrously happy that you even wanted that kind of rela-tionship with me. When I woke up with you, I wanted to wake up with you all the time."

Allie felt a lump in her throat. Her eyes burned. She forced the words out. "But then why did you say you just wanted to be friends? Why did you say it was a mistake?"

"I thought that's what you wanted me to say. I thought you wanted an out."

Allie rolled her eyes, anger welling up. "That's bullshit! You said it before I even had a chance to talk!"

"But you agreed! You agreed, like, *right away*!" Ryan held up one hand helplessly.

"What was I supposed to say? You just decided in the light of day that you didn't feel strongly enough about me for us to have a relationship."

"That's not true!" For the first time in the conversation, he took a step toward her. "That's the furthest thing from the truth. I've liked you all along. I've been into you since—" He looked off to one side, took a deep breath and looked back at her. "Since the first time we met."

"If that's actually true, then seriously, what's your *problem*, Ryan?" The words came out with more poison than she intended. His face crumpled, and she felt a whoosh of sadness.

"Well, since you asked." He stared right into her eyes. "My problem is, I feel like this big, weird *monster* who scares everyone off and doesn't even have a family who wants him around and is just mostly lonely all the time. I feel like most people I have been close to have just . . . never been able to love me."

Allie tried to temper the harshness in her voice. "What about your sister, Ryan?"

"My sister?"

"Yes!" She threw her hands up in the air. "Weeks ago, you said you'd think about writing her a letter. Have you?"

Ryan looked at the floor. "No."

"Well, maybe you should stop pressuring me to face up to complicated people from my past and start facing up to yours. We're never going to find Jessi. It's just dead end after dead end. At least with your sister, you know where she is. At least you could *try!*"

Ryan looked back up at her, not even trying to conceal the tears that were running down his face. He looked helpless, miserable.

Allie's anger deflated. "Oh." She stepped toward him. He backed away.

"I know I screwed up. I didn't know what I was doing. I'm sorry that I hurt your feelings. You deserve better," Ryan mumbled as he turned to leave the kitchen.

She could not handle this. She'd been wrong to think she could.

Well, that's it. Everything you were afraid of has happened. You've lost him.

When she heard the bell ring as the front door closed behind him, she leaned back against the wall by the office and slid to the floor, wiping her eyes with the back of her hand. Ren appeared immediately. They sat down beside Allie.

"Well, that didn't seem to go well."

"You heard?"

"Do you want me to pretend I didn't?"

"I guess not." Allie dropped her face down into her hands and groaned.

Ren put their arm around Allie's shoulders. "I'm sorry. I was rooting for you two."

"Why did I have to start a fucking fight? If none of this had happened, then we'd just be discussing all that new shit that Ayla told me about Jessi."

"Yeah, but you'd still be pining for him, even behind all that friendship. Friendships have an expiry date when what you really want is to take each other's clothes off."

Allie laughed miserably. "That's kind of what George said."

Ren considered this information. "I wouldn't have thought the old guy had it in him, but good work, George. Walking around picturing various ladies at the seniors' center without their bloomers on."

Allie laughed more authentically at that one. "You're impossible."

"Impossible not to love, you mean?" They rolled their head to one side, meeting Allie's eyes and grinning.

"Okay, sure." Allie smiled back. "Impossible not to love."

Ren stood and held their hands out to Allie, who allowed herself to be helped to her feet.

Allie opened the door to the staircase. "If you're okay without me, I'm going to go upstairs for a bit."

"To wallow?"

Allie considered lying but knew that Ren wouldn't buy it. "Yeah. To wallow."

"Only a few hours of wallowing, and then you need to do something else."

"I'm not sure when you became an expert on self-care, but fine. I will limit my wallowing, if possible."

Allie wasn't sure that it would be possible.

Chapter Twenty-Four

Her apartment was darker than usual, thanks to the cloudy conditions outdoors. She didn't turn on her bedside lamp and certainly didn't bother plugging in the string of lights on her tree. A tree that was now making her feel bitter and mildly ashamed of herself.

She wasn't sure what to believe. Ryan's words and actions were so different from each other. Choosing not to think about it, she climbed into her bed and pulled the multiple blankets over her head, listening to her ragged breath. Her eyes filled with tears and ran down the sides of her face, making muffled plops as they hit the pillow. She was exhausted. Within minutes, she was asleep.

She woke to darkness, momentarily confused about where she was. She scrambled out from under her blankets and looked at the clock on her bedside. Eight p.m. Ren had let her sleep through the entire afternoon shift. She could hear them crashing around downstairs as they cleaned up, preparing to close.

The memories of her fight with Ryan came rushing back into her mind, and she sighed deeply. Then something else pushed its way into her thoughts. A melody.

Allie swung her legs over the side of the bed and sat up, humming. Ryan's words were lingering, and her mind was turning them into lyrics.

"*I always feel like a monster . . .*" She sang it under her breath, moving the notes around as she repeated the phrase, bending it to the melody that was playing in her head. She started scrambling for her acoustic guitar and her notebook.

The song was finished after just an hour of her fussing with chord progressions and a particularly tricky rhythm within the bridge. It was undoubtedly a song of love and apology. A song with lyrics pleading for him to find his way to her again. For them to somehow find a way forward together. She worked furiously, scratching out sections that weren't quite good enough, that didn't feel real enough, replacing them with better words and more evocative images. She managed to pack everything in there. Her feelings for Ryan were clear in the lyrics; she'd turned his own words into a metaphor that ran throughout, the complexity complemented by the simple melody she picked out on her guitar strings.

She played it through again and again. Until she could sing it without crying. Until it was perfect. It was such a strange feeling, something so sad also being something so satisfying. She'd missed writing songs and watching them magically turn into what they were meant to be.

She set down her guitar and realized she was hungry. Rooting around in her bar fridge yielded an apple and some crackers and peanut butter, which was about as elaborate as she could manage. As she was arranging her feast on a not-that-dirty plate, her phone rang.

Ryan?

She lunged for it and checked the screen. She didn't recognize the number but answered anyway, feeling daring after her creative triumph.

"Hello?"

"Hi, is this Allie Andrews?"

"Yes, that's me. Who's calling?"

"It's Meera Bukhari, I'm one of the producers of *Mixtape Universe.*

We have you on our list as a performer for our day at the Brooklyn Arts Fest, and I'm calling to talk over the details."

"Oh." Ryan must not have canceled the gig yet. Of course he hadn't. This Meera woman was overly keen, calling people at 9 p.m.

"I know, you probably didn't think you'd be hearing from us so quickly, but we're a bit under the gun, to be honest. Having a festival of any kind in the second week of January is a terrible plan from the jump. And they threw us in there at the last minute and— Oh you don't need to hear all my complaining." Meera laughed. "We just need to get our details sorted as soon as possible. You're Ryan's friend, right? I loved the recording he played us. That cover of 'Borderline' was really a cool take. Is that what you'll be performing for our show?"

Allie opened her mouth to tell Meera that there had been a mistake.

"No, I—" She could still feel the sting in her fingertips where she'd been holding down the strings of her guitar as she played the new song over and over again. *Her* song. "I'm going to play an original. A new song."

"Great!" Meera chirped. "What's it called?"

"Uh—'Monster.' It's called 'Monster.'"

—

Allie went back to sleep after Meera's call, already wondering whether accepting the show was the right move. When she woke early the next morning, she forced it out of her mind. It was Christmas Eve, and one of her favorite days to work in the café. It was always a mob scene, full of last-minute shoppers and people having coffee with visiting friends. The festive season would surround her whether she liked it or not. She was missing the days when her life happened without much effort on her part. She dressed in a long-sleeved forest-green T-shirt and a pair of bright-red corduroy overalls and walked down to the kitchen, yawning as she went.

Alone in the kitchen, she felt a light relief, happy to begin work that was so familiar she hardly had to think about it. She started baking the scones and sticky buns that she knew would sell out, the thick scent of cinnamon like a wool blanket around her. At 7:30 a.m., she turned the lights on at the front and unlocked the doors. There were already two customers waiting, men in suits gazing eagerly through the window. They were the beginning of the avalanche.

By the time Ren strolled in at nine, Allie hadn't had a moment to catch her breath. Ren immediately began busing tables and sorting out the dishes that had been left abandoned in the dishwasher as Allie stood behind the counter, serving pastry after pastry and coffee after coffee. Mindy, normally in for the late shift starting at lunch-time, came in early, knowing what they'd be facing. The three of them fell into their well-worn patterns within the café, running everything with a peaceful efficiency that made the day sail by. Customers were happy; Ren was playing Christmas music, of course, and Allie was just glad to be thinking about anything but Ryan.

Mindy, holding her tongue about the endless Christmas playlists, fell into uncharacteristic nostalgia, thinking about Christmases past at the café.

"There was one year, probably before you were born, Allie, when the power went out. The whole two days, Christmas Eve and Christmas Day, no power at all. That was when I had a giant coffee carafe and a minifridge for sodas. People still came in. I made coffee on the gas stove, ran through my supplies of frozen baked goods and warned anyone who came in that the sodas were warm. People still came. Do you remember that guy Albert who used to come in every day before he moved to Tennessee?" She looked at Allie.

Allie nodded. "Oh yeah, he always had a guitar, and he called me *honey*."

Ren clucked their tongue. Allie laughed. "Not in a disrespectful way. I always thought maybe he just never learned my name and then was too embarrassed to ask."

"Anyway, Albert was around back then, too. He brought his guitar and a bunch of his weird music buddies, and we all stayed up all night. They just played old songs, and they shared a bunch of beer, and we lit candles."

"That sounds nice." Allie stopped arranging the tray of new scones in the display case for a minute. She straightened up and put her hand on Mindy's shoulder.

"It was nice." Mindy sighed. "It's always been nice to be here."

Allie blinked away tears and saw Mindy doing the same. Then a family of six came crashing through the door looking for cookies for the exhausted children, and everything went back to normal again.

During a brief lull at 6 p.m., Ren found Allie in the kitchen unloading the dishwasher for the seventeenth time that day.

"Hey, so, I'm headed to Anisha and Ryan's tonight. I'm going to stay over and then have Christmas with them both tomorrow."

"That sounds nice." Allie stacked saucers, distracted.

"Are you going to come, too?"

"Am I what?" Allie turned away from the dishes and looked at Ren, confused.

"Are you going to come over, too? It would be great. All four of us, eating whatever delicious shit Anisha is going to make? Hanging out?"

"Ren." Allie sighed. "I'm pretty sure I'm not invited. Ryan and I aren't exactly on good terms. I'm not really sure that we can go back to just being friends."

"So don't!" There was a hint of desperation in Ren's voice. "Go back to banging!"

Allie smiled, shaking her head. "I don't think that's going to work, either. We never should have changed things between us. We took a risk that didn't pay off."

"Allie, please don't take this the wrong way, but you're a fucking weirdo."

Allie stared at Ren for a moment, blinking. "Please elaborate."

"You know that normal people talk to each other when they encounter difficulties in their relationships, right? Like, people have fights and disagreements and issues all the time. It's a quality that exists in all human relationships. You don't have to live in absolute harmony with someone else to have a long-term, or even fucking *medium-term*, relationship with them."

"I know that." Allie was indignant.

"*Do you*, though?" Ren threw up their arms. "I didn't know you ten years ago, but it sounds like you were spoiled by this magical band you had, and then when that changed, you just wrote everyone off and walked away. You lost your best friends because of one conflict? It's kind of absurd."

"That was different! They hated me!"

Ren exhaled loudly. "Again, *did they*? If they hated you, then why did Mimi talk to you on Instagram as soon as you messaged her? Why was Ayla so happy to see you the other day? Why was she sad that she didn't have more info to help you find Jessi?"

Allie hadn't considered the situation in that particular light. "Okay, maybe I see your point."

"Ryan doesn't hate you, either. You had an unfortunate stumbling block. He acted like a dingus, you acted like a dingus. It happens. Sometimes that just means there are strong feelings there. Come with me for Christmas. You can make it work."

Allie shook her head but smiled more sincerely. "I'm not going with you now. But I promise to think about what you said."

Ren's dark eyes sized her up. "I'll allow it." They looked back toward the front of the café as the bell on the door rang, signaling a new customer. "And don't think I won't be lecturing Ryan about all this as well."

"Oh, I definitely assumed you would also be lecturing Ryan."

Ren nodded and turned on their heel, loping back out to the front to help Mindy serve a new crowd of customers who had just come through the door.

Chapter Twenty-Five

Allie had made plans to spend Christmas with Mindy, who hated Christmas. It made her the perfect person to spend the holiday with when one was feeling slightly miserable about it.

It was not the first time Allie had felt despondent at Christmas over the years she'd been in Brooklyn, and it wasn't the worst. Nothing would ever compare to the first Christmas she'd been there, her life upended, an orphan trying to start over without the friends who'd made her life worthwhile. She'd spent that Christmas with Mindy as well, the two of them barely speaking. Allie didn't even complain when Mindy decided to play all of her Joni Mitchell records one after the other. For once in her life, she didn't care about the music that surrounded her. She didn't think she'd ever get over the feelings of loss that seemed to have embedded themselves permanently in her heart after she'd left that last band practice.

She thought again about her conversation with Ren and felt a heavy clutch of doom in her stomach. What if Ren was right? What if she'd wasted all those years assuming her bandmates hated her when she could have just worked harder to save the relationship? What if Jessi had stayed in her life instead of eventually becoming the focus of a mystery that she wasn't sure would ever be solved?

When Allie arrived at the door, Mindy flung it open and regarded Allie with concerned eyes.

"How are you doing?"

Allie shrugged. "Fine, I guess."

"I'm worried about you."

"Well, don't be."

Allie knew Mindy wouldn't push it. Strong feelings—her own or anyone else's—made Mindy uncomfortable when she was confronted by them one on one.

Mindy's apartment, two blocks from the café, was a cozy and comfortable one-bedroom above a laundromat. Its radiators hissed and clanked in the cold weather. The whole place always smelled vaguely of fabric softener. Mindy had lived there for almost twenty years now, and Allie was saddened to see that the decluttering and packing efforts had already begun, in preparation for her aunt's pending departure. There were cardboard boxes marked Donate in each room, and all the bookshelves, once crammed, were empty.

"I brought you something." Allie dug around in the pockets of her coat and pulled out a cassette. She handed it to Mindy, who looked at the handwritten song list curiously.

Allie had decided that the final form of her covers project had to be a cassette. It seemed only right, given the inspiration for the project in the first place. She'd made three copies, for the three people she knew who still owned cassette players. One for George, one for Mindy. And one for Ryan. But it was looking as if that last one wasn't going to be gifted after all.

"You finished it! Allie, this looks amazing." Mindy turned the small plastic case over in her hands. "Your dad would have gotten a real kick out of it."

Allie smiled. "Yeah, I think he would have."

Mindy made spaghetti, and they ate it on the soft, tweedy sofa. Snow was falling outside the tall, uncurtained windows, flakes illuminated as they moved through the beam of a streetlamp.

Mindy let Allie choose the movie, stipulating that anything that wasn't Christmasy was fine with her. After a bit of thought, Allie chose *Funny Face*, knowing how much Mindy loved Audrey Hepburn and figuring the scenes in Paris would amplify Mindy's excitement about her upcoming travels. But when the characters arrived in Paris, Allie glanced over at her aunt and saw that her face was wet with tears. Allie scrambled to pull the remote control from the sofa cushions and hit Pause.

"Holy shit, what's wrong?"

Mindy managed a small smile and wiped her cheeks with the back of her hand. She sighed and looked away from Allie. "I'm just sad, I guess."

"Sad about what?" Allie was mystified. She'd seen her aunt cry at the occasional funeral they'd attended over the years, but never just randomly in the middle of a movie like this.

"About leaving the café. And about leaving you and Ren and . . . everything, I guess."

"Do you not want to go anymore?" Allie hated herself for feeling a flicker of hope.

"No, no." Mindy waved her hand, as if batting Allie's words out of the air. "Of course I want to go. I'm just . . . I guess I'm just having feelings about it. Perfectly normal feelings."

"Maybe for other people." Allie was pleased when Mindy gave a gentle laugh.

"I have *feelings*, Allie. And I'm allowed to be slightly conflicted about this massive life change." Mindy laid her head back against the wall behind the sofa. "I just keep thinking about how if someone asked me who I am, right now I would say I'm a New Yorker and a café owner. When I leave, then who will I be?"

Allie didn't have an answer. They sat in silence for several minutes, and then Mindy reached for the remote control and wordlessly pressed Play.

When the movie finished, Mindy was fast asleep. Rather than wake her, Allie covered her aunt with a plaid wool blanket and let herself out. The streets were quiet, and the air was cold and fresh. Something about being out there walking, with few other people around and without anyone she knew anywhere near her, made Allie feel pleasantly untethered. She walked slowly, feeling as if she were the only person on earth. As if whatever she chose to do, now or in the future, would have no consequences for anyone but herself.

"That's some weird Ayn Rand shit right there," she muttered aloud as she crossed the road toward the darkened café. Still, something about that moment of freedom allowed her to think about what she would be choosing for herself if she weren't worried about what anyone else would think or feel about it.

She let herself into the café and locked the door behind her, grabbed a cookie from the kitchen and headed up the stairs to her apartment. Immediately, she picked up her guitar. She played her new song once, twice, and then a third time, changing a few lyrics and adding a more complex melody for the bridge. She was just thinking about recording it when she heard someone enter the kitchen downstairs through the back door.

"Allie? You up there?"

Ren's voice floated up the stairs. Allie laid her guitar down and quickly opened the door. Ren was staring at her from the bottom of the staircase.

"Yeah, I'm here. Is everything okay? I thought you'd be at Anisha's."

"Can I come up?"

"Of course."

Allie backed into her apartment and waited for Ren to climb the staircase. Once Ren had removed their coat and boots, they sat on the stool by Allie's recording setup and gestured for Allie to sit on the bed.

"Ren, what's going on? You're freaking me out."

Ren took a deep breath.

"Did you tell Anisha not to get involved with me?"

Allie wasn't sure what she'd been expecting to hear, but it certainly wasn't that. She felt a tickle of panic in her belly.

"What?"

"Did you tell Anisha not to get involved with me? At our Thanksgiving dinner?"

Allie remembered. The conversation with Anisha. Conspiring with Mindy to avoid another heartbroken paramour banging on the café door in the wee hours, looking for Ren.

Shit.

Allie took a deep breath. "Yes. I did. Mindy and I—Uh . . . Well, it was mostly me."

Ren was very still. "Do you want to explain why?"

"I'm sorry, Ren. Anisha was asking me about you and—god, I really do feel terrible about this now—I told her that you were a heartbreaker. I told her about all the girls that have been hurt and showed up here." This was all hard to say. Allie forced herself to get the full truth out. "And I did, I recommended that she not get involved with you."

Ren stood up. "Allie." Their voice was disturbingly calm. "I am very angry about this. I am angry at you."

"Why are you saying it like that?"

"Like what?"

"Like you're a robot?"

Ren smiled, just a bit, with one corner of their mouth. "I'm showing you that we can get through this without it being a giant bust-up. I am *setting an example*."

"Oh." Allie blinked, startled by this left turn in the conversation. "Okay, then. What happens next?"

"What happens next is that I leave and go for a walk around the block. That will help me get some perspective and be less mad. Then I'll come back here, and we'll have a conversation about how we can move forward from this experience."

Allie wasn't sure what to say. "Uh . . . okay, sure?"

Ren nodded and rose, stepping into their boots and pulling their thick winter coat back on. They disappeared down the stairs, and Allie sat back down on her bed. She wanted to play guitar again, but that seemed inappropriate. So she sat still and waited, watching the bare branches on the tree outside her window sway in the wind.

Ren returned ten minutes later, their boots clomping up the stairs. Allie could feel her jaw tightening. Ren being upset made her stressed. Even though this fight—if that was even what was happening—did not feel like any conflict she'd had before.

Ren took off their coat and boots again and sat back down on the stool, facing Allie. They clapped their palms down flat on their legs and looked Allie in the eye. "What you said to Anisha made me upset. It hit a nerve for me because I *have* been worried that I'm not good enough for Anisha. So to know that you thought the same thing felt really bad."

Allie started to speak, but Ren held up one hand to stop her. "I understand what you said and why you said it, and I know that Anisha was probably a bit . . . *relentless* in her questioning, so I don't think that you did it to be intentionally hurtful. But it did hurt me. And I wanted you to hear how I feel."

Allie stared at Ren. An awkward, prolonged silence enveloped the room. Finally, Ren seemed to realize that Allie needed permission to speak. "Oh, you can go ahead and talk now."

"Okay." Allie smoothed her sweaty hands over her bedspread. Her heart was pounding. "This is really hard for me. Right now, I feel like I want to just hide. I hate that I hurt your feelings. I think you're amazing. I also think, for the record, that you are absolutely, without question, good enough for Anisha. I am really happy you found each other. I based what I said that night on your past, on those situations that happened with the other people you'd dated. I should have known that a person's past doesn't always equal who they are in the present. I was worried that if something went wrong with you and Anisha, I wouldn't get to have Ryan and Anisha in my life anymore, and that was so scary to me. What I told Anisha was about my own fear, not about your prospects as a good partner."

Allie finished and forced herself to look at Ren, who was smiling.

"Thank you, Allie. Good use of *I* statements, by the way."

"I don't know what you're talking about, but I will look it up."

Ren laughed. "Wow, you really haven't been in a healthy relationship before, have you?"

Allie shook her head. "Not yet, I guess."

"Well, I'm going to head back to Anisha's." Ren got up and retrieved their coat and boots.

"Ren, thank you for coming here, in the middle of the night on Christmas, to tell me what you needed me to hear. And to help me with all of this."

"Well"—Ren shrugged—"I couldn't sleep for thinking about it. So, you're welcome. I'd say *anytime*, but I don't really want to do this again."

Allie laughed. "Do you want me to walk you?"

"Naw, I'll get an Uber. I'll tip big."

"Merry Christmas, Ren."

"Merry Christmas, Allie."

Allie listened to Ren's boots on the stairs and the ringing of the bell on the front door as they let themselves out and locked it behind them. Allie was alone, again. The conversation had been a success, but she still felt like a failure. She'd ultimately chickened out and hadn't told Ren that she was having doubts about taking over the café, for fear that it would disrupt the harmony they'd just established.

I'll tell them soon.

She made this promise to herself as she flopped back onto her bed, exhausted. Within a few minutes, she was asleep.

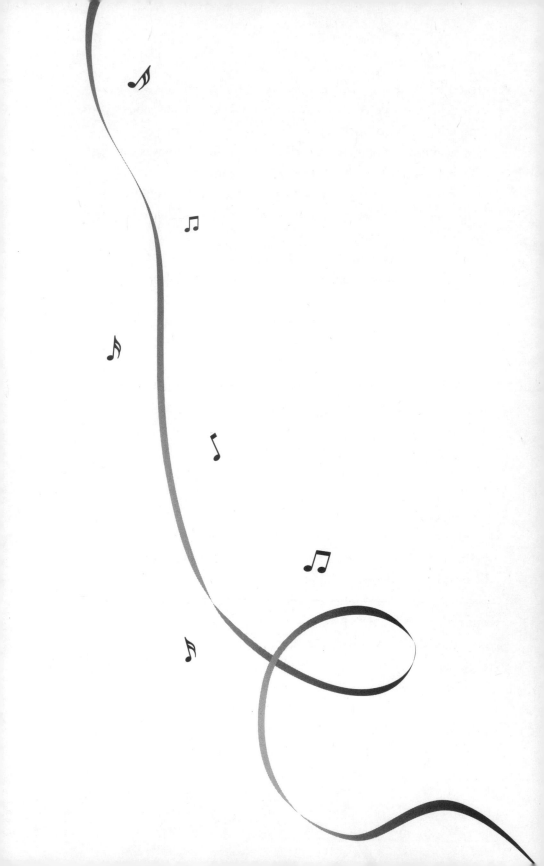

JANUARY

True Colors

Chapter Twenty-Six

The Brooklyn Arts Fest was mobbed.

As Allie made her way into the Brooklyn Academy of Music build-ing for the show, she tried her best not to wield her guitar case like a battering ram. She checked in at the front desk, as per Meera's detailed instructions, and received a name tag and lanyard from the frazzled volunteer. Allie could not shake the feeling that someone would soon be stepping out from the shadows and declaring that she actually had no right to be there and asking her to please leave.

She forced herself to gulp down a deep breath and push ahead through the crowded hallway toward the theater doors, which bore a Talent Only sign that made Allie feel more intimidated. The idea of barging through the doors and presenting herself as "Talent" was so thoroughly ridiculous she felt an urge to drop her guitar and flee. Before she could make that call, the door opened, and a woman with chin-length black hair and a gorgeous embroidered dress poked her head out.

"Oh, hi, are you coming in here?"

Allie recognized her voice from the phone call. This had to be Meera. Her efficient confidence was unmistakable. Meera looked quickly at Allie's name tag and guitar and then flung the door open wider.

"You're Allie! Hello! I'm Meera." They shook hands. "Come on in. People are still arriving, and we're doing some really rudimentary sound checks. You can head backstage through that door on the left. Our tech people will figure out how to mic you."

Meera's phone rang, and she answered it before Allie could ask, casually, what the names of the tech people were who would be helping her with her sound needs. For the second time in as many minutes, she fought the urge to flee.

Backstage was a flurry of activity, with musicians of all varieties clustered in various positions around the space. The sound tech who greeted her was absolutely not Ryan—she was a Black woman wearing overalls with mic cables looped over both of her shoulders—and Allie felt herself caught between relief and disappointment.

To her left, two women stared intently at each other as they sang an imperfect line of harmony repeatedly, getting closer to having it work each time. A guy with an electric guitar was in the middle of some kind of heated debate with a guy holding a snare drum. They looked like they could be twins, or at least brothers. Allie was happy to be performing alone; she had enough potential drama at this event without having to negotiate with another nervous, ego-driven musician.

"Okay, everyone, can I have your attention?" The sound tech cupped her hands to her mouth and called out to everyone. It took almost a full minute and two more calls before everyone stopped singing, arguing, chatting and strumming. When the group was quiet, she went on.

"Thank you all for coming. I'm Mel. I'm your tech for this wild ride. We have two spots set up on the stage. You can see the borders of each marked off with tape. We've set up the backline and the basic mics at each, and you'll be given either number one or two to know where to stand and play when you go onstage. This way, we can get one spot set up for the next act while the other act is playing." There was a murmur from the crowd. "We'll be discreet, I promise. We are not out here trying to take attention away from your performance. This is just the only way we could do this bananas mixtape-style show without it taking five hours and boring everyone to death. You have"—she looked at her watch—"seven minutes until we start letting people in. Use it wisely. Have a great show!"

Allie used her seven minutes to go hide in the bathroom. She didn't want to talk to anyone. Her guitar had been checked by Mel's assistant and was secure in a stand, waiting for her to grab it when it was her turn onstage. She had nothing to do, so she sat in a stall and took deep, gulping breaths.

It's one song. Just one song. If you hate playing music onstage today, you never have to do it again. You can find something else to do with your life. There are other things. It will be fine.

When Allie emerged from the stall, Meera was standing at the sinks, looking into the mirror.

"Hey, there!" She smiled and then went back to smoothing her hair and squinting at her reflection. "I'm really glad I only have to be onstage for a minute to introduce the host. My hair is starting to reflect my nerves."

Allie laughed and turned her head to check her own hair in the mirror. "Well, I think you look great."

"Thanks." Meera grinned and took a plastic bottle from her purse. She squeezed a small amount of whatever it was into her palms and started working it into her hair. "Ryan said you didn't want to do the show at first. I'm glad you changed your mind. He said you're really talented."

"He did?"

"Yeah, of course. He's a big fan, I gather." Meera's voice was maddeningly neutral.

Allie arranged her features into what she hoped was a casual expression. "Did he say that . . . recently?"

Meera laughed, her eyes meeting Allie's in the mirror. "Do you think he's changed his mind?"

Allie looked down and muttered, "Not sure."

"Well, he was just telling me earlier how great you were going to be, so I don't think he's had a change of heart."

"He's here?" It was getting harder to be casual as this conversation progressed. "I haven't seen him yet."

"Yeah, he had to run back to the studio to get two more patch cables, but he should be back now. He's running the soundboard. You'll see him in the theater. He's hard to miss."

Allie laughed. Her voice sounded weird and tense, but Meera did not seem to notice anything peculiar. She put her hair product back in her purse and looped it over her shoulder. "Okay, they're letting people in now. I'm gonna go make sure it's all running smoothly. Break a leg, Allie."

"Thanks."

Allie left the bathroom and waited in the wings for her turn. There were fifteen acts, and she was on seventh. After the introduction, the first act took the stage, and Allie had to work hard to keep breathing.

Her song was good. She knew it was good. And there was only one person in the audience whose opinion she was concerned about, anyway. Time crawled by. When she'd toured with the Jetskis, she'd always loved watching the other bands they played with. But now the music just washed over her as she marinated in her own anxiety.

When the sixth performers—the women who were working on their harmonies when she first arrived—took the stage, Allie retrieved her guitar from its stand and waited for the sound tech to signal her. When the signal came, she quietly took her place on the darkened side of the stage, her heart beating wildly.

The house lights were dim, but they illuminated the audience enough for her to see him, the small desk lamp beside the soundboard in the middle of the theater throwing shadows across his face. She felt

MAKE ME A MIXTAPE

for a moment as if someone had punched her in the stomach. She breathed in through her nose, forcing herself to hold it for a count of three, then released the breath and closed her eyes for a moment longer than a normal blink. As the two women finished their song and took a bow, the lights went down on them and came up on Allie.

They'd all been warned that they wouldn't have a proper sound check once they hit the stage. There was no time for that. Instead, she'd been told to strum her guitar once, speak into the mic for a quick introduction, and then start playing. She strummed her guitar and heard its comforting tone ring back through the monitor. So far, so good. Ryan was looking down at the board. Leaning in toward the mic, she took a final deep breath and then spoke.

"Hi. I'm Allie Andrews. This song is called 'Monster.' It's about someone I like very much."

There was a second, right before she started playing, when their eyes met. When it was as if he was the only person in the theater and she was about to play the song just for him. The same way she'd done in the past as they sat in her bedroom or in his living room. As if only the two of them mattered.

Allie had to look away from him or she'd never get through it. She strummed her first chord and let the song carry her off. She could hear her own voice through the monitor, and she closed her eyes as she sang, her words and guitar filling the theater. The nerves that had plagued her before the performance vanished, and she put everything she had into the song, desperate to get the emotion across.

When her last chord rang out, she opened her eyes. People were clapping, and she even heard a few whoops. Then, her side of the stage went dark, and her time was up.

She wanted more. This was it. She wanted to be onstage, singing songs she'd written. That was all she wanted out of her future.

Except, she also wanted to find Ryan.

"Hey, Meera?"

Meera was staring intently at a clipboard backstage when Allie found her. She looked up, startled. "Oh, hey, Allie. Great song! I actually snuck out to watch you, and it was worth it. I'm glad Ryan had us book you, and I'll keep you in mind for future events. Your payment should be in your account by end of day tomorrow."

"Oh. Thanks." Allie hadn't actually been looking for any comments about her performance, and she felt slightly ashamed for not thinking of it. "I really appreciate that. Do you happen to know where Ryan is?"

"Oh yeah, he had to leave. I think he stayed for your song, but then he left Yusef in charge and ran out pretty quickly. Was he supposed to wait for you?"

"No." Allie made a Herculean effort to hide her disappointment. "I was just seeing if I could check in with him before I left. But that's cool. I'll catch him, uh, later."

"Take care, Allie. See you again soon." Meera went back to her clipboard, leaving Allie to pick up her guitar case and walk alone out the front doors of the building, into the harsh winter light.

Well, that was it. Ryan didn't want anything to do with her.

I'm Sheila now. I'm fucking Sheila.

She'd sung her song, her heartfelt words that were unmistakably a message only for Ryan. And he'd heard those words and pretty much instantly bailed, not wanting to talk to her afterward at all.

Allie walked home, the streets full of people attending to their weekend errands and social engagements. She didn't notice that she was crying until the wind blew, stinging her wet cheeks. Sniffling, she dragged her mittened hand across her eyes and told herself to get it together. It didn't help. The tears came more readily, streaming down her face and mingling with the snot now dripping from her nose. She gave up trying to preserve her mittens and just pulled the left one off, using it to mop her face as she stood on a street corner, her guitar case resting on the wet and slushy sidewalk.

This is what it feels like. This is a broken heart.

She didn't think she'd ever had one before. The closest she'd come was losing her band. And that was different from the misery she was feeling now, thinking about how things were never going to be the same between her and Ryan again. Losing the band meant losing the music and friendships that had meant so much to her. Losing Ryan made her feel unmoored, as if she were floating through space with nothing to hold on to. As if she'd lost everything.

She reached the café and took a deep breath before walking in. She knew her swollen eyes and red face would make it impossible to hide the fact that she'd been crying. Mindy and Ren would have questions.

The bell on the door rang as she entered, and Mindy looked up from her spot behind the counter and yelled, "Ren! She's back!"

Ren came skidding into the café from the kitchen, wiping their hands on a tea towel.

"How did it go? Tell me everything. Wait, why are you crying?" Mindy dropped the spoon she was holding and moved around the counter to get closer to Allie. "What happened? Did something happen?"

Allie, who seldom cried in front of anyone, knew she was freaking them out but couldn't stop her tears. Ren linked their arm through hers and began to steer her toward the kitchen. "Come into the back." Allie saw Mindy looking from the busy café to the kitchen door, torn. Ren noticed, too. "I got her. We'll call you if we need you."

When they got to the back, Allie slumped down on a stool and surrendered to her sobbing. Ren filled a glass with cold water and handed it to her, then waited, looking at her with patient concern.

Drinking the water allowed her to regulate her breathing and brought on a slow calming of her nerves.

"Jesus, I'm sorry about this," she gasped to Ren.

"Allie, don't apologize. You're allowed to be upset. I've just never seen you like this. Can you tell me what happened? Was the show bad?"

Allie shook her head. "No, actually. The show was great. I sang well, I felt . . . I felt *wonderful*."

"Okay." Ren spoke slowly, tilting their head to one side. "Then, what was it?"

"It was . . ." Allie heaved a long sigh. "It was Ryan." She felt her throat tightening again, and tears welled in her eyes. "Fuck, here I go again."

"Okay, okay. It's okay." Ren's cool demeanor was beginning to crack. "It's going to be fine. Uh—Mindy!"

It was only a few seconds before Mindy poked her head through the doorway. "Yes?"

"Switch, please." Ren's eyes were wide.

"Sure, go out front. I'll stay here. The lady at the counter just ordered an oat milk latte and two chocolate tarts."

Ren nodded and fled the kitchen, leaving Mindy to stare at her sobbing niece, attempting to assess the situation.

"I'm sorry." Allie managed to squeeze out the words between gasps.

"Allie, I'm sure Ren already told you not to apologize for being upset. Now"—she pulled up a second stool and sat in front of Allie, holding her hands tightly—"try to breathe, and go ahead and tell me what's happening. Whatever it is, you'll get through it. And honestly, you've probably been through worse."

Allie managed a small smile.

"See? You're feeling better already." She released Allie's hands and sat back slightly. "Now *talk*."

Chapter Twenty-Seven

It had been exactly one week since the show, and Allie still hadn't heard anything from Ryan, further solidifying her belief that he was set on avoiding her forever. It was embarrassing.

She made a playlist called Humiliating Heartbreak Songs and sang along as she worked. Ren made a few gentle cracks about how much Fleetwood Mac was too much Fleetwood Mac, but otherwise, no one commented, and Allie was grateful. The music soothed her, but in a new way. Instead of just letting the songs carry her into a state where she wasn't thinking about her problems, they showed her that other people had the *same* problems.

She tried not to pester Ren for inside info, but regardless, Ren volunteered whatever they had, and it wasn't much. Word from Anisha was that Ryan had been either absent or quiet for the past week. He'd missed dinner two nights in a row, and when asked, just said he was doing "research." That was the most detail Ren could provide. But of course, they had opinions to heap on top of the minimal facts.

"I think he's heartbroken, too," Ren posited one afternoon when Anisha had come to the café for a tea and Allie came briefly out of the kitchen to say hello.

Anisha, wearing a dress made of rainbow-hued velvet, stood at the counter, looking at Ren like a lovesick exotic bird. "I think Ren is right, Allie. I can't get him to talk to me about it, which is a sure sign that he's feeling . . . something? He usually won't shut up about whatever is going on in his life."

"Ugh." Allie turned and gently hit her forehead against the wall. She was glad that the café was surprisingly empty for a Sunday afternoon, so she wasn't entertaining a bunch of curious customers with her angst. "I'm sorry. Now whatever this is is affecting your friendship. This is so awful. I made such a huge mistake."

"You both made that mistake together." Anisha put her teacup down gently on the counter. "And honestly, who knows if it was a mistake, anyway?"

"Anisha," Allie huffed. "It was obviously a mistake. Ryan won't even talk to me. And now he will hardly talk to you. I don't get to hang out at your place anymore, and I miss your food. And your company. But you know, *the food*."

Anisha laughed. "And I miss feeding you. You should just come over, anyway. Fuck that guy. You're my friend, too."

"No." Allie shook her head. "Too awkward."

"Yeah, babe," Ren chimed in. "What's she supposed to do? Sit beside him at the dinner table and say *Hey this is great soup, and wasn't it weird that we boned that time and then stopped talking?*"

Anisha rolled her eyes but offered no further protest.

Allie retreated to the kitchen to mix batter for scones and left Ren and Anisha making eyes at each other in between customers. She was just setting the batter aside to rest when she heard the bell on the front door ring and Ren's loud, confused voice.

"Ryan?"

Allie went still.

My Ryan?

Hardly breathing, she walked to the door of the kitchen and looked out into the café.

There he was. His hair neatly combed and his usual shirt and jeans combination unchanged. He was looking at Ren and Anisha when Allie first saw him, but he quickly shifted his gaze to her.

"Hi." His voice was soft.

Allie's face drew into a suspicious pout. "Hi."

"What are you doing here?" Anisha was the one to finally ask what they were all wondering.

"I'm, uh, meeting someone."

Was he bringing a date to her café? Was he legitimately that ridiculous? From the horrified look on Ren's face, Allie knew they were thinking the same thing. Before any of them could ask any follow-up questions, the door opened again, and three children tumbled in, obviously siblings, laughing and shoving each other. They all had the same dark hair and wide smiles. They went right for the pastry case and started poking fingers at the glass, exclaiming over the tarts and slices of cake.

"I think this is them now." Ryan looked at the kids and then back to the door. Allie followed his gaze.

The door opened again.

"*Jessi?*"

Allie's voice came out as a croak.

Jessi Jetski had just walked through the door of Mindy's Café. Allie looked at Ryan, who had an unreadable expression on his face, and then to Jessi again.

Jessi looked right into Allie's eyes.

"Allie." Her voice was full of warmth and so, *so* familiar.

They stared at each other for a moment. When Allie saw tears start to spill out of Jessi's eyes, she started to cry as well. Jessi stepped around the children—*her* children, Allie now realized—and grabbed Allie into a bone-crushing hug. Allie had forgotten what it was like to receive a hug from Jessi, but in that moment, everything felt so good. She squeezed back and closed her eyes tightly, not wanting to let go.

"Holy shit," Jessi murmured into Allie's ear, squeezing tighter, then releasing her.

Allie stared at Jessi's face and shook her head in disbelief. "Holy shit is right."

The hug was interrupted by the front door opening again. Allie recognized Jasmine immediately. She also recognized the box that Jasmine was carrying.

"Babe! Thanks for grabbing the tapes!" Jessi moved toward her wife to grab the overflowing cardboard bootbox. It had seen better days and needed to be clutched against Jessi's body to keep it from falling apart.

"I can't believe you still have the tapes!" Allie said. "And, uh, hi, Jasmine."

Jasmine's smile was wide. "Hey, Allie. Good to see you."

As Jessi laid the box on an empty café table, Allie took a moment to look at her bandmate and her wife. Jessi looked almost exactly as she had when Allie last saw her, minus the half-shaved head and torn black clothes. Both she and Jasmine wore jeans, Jessi with a plaid shirt and Jasmine with a loose gray sweater. Jasmine's coat was long and woolly, Jessi's was a khaki parka. Their cheeks were red from the cold. Allie turned to look at the kids, who were now squabbling over who would get the last lemon square in the display case.

"Wow," Allie murmured.

"You okay?" Ryan was beside her. She'd forgotten about Ryan.

"It's just, this is . . . a lot."

Jasmine stepped forward and gave Allie a warm hug, then moved past her toward the kids.

Allie looked from Jessi to Ryan. "How? I mean . . . did you find her? How did you find her? How did he find you?"

Jessi grinned at Allie. "He was a pretty good detective, I'll give him that. And very convincing when it came to getting us all to come into the city as a surprise."

Allie turned to Ryan. "How did you do it?"

Ryan broke into a cautious smile. "Ren told me that Ayla said Jessi and Jasmine got married. And one day, I just randomly stopped looking for 'Jessi Jetski' online, and I typed in 'Jasmine Jetski' instead."

Jessi rolled her eyes. "It's her Instagram name. She really wanted an account, even though I was *not* into it. She agreed to use a fake name."

"I always wanted to be a Jetski, anyway." Jasmine smirked at them from the counter, where she was paying Ren for the kids' treats.

Jessi laughed. "But anyway, it's fine. She doesn't post any photos of me or the kids. And she never looks at her DMs."

"Can confirm." Ryan nodded. "That account was not very useful."

"Hey!" Jasmine frowned. "I'm right here!"

"Sorry!" Ryan laughed. "Pretty photos, though. Lots of sunsets and flowers and that kind of garbage." He looked at Jasmine, who was still staring at him. "Good garbage! Nice garbage! I mean . . ." Color rose in his cheeks.

"It's okay," Jessi said to him, grinning. "She's not as mean as she looks."

"Anyway." Ryan gave Jasmine another cautious look before turning back to Allie. "One of her posts did say that she and her family were moving to a new house. Photos of stuff packed in boxes and all that. No identifying info about where they were moving to. Except at the end of the post, she said that the house was special because it had been in her wife's family for a long time."

Allie wheeled around and looked at Jessi. "Your grandma's house?" Jessi nodded.

Allie felt a whoosh of emotion sweep through her. "Oh my god, that's incredible." She turned back to Ryan. "But you wouldn't have known where that house was! I never told you."

"You didn't. But you did say that the photo on the album cover was taken outside of the house."

"Holy shit, Nancy Drew!" Anisha, who'd been uncharacteristically quiet up until then, stepped forward and patted Ryan on the back. She then glanced back at Jessi and Jasmine's kids, who were staring at her. "Sorry! I meant 'holy shoot.' *Holy shoot!*"

"It was really just a reverse photo search." Ryan was modest but smiling. "And then when I found the street, I had to knock on a few doors—"

"He charmed our neighbor so much she basically gave him a whole cake and almost didn't let him leave," Jessi added.

"True," Ryan confirmed, nodding. "Mrs. Evanstein makes a very good lemon Bundt."

"Anyway, then we got this knock on our door, and I was very suspicious because we definitely don't get weird strangers knocking at our door very often. I thought he was the guy who used to refinish my grandma's deck every few years. But he wasn't. He was your Ryan."

Allie felt her heart jump.

Her Ryan.

"He told us all about your whole thing, how you were looking for me in places where I definitely wasn't. I was just sitting out there in Fort Lee, picking my kids up from school and working part-time at an insurance broker."

"That's what you do?" Allie stared wide-eyed at her friend.

"Yep." Jessi nodded. "I kind of love it. My coworkers are nice. The work isn't too hard, and I have a ton of time to be with the kids and work on the house."

"We're putting in a new bathroom and finishing the basement," Jasmine piped up. "Jessi won't let us change the kitchen. But she's going to do most of the other work herself."

"Really? I used to have to plug in your pedals for you because you got confused about the patch cables."

Jessi tucked her hair behind one ear and looked down. "Well, it's been a decade since then, and somehow, I learned how to do stuff for myself. Wasn't that kind of the bigger point behind our DIY punk youth?" She caught Allie's eye and winked.

Allie was silent for a moment, processing. "Hey, can I meet your kids?"

"Oh damn, yes! I forgot about them for a minute." Jessi laughed awkwardly, and for the first time, Allie wondered whether Jessi was just as overwhelmed as she was. They moved over to the table where Jasmine sat with the three children, all of them enthusiastically tucking into the treats in front of them.

"The large one is Emily, she's eight. Middle guy there is Akira, he's six, as of two days ago, right, bud?" Akira looked up from the lemon square he'd scored and nodded solemnly. "And the little one is Farah. She's four. And I think we can all agree, she is the boss of us all." Farah looked up with a smile that was verging on painfully adorable. Her siblings nodded, agreeing with Jessi.

"So, folks? This is my friend Allie. Remember how Mama was in a band a long time ago? Allie was in the band with me."

"And you had a fight." Emily looked from Allie to Jessi. "Right?"

"Uh, yeah." Allie pushed her hand through her hair. "We did. It was my fault."

"Uh, no." Jessi shook her head. "It was definitely my fault."

Allie looked at her in amazement, then decided that was a discussion for another time. Or perhaps for never.

"Well, at least you made up now." Emily looked at Jessi. They had the same eyes. "You can be friends again. Right?"

"Yes." Jessi nodded. "No time like the present."

Happiness flowed through Allie like warm honey. To stop herself from crying again, she turned to the table where Jasmine had dropped the box of mixtapes. "I can't believe you still have these."

They sat down across from each other at the table and started sifting through the cassettes. As they giggled together about one particularly terrible ABBA mix that Mimi had insisted they play often, Allie noticed Ryan standing awkwardly by the counter.

"Ryan! Anisha! Come sit with us." She waved them over.

"You sure?" Anisha asked. "We don't want to intrude."

Jessi snorted. "Oh god, if you won't be bored by two ladies telling obscure stories about weird cassettes, then you are welcome to join us!"

"Allie, actually, can I just talk to you in the kitchen real quick?"

Ryan was shifting from foot to foot. Allie looked at Jessi, who nodded almost imperceptibly, their old telepathy returning as though no years had passed.

"Sure." Allie got up and followed him into the kitchen, not sure whether she could take any more emotional avalanches. When they were alone, he looked down at her.

"Hi. How's it going?"

"*How's it going*? Ryan, you've been here this whole time. You can see how it's going."

"I guess I meant, how are you feeling?"

"About seeing Jessi?"

He hesitated. "Sure, let's start there."

"I feel great." She felt the urge to reach out and grab his arm, but she kept her hands at her sides. "Thank you. Thank you so much for this. I don't know why you did it, but I definitely appreciate it."

"You don't know why I did it?" Ryan's face contorted into a mix of surprise and frustration. "Allie, I did it *for you*. I heard your song last week, and I feel the same. I always have."

She turned her face toward the floor. "You don't have to say that now. I know you only thought of me as a friend. And I blame myself for pushing you into more. It's okay. You don't have to compensate."

Ryan huffed out a frustrated breath. "No, Allie, seriously, listen to me. I panicked the day after the party. I choked. I was so used to women not wanting to be with me, women thinking that sleeping with me was a mistake. I was in so deep with my feelings for you, I couldn't take it if you rejected me, so I rejected you first. Which was so ridiculous. And then you wrote that song, and it made me think you still wanted me in your life, and I was so relieved. Killer song, too.

That line about us both being monsters just trying to learn how to live like humans? Heartbreaking."

Allie's emotions were a jumble of relief and confusion. "Why did you leave, though?" Her eyes searched his. "Why did you bail right after my performance? Why did you not even contact me for a *week*?"

"To find Jessi!" He was emphatic. "I literally went home and started searching and didn't stop until I'd found her. You wrote me a song. I couldn't come back to you with nothing."

Allie stared at him, unsure whether to be charmed or frustrated. "You *could have*, though. You could have just come to talk to me. That was all I wanted. You left and you didn't talk to me, and it just made me feel like . . ." Her voice got quieter. "Like you didn't want me at all."

They stood and stared at each other. Her heart plummeted.

"Well, damn." Ryan's voice was soft. "What do we do now?" He sounded as defeated as she felt.

"I don't know. Maybe we can go back to where we started from? Act like we just met? See how things go from there?"

"I should have asked you out the minute you walked into the studio with my coffee." Ryan sighed.

"You didn't know how great I was." She managed a cautious grin.

"Yes, I did." Ryan smiled back. "Don't you mess with me, Allie Jetski. I've had a crush on you for fifteen years."

Allie snorted, grateful for the moment of levity. "Even you aren't charming enough to pull off *that* lie." They shared another uneasy smile. She had no idea what to do next.

"Oh!" Allie said finally, desperate to break the tension. "I finished my covers project."

Ryan's expression brightened. "You did? Nice!"

Allie stepped into the office and pulled her purse off the coat rack. She rummaged inside until her hand found the smooth plastic rectangle. "I gave one to Mindy and one to George, of course. And I saved this one for you."

Ryan took the cassette when she held it out to him. He looked at the track listing and smiled, his eyes soft and sad.

"Thanks, Allie." He looked up at her. "This is really something special."

Allie swallowed the lump in her throat.

Unable to think of anything else to say, she led the way back out to the café, where Jasmine had joined the table of adults and was sifting through the tapes with Anisha and Jessi. The kids were happily coloring and chatting by themselves.

"So, people just made these for you? What people?" Anisha was asking as Allie sat down.

"So many people!" Jessi shook her head, looking amazed. "Promoters, sound techs, fans. I mean, to be fair, we did *beg* for tapes everywhere we went." She picked up a cassette from the pile. Its scratched plastic case had the title of the mix written in black marker directly on it, with no paper liner or any other list of songs. "Oh, Allie, look at this one. Remember the tape we listened to when we drove home from Chicago in that snowstorm?"

"I was so scared that if we both weren't watching the road, we were all going to die."

"Yes!" Jessi was giddy, obviously enjoying dredging up these memories. "So you wouldn't let me look down to change the tape. We listened to"—she paused to check the writing—"*Midwest Hardcore Scene Report VII*, what, like, seventeen times?"

Allie could not help giggling at the memory. "There wasn't much worth reporting, if I remember correctly."

Jessi laughed, too, and kept pawing through the well-worn tape cases. She pulled out a nondescript case with a plain blue cover.

"Oh, here's the *Allie Crush* tape."

"The what?" Allie leaned in, confused.

"The tape with all the songs with your name in them? We all teased you about it."

Allie scoffed. "You're lying. I don't remember this at all."

Jessi was incredulous. "What do you mean? How can you *not* remember this tape? Look: 'Alison.' Elvis Costello. 'Alison's Starting to Happen.' The Lemonheads. 'Alison.' Slowdive. 'Allison.' Pixies . . ."

Allie laughed, amazed that she didn't remember the mix. She had been so focused on the band in those days, definitely never looking for crushes. "What else is on there? There aren't enough Allison songs to fill a whole tape."

"There's other good stuff on here." Jessi opened the case and pulled out the liner. "Some Talking Heads, some Velvet Underground. A few weird churchy songs that I used to just fast-forward through. Ha, oh yeah, that funny 'Doctor Worm' song . . ."

Allie felt a jolt of adrenaline shoot through her.

Church songs.

'Doctor Worm.'

She looked at Ryan. He was fiddling with a spoon on the table in front of him. His cheeks were bright red. Allie reached for the cassette liner. "Let me see that."

The handwriting was so familiar it might as well have been her own. She flipped the notes over and saw a tiny heart and an "R.A." penned in the bottom corner. She could hardly get the words out.

"Ryan, can I see you in the kitchen again for a minute?"

Chapter Twenty-Eight

Allie walked quickly into the kitchen, Ryan at her heels.

"Look, Allie, are you mad? I didn't tell you about the tape because I didn't want you to think that I was some creepy stalker. I really never thought I would see you again after the band stopped playing and then you just walked into the studio with that coffee and I swear I didn't mean for anything weird to happen and I should have told you and—"

Ryan's babbling speech abruptly halted as Allie gripped and twisted his shirtfront, pulling him toward her. Their lips met and he abandoned his protests. Allie's thoughts were reeling.

He liked me all along.

She wrapped both arms around him, pulling his body into hers. He'd liked her when she was a twenty-year-old punk singer who was always sweaty from sleeping in a van. He'd liked her when she was an ex-musician who delivered coffee. And he still liked her now, when she was— What was she exactly? She felt close to figuring it out. For now, she was someone who was very happily making out with the man of her choice in the kitchen of her workplace.

Panting, Ryan broke the kiss for a moment. "Allie, I really am sorry. About all of it."

"Shhhhhhh." She kept her forehead against his, her hand now

cupping the back of his neck. "You are forgiven. Please stop apologizing for liking me for over a decade."

Ryan laughed. "It's more than that, Allie." She could see tears starting in his eyes and blinked her own rapidly, trying to avoid the weeping that was coming far too easily to her lately.

"Allie, I *love* you. I used to just imagine how cool you were after I saw you onstage, but now that I actually know you, you're even better than anything I came up with in my head. You're creative, and stubborn, and every time I see you, I can't wait to find out what's going to happen next. You're the person I want to sit beside on my couch at all hours of the day and the only person I would drive to a stinky punk club in New Jersey in the interest of solving a mystery."

Allie laughed, sniffling slightly but maintaining her composure by sheer force of will. Her voice shook when she spoke.

"I love you, too. I actually need to talk to you every day or I just don't feel right. When I thought you were through with me, I could hardly handle it. You've turned my life into a chaotic mess. A really nice, chaotic mess."

He kissed her again. Gently this time. "Look, as much as it pains me—like, *physically*—to say this, we need to go back out there. You have some special guests, and our friends are all probably wondering if we're pulling a Ren-and-Anisha in here, which I'd rather them not be picturing."

Allie snorted with laughter and grabbed him in a fierce hug. "Do you want to come upstairs later?" she whispered in his ear, her heart pounding.

"Yes indeed," he whispered back. "Except, as you've pointed out, I'm too large for your apartment."

She released him from the embrace and slid her hand into his. "You won't be standing up. It will be fine."

Ryan emitted a strangled moan and adjusted his pants with his free hand. "Ma'am, there are children present. Get a hold of yourself."

She grinned at him. "You ready to go back out there?"

He beamed back. "Ready when you are."

—

Jessi and her family stayed at the café almost until closing. Ren made grilled cheese for the kids, and the adults ate soup and fresh bread and desserts and drank too much tea and coffee.

"I'm going to be up all night." Jessi set her empty cup on the table.

"Well, they won't be." Jasmine nodded toward the kids' table, where all three of them were watching a video on Jessi's phone with heavy-lidded eyes. "That group will be fast asleep as soon as we cross the state line."

"If we can carry them in from the car without waking them, we'll have time to watch grown-up television before *we* fall asleep," Jessi explained to Allie. She was leaning in, her arm across the back of Allie's chair, as though they were conspiring. It was a familiar feeling that Allie couldn't get enough of.

People say all the time that things feel like a dream, but this actually does.

It was like a weird melding of her past and her present, and she couldn't get enough of the trippy, dreamy feeling.

At 9 p.m., Ren locked the café doors and asked the kids whether they wanted to see the big ovens in the kitchen. Jasmine went with them, and Ryan and Anisha were having some kind of murmured conversation at the end of the table, looking at each other in an almost exact copy of the way Allie and Jessi were staring at each other.

"Damn, I missed you." Jessi pulled Allie into a half hug, half head-lock and kissed the top of her head. It was something she used to do if Allie was nervous before they went onstage.

"I missed you, too. I'm so sorry about everything. About setting us up to waste all these years not talking to each other."

Jessi made a *fft* sound and waved her hand dismissively. "We were young. I know we felt like grizzled old broads, but we were actually tiny babies."

Allie laughed. "True. But I didn't have to be such a dick about everything."

"Hey, I was also a dick. I was in love with Jasmine, and I just wanted to stop touring and be with her. But I didn't really try to explain to you what would make me happy. I just wanted to be cool, like you. To be dedicated to the band and be on the road. I was so jealous of that. But I just acted like a stuck-up bitch and let the band implode and then fucked right off to the suburbs and started having babies."

"Jessi, your babies are amazing. And you and Jasmine are amazing, and the fact that you live in your amazing grandma's amazing house is amazing."

Jessi laughed. "Well, thank you. This place is also amazing." She leaned in closer and spoke into Allie's ear. "Ryan seems kind of amazing, as well."

Allie could feel herself blushing. "Yeah, I mean, he is. He's turned my life into a total shitshow, to be honest, but this shitshow is so much better than the non-shitshow it was before."

"And he fucking made the *Allie Crush* tape. What a trip!"

Allie glanced over at Ryan. He looked up and winked at her.

"He made the *Allie Crush* tape," Allie repeated, nodding slowly. Her heart felt as if it were going to explode.

Jasmine approached their table and started putting on her coat. "We gotta get going or the kids are going to turn into pumpkins. And by *pumpkins*, I mean assholes."

Jessi stood up and kissed her wife's cheek. "Okay, babe. Let's get going. But, Allie, you have to come visit us soon. Bring Ryan. Hell, bring Ren and Anisha, too."

"Careful," Allie said. "They'll all totally want to come."

"Everyone is welcome." Jasmine helped Jessi on with her coat. "Kids! We're heading out!"

A collective disappointed "Aww" went up from the children, but they collected their coats and filed out with their moms.

"Keep the tapes!" Jessi called as the door closed behind them. Allie stood by the window and waved until she saw their car drive away into the darkness.

Allie turned around and looked at Ryan. She felt a jolt of electricity zinging between them across the almost empty café. Ren and Anisha saw what was happening.

"Well, honey? Nothing else to do here? Are you ready to go?" Anisha asked, her voice a note higher than usual.

"What? Oh yeah. Right. Nothing else to do. I'll just"—they grabbed their coat from a hook by the door—"put this on and, uh . . ." They looked around the café. "Yep, ready to go."

The two of them left without saying goodbye, their giggles silenced by the closing door.

Ryan looked at Allie across the empty café as she locked the door behind the rapidly retreating figures of their friends. She turned the café lights off and grinned at him. The weak glow of the kitchen light was illuminating his face. He looked over at the staircase that led to her apartment and then turned back to her.

"Race you."

They both broke into a run, laughing.

"Don't hit your head!" Allie shouted as her feet pounded up the stairs. Ryan was close behind her. So close that, as she paused to unlock her door, he pressed his body to hers from behind. She shivered in anticipation and pushed the door open, tumbling in. "I win!"

They each paused to kick off their shoes. "It wasn't really a competition, Jetski." Ryan smiled as he approached her, ducking slightly to protect his head. "We both win."

She grabbed his shirt and pulled him toward her. His lips were warm against hers, their bodies as close as they could get them. She didn't want to let him go. But she did want him to take off all his clothes.

Her fingers fumbled with the buttons of his shirt as they kissed, his hands moving down the sides of her body to cup her ass. He found the hem of her dress and pulled it up over her head in one motion, leaving her standing in decidedly unsexy wool tights and a plain black bra. It was hardly seductive lingerie. But then, when she'd dressed that morning, she and Ryan hadn't even been speaking to one another. She took one moment away from thoughts of removing Ryan's clothes to ponder how much of a left turn her day had taken. How much better the night was than the morning.

Ryan leaned over her crate of cassettes and selected one. Cyndi Lauper. She admired his dedication to setting the mood. She was still impatiently wanting to jump him.

As the opening strains of the first song flowed quietly from the speakers of her boombox, she wiggled out of her tights, her body now warm enough without them. Ryan looked up from the cassettes and barely suppressed a moan when he looked at her.

"Dang, you look good."

She considered saying something sarcastic, to deflect the compliment, but decided she liked how he saw her. "Thank you." She smirked. "Your turn."

Ryan did not need telling twice. He shed his now-unbuttoned shirt, and his jeans and socks, and faced her in his T-shirt and boxers.

"Dang." She laughed. "You *also* look good."

He blushed and took one long step toward her, pulling her into an embrace and leaning down to kiss her neck. "I believe you promised that I would be lying down?" he murmured, his voice muffled by her hair as his fingers worked on her bra's clasp behind her back. Allie felt it release and pulled it free from her body, dropping it at their feet. She grasped the hem of Ryan's T-shirt and pushed it upward. He ducked his head and pulled it off, adding it to the pile of clothes on the floor. His hands went quickly to her breasts. Allie groaned.

"Oh yes. Let's lie down," she said breathlessly. "Let's lie down right now."

For once, she was relieved that her apartment was so small, her bed was almost unavoidable. Ryan lay down first, and she lay beside him, her hand going immediately for his hardness.

"Why are we even wearing any clothes?" Ryan asked, as he urgently pulled off his own underwear and then hers. He lay down on his side, one arm above his head and the other pulling Allie close to him. His nakedness pressed against hers made Allie's whole body buzz with excitement. He slid his fingers down and moved them inside her.

"Oh . . . Ryan." She moaned, arching her back and letting her eyes flutter closed.

"You feel good," he whispered into her ear. She stretched her arms above her head and tangled her fingers with his. He held her hands there, firmly, as his other hand continued to touch her. It wasn't long before she felt her orgasm building. She cried out, saying his name and some other jumble of words she was barely aware of, her body twisting in pleasure.

As she came down from the high of climax, she was aware of Ryan holding her, stroking her skin sweetly. She opened her eyes and turned to him.

"I'm so glad you're here," she told him.

"I wouldn't want to be anywhere else." He smiled at her, his eyes full of tenderness.

She rolled to her right and pulled open the drawer of her night-stand, relieved to find a few condoms in there. They'd been tossed at her when she and Ren had gone to the Pride parade in June, and she'd stowed them in her bedside drawer thinking she was being remarkably optimistic.

Sending a quick thank-you to Allie from the Past, she opened the package and helped Ryan roll it on, slowly. He exhaled deeply, looking into her eyes with an affection that made her insides melt.

She climbed on top of him, and he grabbed her hips.

"I meant it, Allie," he gasped between moans, his eyes closing. "I *love* you. I love everything about you."

His hands were so strong and warm on her body, holding her hips, rubbing up and down her thighs. She sighed and adjusted her body so he was deeper inside her.

"I love you, too." She moved herself faster up and down on top of him, her hands finding his hands and gripping them, fingers laced between his. "So fucking much." She tipped her head back and closed her eyes, drunk with the feeling of his skin against hers.

It wasn't long before he was bucking his hips and shouting her name into the darkness of her room. As he finished, she collapsed on top of him, their sweaty, warm bodies tangled and panting.

As their breathing slowed and their bodies stilled, Allie became aware of the song playing quietly on her boombox by the door.

"True Colors."

Fucking perfect.

The song lit up her heart with more intensity than it ever had before. She lay beside Ryan's warm body, her head on his forearm. She did not remember ever feeling this safe.

As the final notes of the song faded in the darkness, Ryan rose and moved sluggishly around the chilly, dark room, disposing of the condom, pulling his underwear and T-shirt back on. When he slid back in beside her, she pulled the covers up over them both, lying close to him again, her arm thrown across his belly.

"Dammit, Allie." His voice was raspy, his chest still rising and falling rapidly. "I'm so happy right now. This might be the happiest I've ever been."

Allie moved even closer to him, heart full, eyelids heavy.

"Me too."

Allie held on to him tightly. She never wanted to let him go again. The music finished, and she heard the soft *cachunk* of the cassette stopping.

Within minutes, they were both asleep.

Chapter Twenty-Nine

After several weeks of spending most of their free time in bed, Allie and Ryan began to explore a less naked collaboration. Ryan hadn't been lying when he'd said that his drumming was coming along. Allie felt herself inspired, for the first time in years, to write song after song. They were creating something that made her so excited she had trouble sleeping at night. She woke up with their songs running through her head and sang them all day at the café.

They were practicing in the tiny, windowless room in the basement of Ryan and Anisha's apartment building. The sign on the door, written in Ryan's almost illegible scrawl, read Dr. Worm's Drum Studio. It smelled a bit damp, and Ryan had to duck to avoid smashing his head on the doorframe, but Allie was always eager to go there.

They took a break from rehearsing the bridge to a new song, and Allie inspected her guitar in the dim light. She was worried that her enthusiastic strumming was going to scratch the wood of her beloved acoustic. She hadn't expected to want to play loud, but she did. It was a different kind of loud than it had been with the Jetskis. Ryan as her steady—and only—backup made her feel more courageous, as if she could take these songs in whatever directions she wanted and he would happily support her as she did it. That seemed worth being loud about.

"I think I should get an electric guitar." She rubbed her fingers over the wood and frowned. "I don't want to fuck this one up. Plus, it will be easier to get the sound we want at a show, like there's more than just two of us."

"Is that your way of telling me that you finally want us to book a show?" Ryan grinned. He'd been a typical first-time band participant, thinking they were ready for a show immediately, so eager to show the world what they'd come up with.

Allie smiled back at him. "Soon, my eager friend. Soon."

"You know I just want everyone to see how cool my lady friend is."

"You're no slouch, either. Those fills are really coming along."

She could see him blushing and felt her heart warm.

"Thanks." He pulled his phone from his pocket to check the time. With it came a folded envelope. A smile bloomed across his face. "Hey, I wanna show you something."

Allie put her guitar in its stand and stepped closer to him. "What is it?"

"I got a letter from Rachel."

Allie's eyebrows shot up. "You wrote to her? You really finally did it?"

Ryan bit his lip and nodded. He smoothed out the envelope and took out the folded paper inside. "I wrote to her at her work. She owns an ice cream shop, so I was sure she wouldn't have any family around when she got the letter. And she wrote back."

"What did she say?" Allie put her arm around Ryan's shoulders and leaned closer to see the letter.

"She was glad I wrote. She didn't say much, but she did say she misses me. And that I should let her know if I'm ever visiting anywhere close by so we can meet for coffee."

"Ryan, that's amazing." Allie's eyes skimmed the one page of scratchy writing, tearing up when she saw that it was signed "Love, Rachel." She put an arm around his neck and pulled him close to her. "I'm so happy for you."

Ryan smiled and kissed her cheek, then folded the letter back into the envelope and slid it into his pocket. She released him from her embrace and stretched both arms in the air, yawning. "Should we run it again?"

"I wish we could, but if you want to stay in Ren's good graces, we should get you back to the café. Our two hours are up."

Ren had been crushed when Allie let them know that she would not actually be taking over the café. Mindy hadn't exactly jumped for joy, either. The other offer she'd gotten at Christmas was no longer on the table. It had been a quiet few days at work. But Allie knew that both of them wanted the best for her, and Ren had eventually— grudgingly—admitted that they'd never seen Allie this happy, so the decision seemed to be the right one. Mindy, for her part, had agreed that Ren's opinion of any prospective owner mattered, so both of them could often be found discussing the qualities they each wanted in a new proprietor, animated and occasionally ridiculous discussions that Allie happily ignored.

She put her guitar back in its case, and Ryan rose from his drum kit and took the case in his hand. It weighed a ton, and she had quickly grown tired of hauling it back and forth between her home and his. She'd begun reluctantly accepting Ryan's help for small things like this. If the guy liked her enough to carry her guitar through the cold Brooklyn streets several times a week, who was she to argue?

She pulled on her coat and glanced at Ryan. "Ready to go?"

He nodded, and she walked to the door, opening it toward herself with her free hand.

Anisha was standing on the other side, hand poised in the air as though she was about to knock. Allie screamed. Then Anisha screamed. Ryan, for his part, skipped the screaming and went straight to laughter.

"Jesus." Allie clutched her chest. She could feel her heart pounding. "You scared the crap out of me! Why are you lurking behind the door like a serial killer?"

"I wasn't expecting you to fling it open and scream in my face!" Anisha wiped her brow with a handkerchief she'd produced from the pocket of her dress. "Holy crap. Simmer down, everyone. I just wanted to walk with you to the café."

They left the practice room and locked the door behind them.

It was freezing outside. Ryan wrapped one arm around Allie's shoulders to calm her shivering. She felt his warmth radiate through her and leaned in closer. All those years walking alone on the street had been fine, but this was better.

The café was almost empty when they got there, the post-lunch lull having arrived just as it always did. Ren was wiping down the counters when they all hustled in from the cold. Anisha moved toward the counter quickly, and Ren's face lit up. They looked, Allie noted, just as happy as they had every other time she'd seen the two of them together. So much for all the worries about Anisha ending up another broken heart. It seemed implausible now, looking at them together. But then, so many things that she'd thought to be true mere months ago now seemed absurd.

"Oh good, you're all here." Mindy emerged from the kitchen, wiping her hands on a towel. She was looking at Anisha, not Allie.

"Were you expecting Anisha?" Allie asked, shrugging out of her coat and taking Ryan's from him to go hang them up by the office. She'd thought Anisha's visit was spontaneous.

Mindy turned to her. "Yes, I was, actually. I need to have a chat with the three of you in the kitchen, briefly. Ryan, you can come, too, I guess."

"Can't pass up an enthusiastic invite." Ryan grinned.

"Quickly." Mindy ignored his joke. "Before we get a bunch of customers."

The five of them entered the kitchen, Ren standing by the door so they could keep an eye on the front.

"I have good news." Mindy looked from Allie to Ren. "I've found a buyer for the café."

"A buyer!" Allie's eyes widened. She hadn't expected Mindy to find someone so soon. "Holy shit! Wow. Okay." A mix of contradictory feelings rushed through her.

I should be used to big changes by now.

Still, she couldn't help but be unnerved by the news.

"Are they going to keep running it as a café?" Allie glanced nervously at Ren, whose eyes were locked on Mindy, waiting for the answer to this very question.

"I don't know." Mindy spoke slowly. The tension in the room heightened. She turned to Anisha. Her face broke into a smile. "Are you going to keep running it as a café?"

Ryan, Allie and Ren whipped their heads toward Anisha, who had been patiently and silently standing against the counter. Anisha's smile was as wide as Mindy's was. "Yes." She nodded. "I absolutely will keep running it as a café."

Ren left their spot by the door and walked, looking dazed, toward Anisha. "You? You bought the café?"

Anisha took both of Ren's hands and nodded again, looking right into their eyes. "I did. Making food for people is the thing that's always made me the happiest. Until I met you. This just makes sense. Will you—" Anisha stopped and grinned. "Will you, Ren Zhao, do me the honor of . . . running a small community-based coffee shop with me? As long as we both shall, uh, want to?"

Ren nodded. Allie thought she saw some rare tears in her friend's eyes. "I will." Ren grabbed Anisha in a hug, and Allie and Ryan applauded. Relief and happiness washed over Mindy's face. Allie knew that this whole process had been stressful for her aunt as well. Despite Mindy's clear desire to leave the café portion of her life behind, it was obvious that she wanted to know she was leaving it in good hands.

"And you"—Anisha pointed at Allie over Ren's shoulder—"can work here whenever you want. If you two take your show on the road, we'll just hire someone else for a bit. You'll always have a place here."

"Thank you." Allie's heart swelled. "We're not going anywhere for a while, but it's good to know that we'll be able to eventually. Plus, it will take me months to teach you how to make George's tea."

"Oh god." Anisha rolled her eyes. "I forgot about George's tea. Is it too late to back out of this deal?"

"Sorry." Mindy grinned. "We signed the papers. No turning back now."

"Well"—Anisha leaned her head on Ren's shoulder and looked around the kitchen—"I guess we'll just have to figure things out. George included."

Mindy looked at the four of them. "I have faith in you." She caught Allie's eye and winked. Allie fought back the tears. "You're all amazing."

It was true, Allie thought, a rush of joy flooding her heart. They were all amazing.

Epilogue

TWO YEARS LATER

The Las Vegas sun was relentless. Allie squinted as their tour van left the hotel's underground parking garage. She fumbled in her bag for her sunglasses and put them on, sighing with relief. Ryan maneuvered their tour van onto the Strip and glanced quickly over to her, smiling as he caught her eye.

"Vegas in August is no joke." He leaned forward slightly to increase the power of the air conditioning that was already blowing at them, hardly making a dent in the blazing afternoon heat.

Allie nodded, settling comfortably back into the passenger seat, watching the overwhelming architecture tower on all sides of them. There was no choice but to drive slowly; the streets were crowded with cars and tourists, everyone moving sluggishly through the heat.

They had been on tour all summer, which was when the podcast production schedule tended to slow down and summer students were available to fill temporary positions at the studio. Ryan still loved his job, and Allie didn't want him to quit, even as Lake Fever—their two-person band—started to gain momentum. Their first album, picked up by an indie label on the strength of Allie's past with the Jetskis, had done respectably well on vinyl and through streaming services. Allie's heartbreak anthem, "Monster," now fleshed out with Ryan's subtle drums and harmonies, had been selected as the background music for a particularly notable scene in a popular TV drama. They had now almost finished enough new songs to record again, with a bigger budget this time. The recording sessions were booked in New York over the winter.

Allie watched the strange sights of Vegas pass by her window. She'd been relieved to discover that she still loved touring and was always excited to hit the road, especially now that she had Ryan with her. His steady mood and general kindness made spending long days and nights with him an actual treat. She couldn't imagine a better life for herself.

They had six more shows left on the tour and they'd be back home. Ryan would go back to his day job, and Allie would put the finishing touches on the new songs, sketching out her ideas for the recording setup in between random shifts at the café. That life wasn't bad, either. As much as she loved the road, she also didn't feel sad about going home again.

But before they played any more shows and before they returned to Brooklyn, they had something important to do.

Ryan looked at her as they stopped to allow a flock of tourists in matching visors to cross the street in front of the van.

"You still want to marry me?" His eyes were sparkling with excitement.

"Yep." Allie's heart fluttered. She grinned at him. "You still want to marry me?"

"More than just about anything on earth."

When Ryan had proposed at the beginning of the tour, she'd felt a kind of calm certainty that she hadn't expected to feel in that moment. She'd thought the prospect of spending the rest of her life with someone would leave her rattled and nervous. But she didn't feel any of that. She'd already decided that she wanted to spend the rest of her days with the loyal and sweet man who backed her up on the drums every night and shared driving duties and made sure that she ate something other than french fries every day. Not having strong feelings about conventional matrimony either way, she hadn't been sitting around waiting for him to ask. But then he had. It mattered to him; his traditional side wanted to make it official.

They'd gotten their marriage license after their show the previous night. The marriage office was open twenty-four hours a day. They were by far the most sober people in line at 2 a.m.

"Okay, this is it!" Ryan steered the van sharply into a parking lot. "Can you text the video conference link to everyone?"

Allie giggled as she pulled out her phone, already imagining their friends' reactions. "They're gonna kill us."

Ryan laughed. "They can't kill us long distance. They'll have to wait until we get home."

He steered the car into a parking space and hopped out, smoothing the dark-blue pants he'd bought the day before at a weird mall near their hotel. He'd chosen a vest instead of a jacket, because of the heat, and a shirt patterned with tiny flowers. Allie thought it was adorable, and Ryan thought it might not show the sweat. His bow tie was forest green.

Allie had combed the same strange, crowded mall for something she wanted to wear and had been overjoyed to discover a quirky, punky shop tucked away by the food court that seemed to specialize in dresses that were new but looked old. The one she chose was light blue with a full skirt and crinoline. She'd sprung for some platform heels in a similar color, wanting to reduce the height difference between herself and her groom, at least for the sake of the wedding photos.

She and Ryan walked into the main office to let the chapel attendants know they'd arrived. Souvenir Elvis wigs hung on a rack to the left of the smiling older woman behind the counter.

Allie's phone buzzed in the pocket of her dress. The text was from Ren. "WTF is this shady link? Is this really you? Have you been kidnapped and someone is trying to scam me with your phone?"

"It's really me," she texted back. "And it's a normal video call link. Just click it at 4 p.m. like I said. And make sure Anisha is with you."

"As long as it's not a scam," Ren texted back. And then added, "We miss you both BTW." Three heart emojis followed.

"Yep. They're gonna kill us," Allie muttered under her breath.

She was the most nervous about reaching Mindy, since Paris was nine hours ahead of them. The chances of Mindy being awake at 1 a.m. were strong, but Allie was still flooded with relief when her aunt texted back. "Just getting in from dinner/drinks. Was going to bed. But I'll join your call thing if you need me."

Allie and Ryan had ten minutes to collect themselves at the back of the tiny chapel. Ryan took her hand and leaned in to kiss her.

"I'm glad they can all watch it live. But I just want you to know that all that really matters to me today is you and me. We could get married on Mars and I wouldn't care, as long as I was with you."

Allie put her arms around him and squeezed. "Probably hard to find an Elvis impersonator on Mars, though."

As if on cue, their Elvis—his real name was Brian, they'd learned from the chatty lady at the booking desk—slid into the chapel and took up his place at the front.

"Allison Andrews and Ryan Abernathy?" Brian/Elvis called out. Allie and Ryan nodded. "You got a device? For video?" Allie nodded and looked down at her phone to log on to the video call. She checked the time: 3:57 p.m. Everyone else would be logging on any minute now. She set the phone on a shelf beside a miniature golden bust of Elvis and a pink ceramic flamingo, and angled it toward Elvis. She and Ryan watched as their friends appeared square by square, like a motley Brady Bunch.

First, Mindy's face popped into the frame, the cluttered kitchen of her Paris flat behind her. Allie noted that her aunt looked relaxed, possibly even buzzed from the no-doubt plentiful wine at the dinner she'd just returned from. She'd been in Paris for more than a year and showed no signs of wanting to leave. The city suited her, and she always seemed to be aglow with the pleasures of her foreign retirement. Anisha and Ren appeared next, waving frantically from their spots behind the counter. Ren walked with their phone over to the table where, to Allie's delight, George was seated, having his tea. She waved at him and felt a tug of joy and envy as she watched Anisha and Ren slide in beside him on the bench, all three of them smiling. She missed them all. A third square flickered, and Jessi's face appeared, frowning in concentration as she adjusted the camera, then backing up to allow Jasmine, Emily, Akira and Farah to fill the frame. The five of them called out a jumble of greetings.

One minute later, a fourth square appeared, at first showing only a large ice cream shop menu, but after a moment, Rachel's face appeared and broke into a smile when she caught sight of Ryan. Allie heard him exhale. Rachel was quieter and less animated than the rest of their oddball found family, but she was there, and she was grinning at her brother and his bride.

Emily was the one who spat out the questions everyone was thinking. "Hi, Allie! What's the surprise? What's going on? Where are you?"

"Just hang on a minute, friend." Allie laughed. "It will be clear in a minute." She backed away from the camera, allowing them a full view of Elvis. She nodded to the officiant and stepped closer to Ryan, sliding her hand into his. He looked down at her with shining eyes.

"Ready?" He squeezed her hand.

"Ready." She squeezed back.

Ryan took a deep breath. "Here we go."

Elvis began to sing "Love Me Tender." Allie looped her arm through Ryan's, and they walked forward. She could hear her friends hooting through the tinny phone speaker as they came into view and everyone figured out what was happening.

She took a moment to look around, to appreciate this unconventional wedding, with no in-person guests, with Brian the Elvis Impersonator singing along to an instrumental track he was playing on YouTube on a laptop hidden in one of the empty, scratched wooden pews. All the chaos and unpredictability of the situation didn't matter. Ryan was right. They could have been getting married on Mars and she wouldn't have cared. All that mattered was that he was there beside her, holding her hand.

She couldn't wait to see what would happen next.

Allie and Ryan's Mixtape

(Find it on Spotify, too!)

"Make Me a Mixtape" —The Promise Ring
"We Belong" —Pat Benatar
"Borderline" —Madonna
"Love Shack" —The B-52's
"Alone" —Heart
"I Want You to Want Me" —Letters to Cleo
"Straight Up" —Paula Abdul
"She's a Rainbow" —The Rolling Stones
"Life During Wartime" —Talking Heads
"Go Tell It on the Mountain" —Mahalia Jackson
"When Will I Be Loved" —Linda Ronstadt
"Hazy Shade of Winter" —The Bangles
"True Colors" —Cyndi Lauper

Turn the page for a secret surprise . . .

SPOILER WARNING

Follow the QR code for bonus musical content!

Acknowledgments

No book is written in isolation, least of all this one. Thanks to my friends who read chapters as I wrote them: Elizabeth Race, Katrina Diamond, Jeff Miller (beret toss!), Jess Carfagnini, Mona Venkateswaran, Devin Cook, Danny Bailey, Shannon Roche, Jenn Huzera, Katrina MacKay, David Hadadd, Jessica Gilmore and Kaia Ambrose.

Extra-special thanks to Martha Copestake, chapter reader, cheer-leader and text wife, who shows her love by being enraged on my behalf every time anything I write is rejected.

Thanks also to Todd Taylor for reading the first draft and suggest-ing that I "put more punk in it" (I did), and thanks to Hallie Bulliet for reading a later draft and making sure I didn't fuck up Brooklyn.

Thanks to Sophie Raniere, who used her therapist skills to help me analyze Allie.

Thanks also to Tavis Maplesden for his ongoing cantankerous support and for being the first person I met who carried around a list of possible karaoke songs. And thanks to Trevor Thompson for giving me the idea of "Love Shack" as a perfect karaoke number.

Luke Martin always answers my panicked music questions promptly and with admirable patience and expertise. But also, before I even started this book, he sat with me in the hottest restaurant in the city (the one with the wood-burning naan oven) on the hottest day of the year and listened to me talk through the entire plot, without complaint. That's friendship.

And even though I already dedicated the book to them, Megan Butcher deserves another thanks for being the most amazing, noble land-mermaid of a friend. They read so many drafts of this that I've lost count. No one supports me the way they do, and I am endlessly endeavoring to deserve them.

Thank you to my agent, Samantha Haywood, for believing in this book and in me.

Thanks to Anna MacDiarmid for miraculous editing and unflagging support, and to Megan Kwan for joyful line edits and her uncanny ability to catch all the times I repeated myself in early drafts. They both made the strange and overwhelming world of publishing so much more manageable. Thanks to Maggie Morris, who somehow made the copyedit fun to do. And thank you to everyone else at Doubleday Canada. I couldn't have asked for a better publisher.

I wouldn't have been able to write this story if I hadn't been a member of the flawed-but-adorable all-girl punk band Sophomore Level Psychology with a bunch of very fun ladies in the early 2000s. We were no Jetskis, but we sure have some great stories to tell.

If you're ever in Ottawa, please go to Planet Coffee (where I wrote so much of this) and also to Octopus Books, which is owned by my longtime friend Lisa Greaves, who is one of my absolute favorite people.

Bringing back the spirit of my grandad George Blackwell as a gentle, tea-drinking customer at Mindy's Café allowed me to spend a bit of time with his memory. I am always grateful to have had him in my life for as long as I did.

And absolutely most of all, thank you to David (who married me in Las Vegas), Milo, Joey and Betty, who all live with and love me, and to the extended family members who offer us so much support. I love you all so much.

Make Me a Mixtape

Questions and Topics for Discussion

1. In *Make Me a Mixtape*, Allie must choose between taking over her aunt's café or pursuing a career in music. Do you think Allie made the right decision? If you were in her position, which option would you choose?

2. How did the breakup of the Jetskis shape Allie's relationship with music? How did it shape her sense of self?

3. *Make Me a Mixtape* is full of nostalgic references to artists and bands of the past, from Pat Benatar to the Bangles. Were there any artists mentioned that you hadn't heard of before? Are there any you are curious to check out?

4. Ryan is a huge fan of the Jetskis even before meeting Allie. How does this dynamic shape their relationship?

5. Do you think Ryan is Allie's creative muse? Why or why not?

6. For Allie and Ryan, music acts as a shared love language. How do they both express their feelings through music?

7. Have you ever made a mixtape or a playlist for a loved one? What songs did you include?

8. While Allie is nostalgic for the punk scene of her youth, she gravitates to other genres of music as an adult. In what other ways does Allie evolve as an artist over the course of the novel?

9. Throughout the novel, author Jennifer Whiteford associates each month in which the story takes place with a different song. October is Pat Benatar's "We Belong," November is Madonna's "Borderline," December is Paula Abdul's "Straight Up" and January is Cyndi Lauper's "True Colors." How do these songs complement the different stages of Allie and Ryan's relationship?

10. Which song would you choose to best represent Allie and Ryan's love story?

JENNIFER WHITEFORD (she/her) lives in Ottawa, Ontario, with her partner, children, dog and record collection. She writes regularly for *Razorcake*, a long-standing punk publication. She was also a founding member of the "all girl, all rock" band Sophomore Level Psychology. With those rock 'n' roll days behind her, she now mostly stays home and reads. Find her on Instagram at @jenniferwhitefordwrites.